AFTER HOURS

LITISHA KIWAIN

AFTERTHOUGHT PRESS

Published by Afterthought Press

First edition

ISBN: 979-8-218-90146-2

Printed in the United States of America

ACT ONE: DOUBLE LIFE

CHAPTER 1
THE PRESENTATION

THE CONFERENCE ROOM fell silent as Sadie Monroe clicked to the final slide of her presentation. Twenty-three pairs of eyes fixed on her, waiting. She let the silence stretch—three seconds, four—before she spoke.

"Gentlemen," she said, her voice smooth as aged whiskey, "the question isn't whether you can afford to invest in this initiative. The question is whether you can afford not to."

She moved from behind the podium with the fluid grace of a woman who knew exactly how much space her body commanded. The Armani pencil skirt hugged her curves like a second skin, the slit at her thigh offering just a whisper of suggestion as she walked. Her silk blouse—burgundy, the color of expensive wine—draped perfectly across her shoulders and décolletage. Professional. Powerful. Untouchable.

The CFO leaned forward. "Ms. Monroe, these projections seem aggressive—"

"Aggressive?" Sadie tilted her head slightly, and a strand of her honey-highlighted hair slipped from behind her ear. She didn't fix it. "Mr. Patterson, I don't deal in aggressive. I deal in inevitable." She clicked her remote, pulling up the data analysis. "Three comparable markets. Three successful implementations. Thirty-seven percent ROI within the first fiscal year."

She watched him swallow. They always did.

For the next ten minutes, she dismantled every objection with surgical precision, her heels clicking against the hardwood floor as she moved around the table, making eye contact with each decision-maker. She knew the power of proximity, of letting her presence fill their personal space just long enough to make them uncomfortable in the best possible way.

When the senior VP finally said, "I think we've heard enough. Ms. Monroe, you've got your budget," Sadie allowed herself the smallest smile—the kind that promised everything and nothing at all.

"Pleasure doing business with you, gentlemen."

Three hours later, Sadie sat in her corner office on the forty-second floor, the city sprawling beneath her like a kingdom waiting to be conquered. Her fingers drummed against the mahogany desk as she reviewed the contract terms one final time. Perfect. Everything was always perfect in this world—her world of board meetings and business lunches, of quarterly reports and strategic initiatives.

Her phone buzzed. A text from LaKrecia: "Closing deals and breaking hearts. That's my girl. Drinks later?"

Sadie smiled and typed back: "Can't tonight. Have plans."

Three dots appeared, then: "Those kind of plans? Girl, be careful."

Sadie didn't respond. Instead, she closed her laptop and turned to the floor-to-ceiling windows. The sun was setting, painting the sky in shades of amber and rose gold. Her reflection stared back at her—polished, professional and perfectly composed.

But as the last rays of daylight faded, something shifted in her expression. Her shoulders relaxed. Her lips curved into a different kind of smile.

It was time for the transformation.

Sadie's apartment was a sanctuary of calculated luxury. Floor-to-ceiling windows overlooked the city, and the open-concept living space was decorated in shades of cream, gold, and deep charcoal. Everything had its place. Everything was intentional.

She poured herself two fingers of bourbon—Blanton's, because she never settled—and carried it to her bedroom. The master suite was her temple, complete with a walk-in closet that could rival a boutique and a bathroom with a rainfall shower that had seen more than its share of meditation.

Sadie set down her glass and began the ritual.

First, the armor came off. She unbuttoned her blouse slowly, watching herself in the full-length mirror. The corporate Sadie—the one who commanded boardrooms and intimidated vice presidents—slipped away with each piece of clothing that hit the floor. The pencil skirt pooled at her feet. The sensible bra that minimized rather than celebrated. The shape wear that kept everything controlled.

Underneath was the real canvas. Smooth brown skin that glowed like it had been kissed by gold. Curves that demanded attention—full breasts, a waist that dipped in before flaring into hips that swayed with deliberate seduction, thighs that were strong and soft all at once.

She stepped into the shower, letting the hot water cascade over her body. As she massaged jasmine and sandalwood body wash into her skin, she felt the final layers of Corporate Sadie wash away down the drain. This was her meditation—the moment between worlds where she shed one identity and embraced another.

When she emerged, wrapped in a plush towel, she was already different. Her movements were slower and more delicate.

She lotioned every inch of her body with shea butter infused with vanilla and amber—scents that clung to skin and lingered in memory. Then she stood before her closet, considering.

Tonight called for something specific. Not too obvious, but impossible to ignore.

She selected a black dress—not the boring corporate black, but the kind of black that absorbed light and attention. It was backless, with a neckline that plunged just low enough to make people wonder. The fabric was liquid silk that moved when she breathed, skimming over her body like water, like hands. The hem ended mid-thigh, showing off legs that had been toned by years of yoga and genetics blessed by the ancestors.

No bra—the dress wouldn't allow it. Just a black lace thong that made her feel powerful and free.

She kept her makeup simple but flawless. A bronze glow on her cheekbones. Lashes extended and curled until her eyes looked like they held secrets worth dying for. Lips painted a deep burgundy that matched the wine she'd worn earlier—but this shade promised a very different kind of negotiation.

Her hair, which had been pulled into a tight bun all day, now fell in loose waves past her shoulders. She ran her fingers through it, tousling it just enough to look like she'd just rolled out of someone's bed.

The final touches: gold hoops that caught the light when she moved her head. A delicate gold chain that drew the eye to her collarbone. A spritz of Tom Ford Lost Cherry behind each ear, between her breasts, at the pulse point of each wrist.

Sadie stepped back and assessed herself in the mirror.

There she is.

This Sadie didn't command boardrooms. She commanded bodies, desires, the secret thoughts men didn't dare say out loud. This Sadie understood that power came in many forms—and the power to make someone lose control was perhaps the sweetest of all.

She slipped her feet into black Louboutins—the red soles a secret signature that only revealed itself when she walked away.

Her phone buzzed with a message from a number she knew by heart but had never saved: "The usual place. 10 PM."

Sadie's smile was slow and knowing. She texted back a single word: "Eager?"

The response was immediate: "Always. For you."

She checked the time. 9:15. Just enough time to arrive fashionably late—to walk in and make an entrance, to let him watch her cross the room and remember exactly why he couldn't stay away.

Sadie grabbed her clutch—small, elegant, containing only the essentials: lipstick, phone, ID, and a condom. A woman who controlled her own destiny controlled her own protection.

As she walked to her private parking garage, her heels echoing in the concrete space, she felt it—that electric hum that ran through her body when she was about to step into her other life. It was anticipation and power mixed together, a cocktail more intoxicating than any bourbon.

She slid into her black Mercedes coupe, the leather seats cool against her exposed back. As she started the engine, she caught her reflection in the rearview mirror one last time.

Corporate Sadie had left the building. Now, the night belonged to someone else entirely.

CHAPTER 2
THE PLAYGROUND

THE VELVET ROOM wasn't the kind of place you stumbled into by accident. Tucked away on the third floor of a renovated warehouse in the arts district, it had no sign, no advertisement, no Yelp reviews. You either knew about it, or you didn't deserve to.

Sadie stepped out of the private elevator, and immediately the atmosphere wrapped around her like a lover's embrace. Low amber lighting cast everything in a warm, golden glow. The air was thick with the scent of expensive cologne, top-shelf liquor, and something else—possibility. The kind that hummed beneath your skin and made your pulse quicken.

Deep house music pulsed through hidden speakers, the bass line sensual and hypnotic. It wasn't loud enough to prevent conversation, but rhythmic enough to make bodies want to move closer together.

The space was intimate—maybe forty people maximum on any given night. Plush velvet booths lined the walls in shades of deep burgundy and midnight blue. The bar stretched along one side, backlit with amber light that made every bottle look like liquid gold. And in the center, a small dance floor where bodies moved together in ways that would make Sunday morning church-goers clutch their pearls.

This was Sadie's playground. Her sanctuary. The place where she could be the version of herself that didn't fit in conference rooms and shareholder meetings.

She moved through the space slowly, deliberately. She knew the power of an entrance—knew that every eye would track her movement across the room. The dress caught the light with each step, the silk whispering against her thighs. Her hips swayed to the music's rhythm, a metronome of seduction.

A man at the bar turned to watch her pass. She met his gaze for exactly two seconds—long enough to acknowledge his interest, not long enough to invite approach. His friend whispered something to him, probably asking who she was. The answer didn't matter. She was whoever she needed to be.

Sadie slid onto a bar stool with the kind of grace that made the simple act look like choreography. The bartender—Xavier, a man who knew better than to ask questions—appeared immediately.

"The usual, goddess?" His smile was knowing.

"Please." Her voice was different here. Softer. With a rasp that suggested bedroom conversations and tangled sheets.

He poured her a glass of Clase Azul Reposado tequila—smooth, expensive, meant to be savored. She wrapped her fingers around the glass, the crystal cool against her palm, and took a slow sip. The liquid heat slid down her throat, warming her from the inside.

"He's in the back booth," Xavier said quietly, polishing a glass. "Been here since nine-thirty. Ordered a bottle of Hennessy Paradis. Man's got it bad."

Sadie's lips curved. "He always does."

She didn't turn around to look. Not yet. Let him wait. Let him watch her back, the exposed skin, the way her hair cascaded over one shoulder. Anticipation was half the pleasure.

She took another sip of her tequila, crossing her legs slowly. The motion made her dress ride up slightly, revealing more thigh. She felt his eyes on her like a physical touch, burning across the distance between them.

Two minutes. Three. She made him wait.

Then, finally, she turned on the bar stool—a slow pivot that gave him the full view. Her eyes swept across the room as if searching, even though she knew exactly where he was. When her gaze finally landed on him, she let her expression shift. Recognition. Interest. The slightest hint of a smile that promised everything.

Jarod sat in the corner booth, his long frame relaxed but his eyes intense. He was beautiful in that dangerous way—six-foot-three of lean muscle wrapped in a perfectly tailored black shirt and dark jeans. His skin was deep mahogany, his fade sharp enough to cut glass, and his goatee was trimmed with the precision of a man who paid attention to details. But it was his eyes that always got her—dark brown, almost black, and absolutely focused on her like she was the only woman in the world.

He raised his glass slightly. An invitation.

Sadie took her time finishing her tequila. She thanked Xavier, slipped a hundred-dollar bill across the bar, and stood. Every movement was deliberate as she crossed the room toward him.

She could feel the weight of other eyes following her, but they didn't matter. Nothing mattered except the electricity crackling between her and the man watching her approach with barely controlled hunger.

When she reached his booth, she didn't slide in immediately. She stood there, letting him take her in. His eyes traveled slowly up her body—from her red-soled heels, up her legs, over the curves the dress worshipped, lingering on the plunge of her neckline, before finally meeting her gaze.

"Sadie." Her name on his lips sounded like a prayer and a curse.

"Jarod." She let the name roll off her tongue, tasting it.

"You're late."

"I'm worth the wait." She slid into the booth beside him—not across from him, beside him—so their thighs touched. The contact sent electricity straight through her body.

He poured her a glass of cognac without asking. His hands were strong, with long fingers that she knew could be gentle or demanding, depending on what she needed.

"New dress?" His voice was low, meant only for her ears.

"You like it?" She leaned back slightly, letting him look his fill.

"I'd like it better on the floor." His hand found her thigh under the table, his palm hot against her skin. He didn't move higher—not yet. Just rested it there, possessive and patient.

Sadie felt the heat pool low in her belly. This was what she came here for—this feeling of being desired so completely that it made her skin feel too tight. In the boardroom, she was respected, even feared. But here, with Jarod, she was wanted. Craved. Worshipped.

"Confident tonight," she murmured, taking a sip of cognac. The burn was different from tequila—deeper, more complex. Like him.

"Always confident when it comes to you." His thumb traced small circles on her thigh, and she felt her body respond immediately. Her breath hitched slightly, and she saw his smile—the one that said he'd noticed.

"How was your week?" It was the question they always asked, the brief moment of normalcy before they fell into the delicious chaos of desire.

"Long. Tedious. Missing this." His hand moved higher, just an inch, and her breath caught again.

"Missing me, or missing this?" She turned to face him fully, her lips close enough to his that she could smell the cognac on his breath mixed with his cologne—something woody and expensive that made her want to bury her face in his neck.

"Can't they be the same thing?" His free hand came up to cup her face, his thumb brushing across her bottom lip. The touch was gentle, but his eyes were dark with barely restrained need.

"They shouldn't be." But even as she said it, she knew they'd crossed that line months ago. What started as purely physical—two people scratching an itch with no names, no complications—had become something else. Something neither of them wanted to acknowledge because acknowledging it would ruin everything.

"Then let's not complicate it." He leaned in, his lips hovering just above hers. "Let's just feel."

And God, did she want to feel.

Sadie closed the distance between them, pressing her lips to his. The kiss started slow—a gentle exploration, a relearning of familiar territory. His lips were soft but insistent, tasting of cognac and mint.

He kissed the way he did everything—with complete focus, like she was the only thing that existed in this moment.

His hand tightened on her thigh, pulling her closer. She shifted in the booth, turning her body toward his, and his other hand slid into her hair, angling her head to deepen the kiss.

That's when the slow burn ignited.

His tongue swept into her mouth, claiming, tasting, and she met him stroke for stroke. The kiss went from gentle to demanding, from questioning to answering. She felt it everywhere—the heat spreading through her chest, down her spine, pooling between her thighs.

Sadie's hand found his chest, feeling his heart hammer beneath her palm. She dragged her nails lightly down his chest, over his abs—she knew exactly what was under that shirt—and heard his sharp intake of breath.

"Sadie," he growled against her lips. "You keep doing that, and we're not making it out of this booth."

"Who says I want to make it out of this booth?" Her voice was breathy, teasing.

He pulled back just enough to look at her, his eyes so dark they were almost black. "Because I need space for what I want to do to you."

The promise in his voice sent shivers down her spine.

"Then take me somewhere we have space." She bit her bottom lip, watching his eyes track the movement.

Jarod didn't need to be told twice. He threw back the rest of his cognac in one swallow and stood, pulling her up with him. His hand found the small of her back, fingers splaying possessively against her bare skin. The touch was electric—skin on skin, heat on heat.

They moved through the crowd toward the back of the Velvet Room. Sadie knew where they were going—the private suites. Sound-proofed rooms with locked doors where consenting adults could explore whatever pleasures they desired without judgment or inter-ruption.

The hallway was dimly lit, lined with doors marked only with numbers. Jarod stopped at Suite 7—their usual—and pulled out a key card. The lock clicked open with a soft beep.

The suite was exactly as she remembered: a king-sized bed with crisp black sheets, low lighting controlled by dimmer switches, a sitting area with a velvet sofa, and a well-stocked bar. The walls were painted a deep charcoal, and one entire wall was floor-to-ceiling mirrors—for those who liked to watch.

Sadie did.

The door clicked shut behind them, and suddenly they were in their own world. No rules. No judgments. Just two people and the fire that burned between them.

Jarod turned her to face him, his hands on her waist. For a moment, he just looked at her—really looked—and she saw something in his eyes that made her chest tighten. Something that looked dangerously close to tenderness.

"You're so damn beautiful," he said, his voice rough with emotion.

"Jarod—" She started to deflect, to make a joke, because compliments about her beauty were easy. Compliments that felt real were dangerous.

"No." He pulled her closer, until their bodies were flush. She could feel every hard plane of his body against her soft curves, feel the evidence of his desire pressed against her hip. "Let me say it. You walk in a room and everything else disappears. You know that?"

Her heart hammered. This wasn't part of the script. They didn't do vulnerable. They did hot, passionate, uncomplicated.

"We should—"

"We should what? Pretend this is just about sex?" His hand slid up her back, fingers dancing along her spine. "Maybe it started that way. But you and I both know it's more now."

"It can't be more." But even as she said it, her body betrayed her, arching into his touch.

"Then let's not talk about it." His lips found her neck, pressing hot, open-mouthed kisses along the column of her throat. "Let's just show each other."

And oh, the way he showed her.

His hands were everywhere—sliding up her sides, cupping her breasts through the thin silk, thumbs brushing over nipples that hardened immediately at his touch. Sadie gasped, her head falling back, giving him better access to her neck.

He took full advantage, his mouth trailing fire along her skin. He found that spot just below her ear that made her knees weak, and bit down gently. The sharp pleasure made her moan—a sound that came from deep in her chest.

"I love the sounds you make," he murmured against her skin. "Every gasp. Every moan. Music."

His hands found the zipper at the side of her dress and slowly—torturously slowly—pulled it down. The sound of the zipper seemed loud in the quiet room, punctuated only by their heavy breathing.

The dress fell away like water, pooling at her feet and leaving her standing in nothing but her black lace thong and heels.

Jarod stepped back, and she watched his face as he took her in. His jaw clenched. His hands flexed at his sides like he was physically restraining himself from grabbing her.

"Fucking perfection," he breathed.

Sadie felt powerful. Desired. Alive. This—this moment when a man looked at her like she was every fantasy he'd ever had—this was her drug. Better than any boardroom victory. Better than any deal closed.

She reached for his shirt, unbuttoning it with fingers that trembled slightly with anticipation. She pushed it off his shoulders, revealing the body she'd memorized with her hands, her lips, her tongue. Smooth dark skin over defined muscles. Broad shoulders that tapered to a narrow waist. Abs that flexed when she touched them.

She leaned in and pressed her lips to his chest, right over his heart. She felt it pounding—for her. Because of her.

Her hands went to his belt, and she looked up at him through her lashes. "My turn to unwrap my present."

His laugh was strained. "Baby, you keep looking at me like that, this is gonna be over embarrassingly fast."

"Then I better make it worth the wait." She unbuckled his belt with practiced ease, popped the button on his jeans, and slowly—so slowly—pulled down the zipper.

She sank to her knees, and heard his sharp inhale.

"Sadie—"

She looked up at him as she pulled his jeans down, along with his boxer briefs, freeing him. He was already hard, impressively so, and she felt that familiar thrill of power. She did this to him. Her presence. Her touch.

She wrapped her hand around him, stroking slowly, and watched his eyes nearly roll back.

"You're trying to kill me," he groaned.

"Would that be such a bad way to go?" She leaned forward and pressed a kiss to his tip, tasting the salt of his arousal.

His hand tangled in her hair—not pushing, just holding, grounding himself. "Baby, please—"

She took him into her mouth, slowly, savoring the weight of him on her tongue. His groan was deeply satisfying—the sound of a man losing control.

This was her favorite part. Not even the pleasure itself, but the power of giving it. Of watching a man—strong, confident, controlled—come completely undone because of her. Because of what she could do with her mouth, her hands, her body.

She established a rhythm, taking him deeper with each pass, using her hand to stroke what she couldn't fit. His hips flexed slightly, trying not to thrust, trying to maintain some semblance of control.

She loved making him lose that control.

"Sadie—baby—I'm close—" His voice was strained, warning her.

But she didn't stop. She doubled down, taking him deeper, faster, until she felt him pulse in her mouth and heard him cry out—a raw, primal sound that sent pleasure shooting through her own body even though he hadn't touched her yet.

When she finally released him, she looked up to find him staring down at her with an expression that was part awe, part devastation.

"You're incredible," he panted, helping her to her feet.

"I know." She smiled, pleased with herself.

"My turn." His voice held a promise that made her stomach flip.

In one smooth motion, he lifted her—literally swept her off her feet —and carried her to the bed. He laid her down on the black sheets like she was something precious, something to be worshipped.

And then he proceeded to worship every inch of her.

His mouth started at her ankle, pressing kisses up her calf, the inside of her knee, her inner thigh. Sadie's breathing quickened with each kiss, each touch of his lips against her heated skin.

When he reached the apex of her thighs, he paused, his breath hot against her through the lace. "May I?"

Even now, even in the heat of passion, he asked. Consent was always sexy.

"Yes," she breathed. "God, yes."

He hooked his fingers in her thong and slid it down her legs, tossing it aside. And then his mouth was on her—hot and demanding and absolutely perfect.

Sadie's back arched off the bed, her hands fisting in the sheets. His tongue moved with the same focus he brought to everything else—dedicated, thorough, satisfying. He learned her body the way she imagined he learned everything: with complete attention to detail, noting what made her gasp, what made her moan, what made her hips buck against his mouth.

"Jarod—" His name was a plea, a prayer.

He slid two fingers inside her, curling them just right, while his mouth continued its assault on her senses. The combination was overwhelming. She felt the pleasure building, coiling tighter and tighter in her belly, spreading through her limbs.

"That's it, baby," he murmured against her. "Let go. I got you."

And she did. The orgasm crashed over her like a wave, pulling her under, drowning her in sensation. Her whole body tensed and then released, pleasure pulsing through her in waves that seemed endless. She cried out—loud and unrestrained—and distantly heard her own voice calling his name like an incantation.

When she finally came back to herself, she found him watching her with undisguised satisfaction.

"Beautiful," he said simply.

Her body still humming with aftershocks, Sadie reached for him. "I need you. Now."

He didn't need more invitation than that. He positioned himself between her thighs, and she felt him—hot and hard—pressing against her entrance.

"Protection?" he asked, even though they both knew the answer.

She nodded toward her clutch on the nightstand. He grabbed a condom, rolled it on with practiced efficiency, and then he was there again, looking down at her with those intense eyes.

"You ready for me?"

"Always."

He entered her slowly, giving her time to adjust, and Sadie's eyes fluttered closed at the sensation of being filled, stretched, completed. This—this was what she craved. Not just the physical pleasure, but the intimacy of it. The connection. The way their bodies fit together like puzzle pieces.

When he was fully seated inside her, he paused, letting her adjust. Then he began to move—slow, deep strokes that hit every nerve ending and made her toes curl.

"Open your eyes," he commanded softly. "Look at me."

She did, and the intensity in his gaze nearly undid her all over again.

"I want you to see me," he said, his rhythm increasing. "Want you to know who's making you feel this good."

"Jarod—" His name fell from her lips like a mantra as he drove into her harder, faster. The sound of skin against skin filled the room, mixed with their heavy breathing and her increasingly desperate moans.

He hooked her leg over his shoulder, changing the angle, and suddenly he was hitting that perfect spot inside her that made stars burst behind her eyelids.

"Right there," she gasped. "Don't stop—please don't stop—"

"Never," he growled, maintaining that perfect rhythm, that perfect angle. "Could do this forever. Could stay inside you forever."

The words, combined with the relentless pleasure, pushed her toward the edge again. She felt it building—faster this time, more intense.

"Come for me," he commanded, one hand finding her clit and circling with just the right pressure. "Want to feel you come around me."

It was the combination of his voice, his touch, his body claiming hers that sent her over the edge. The second orgasm was even more powerful than the first—a full-body experience that left her shaking and gasping his name.

She felt him follow her over the edge, his body tensing as he found his own release, her name on his lips like a benediction.

He collapsed beside her, both of them breathing hard, skin slick with sweat. For a long moment, neither of them spoke. The only sound was their gradually slowing breathing.

Sadie turned her head to look at him. His eyes were closed, a satisfied smile on his lips. He looked peaceful in a way she'd never seen him before.

Dangerous thoughts started creeping in. Thoughts about what it would be like to wake up next to this man every morning. To build something real with him. To let him see all of her—not just the seductive goddess, but the ambitious executive, the vulnerable woman, the complete package.

But those thoughts were dangerous. She came here to escape complications, not create them.

As if sensing her thoughts, Jarod opened his eyes and turned to look at her. He reached out and tucked a strand of hair behind her ear —such a simple gesture, but so intimate it made her chest ache.

"What are you thinking?" he asked softly.

"That I should probably go." It was what she always said, the script they always followed.

But tonight, his hand caught her wrist gently. "Stay. Just for a while longer."

She should have said no. Should have gotten dressed, kissed him goodbye, and returned to her separate life. But instead, she found herself nodding.

"Just for a while."

He pulled her close, and she rested her head on his chest, listening to his heartbeat slow to normal. His fingers traced lazy patterns on her back, and she felt herself relaxing in a way she rarely allowed.

"Tell me something about you," he said. "Something real."

"We don't do real, remember?" But there was no bite in her words.

"Maybe we should start." His hand stilled on her back. "I know your body, Sadie. Know exactly how to make you come undone. But I don't know your favorite color. Don't know what you do during the day. Don't know what makes you smile when you're alone."

She should have deflected. Should have made a joke. But lying there in his arms, in the comfortable aftermath of great sex, she found herself wanting to give him something real.

"Purple," she said softly. "My favorite color is purple. Deep purple, like twilight right before night falls completely."

She felt him smile against her hair. "That fits you. Beautiful and mysterious."

They lay there in comfortable silence, and Sadie felt the walls she'd so carefully constructed starting to crack. This was supposed to be simple. Physical. Uncomplicated.

But nothing with Jarod felt simple anymore.

And that terrified her more than any boardroom presentation ever could.

Sadie woke to the feeling of fingertips tracing the curve of her spine. For a moment, she forgot where she was—forgot the rules, forgot the script. All she knew was warmth and the scent of sandalwood and man.

Then reality crashed back.

She'd fallen asleep. In his arms. In the suite at the Velvet Room.

That wasn't part of the arrangement.

"Hey," Jarod's voice was soft, still rough from sleep. "Didn't mean to wake you."

Sadie opened her eyes to find the room bathed in the dim amber glow of the bedside lamp. She had no idea what time it was, only that they'd crossed another invisible line she'd drawn for herself.

"What time is it?" She started to sit up, and his arm tightened around her waist.

"Does it matter?" He pressed a kiss to her shoulder blade. "It's late. Or early. Depending on how you look at it."

She should leave. Should gather her dress, slip back into her armor, and return to the world where she had control. But his hand was sliding up her ribcage, his thumb brushing the underside of her breast, and her body—traitorous thing—was already responding.

"Jarod..." It was meant to be a protest, but came out as something else entirely.

"I know." His lips found that spot on her neck again, the one that made her melt. "You have to go. You always have to go. But not yet."

His hand cupped her breast fully now, thumb circling her nipple until it peaked. She arched back against him and felt him—already hard again—pressing against the curve of her ass.

"How are you already—?" She couldn't even finish the sentence as his other hand slid down her stomach, between her thighs.

"It's you." He nipped at her earlobe. "Every time I touch you, every time I even *think* about touching you, I want you all over again. Can't help it."

His fingers found her center, sliding through her wetness— evidence that she wanted him just as badly. She was already slick for him, still sensitive from before, and when he slid two fingers inside her, she gasped.

"Still so wet for me," he murmured, his voice dark with satisfaction. He pumped his fingers slowly, curling them to hit that spot that made her see stars. "Could spend the rest of my life learning every way to make you moan."

"Jarod—" Her hand reached back, finding him, stroking him the way she'd learned he liked.

"Fuck, baby." His forehead dropped to her shoulder. "You're gonna kill me."

"Then we die together." She guided him to her entrance, and he didn't need more invitation than that.

He slid inside her from behind, this new angle making him feel impossibly deeper. One of his hands gripped her hip, holding her steady, while the other slid around to find her clit. The dual sensation —him filling her completely while his fingers worked their magic— was almost too much.

"Look," he commanded, and she realized he'd positioned them so they faced the mirrored wall.

In the low light, she could see their reflection: his dark body wrapped around hers, the contrast of their skin, the way his hand splayed possessively across her stomach. She watched his hips flex as he drove into her, watched her own face transform with pleasure.

"See how beautiful you are?" His eyes met hers in the mirror. "See how perfect we look together?"

She couldn't look away. Watching him take her, watching her body respond, seeing the intimacy of the moment reflected back—it was the most erotic thing she'd ever experienced.

"I want you to watch yourself come," he growled in her ear, his rhythm increasing. "Want you to see what I see when you fall apart."

His fingers on her clit moved faster, matching the pace of his thrusts. The combination was intoxicating. She felt the pressure building again—impossibly, incredibly—even though she'd already come twice tonight.

"That's it," he encouraged, never breaking eye contact in the mirror. "Let go for me, baby. Let me see you."

She watched herself shatter. Watched her mouth fall open in a silent scream, watched her body arch and tremble, watched pleasure wash over her features. And she watched him watch her—his eyes dark and possessive and filled with something that looked dangerously like reverence.

He followed her over the edge moments later, his groan rough against her neck as he buried himself deep and found his release.

They stayed like that for a long moment, both breathing hard, still connected. In the mirror, their eyes met again, and Sadie saw it—that flicker of something real, something tender, something that had no place in a arrangement built on pure physical chemistry.

She looked away first.

This time, when she pulled away, he let her go.

Sadie gathered her clothes in silence, hyper-aware of Jarod watching her from the bed. She found her thong, stepped into it. Located her dress and pulled it on, reaching behind to pull up the zipper but finding it difficult to reach.

"Let me." He was there suddenly, his fingers brushing hers aside to zip her up. But instead of just zipping and stepping away, his hands lingered on her shoulders. He pressed a kiss to the back of her neck— soft, almost tender. "Sadie."

"Don't." She stepped away before she could change her mind about leaving. "We agreed. This is what this is."

"And what if I want it to be more?" The words hung in the air between them, dangerous and tempting.

She turned to face him. He stood there in nothing but his boxer briefs, all that beautiful skin on display, looking at her with an expression that made her chest tight.

"You don't," she said firmly. "You want the fantasy. The woman who shows up here and rocks your world with no complications, no baggage, no real life attached. That's what this is."

"What if you're wrong?" He stepped closer. "What if I want to know the woman behind the fantasy? Want to take you to dinner—a real dinner, where we sit and talk. Want to wake up next to you in a real bed, in a real home, and not have you disappear before sunrise."

Her heart hammered. This was the moment she'd feared—the moment when the lines blurred and everything got complicated.

"You don't know me, Jarod."

"Then let me get to know you."

"You wouldn't like what you found." She grabbed her clutch, needing to escape before she did something stupid like say yes. "I'm not the woman you think I am. This—" she gestured at herself, at the room, at the space between them "—this is the best version of me. The rest is boring meetings and spreadsheets and stress. You don't want that."

"How do you know what I want?" His voice was quiet but intense.

"Because I know men." She forced herself to meet his eyes. "You want the fantasy. Trust me, the reality would disappoint you."

She walked to the door, her hand on the handle, when his voice stopped her.

"What if you're the one who's afraid of being disappointed?"

She didn't turn around. Couldn't. "Goodnight, Jarod."

"Sadie, wait—"

But she was already gone, the door clicking shut behind her.

The hallway felt colder, harsher after the warmth of the suite. Sadie's heels clicked against the floor as she walked back through the Velvet Room. The crowd had thinned—it was nearly 3 AM according to her phone—but there were still a few people scattered around, lost in their own worlds of pleasure and escape.

She didn't look at anyone. Just headed straight for the elevator.

The ride down felt longer than the ride up. She caught her reflection in the mirrored elevator walls—her hair was mussed, her lips slightly swollen, her dress wrinkled. She looked exactly like what she was: a woman who'd just been thoroughly satisfied.

So why did she feel so hollow?

The parking garage was nearly empty, just a few luxury cars scattered throughout. Her Mercedes sat where she'd left it, waiting to carry her back to her other life.

Sadie slid into the driver's seat and just sat there for a moment, hands on the steering wheel, staring straight ahead.

What if I want it to be more?

Jarod's words echoed in her head. She'd heard versions of that before from other men—the ones who thought they wanted more until they realized the fantasy didn't match reality. But something about the way Jarod said it felt different. Felt real.

And that scared her more than anything.

Her phone buzzed. A text from LaKrecia: *"You better be alive. Call me in the morning. We need to talk."*

Sadie smiled despite herself. LaKrecia always knew when she was in her head about something. Best friends had that radar.

She started the car and pulled out of the garage, leaving the Velvet Room behind. But as she drove through the empty city streets, she couldn't shake the feeling that something had shifted tonight. Some line had been crossed that couldn't be uncrossed.

The corporate buildings loomed dark against the night sky, waiting for Monday morning when she'd return to her other identity. The city was quiet at this hour—just the occasional taxi or rideshare passing by, carrying other people home from their own secret lives.

When she finally pulled into her building's garage and took the elevator up to her apartment, exhaustion hit her like a wave. It was nearly 4 AM. She had maybe three hours before she needed to wake up and start her Sunday routine—gym, meal prep, reviewing presentations for the week ahead.

Sadie kicked off her heels and padded through her apartment. Everything was exactly as she'd left it—immaculate, controlled, perfect. The opposite of how she felt inside.

She poured herself a glass of water and stood by the floor-to-ceiling windows, looking out at the city below. Somewhere out there, Jarod was probably still in that suite, or maybe he'd gone home too. Was he thinking about her? Replaying the night? Regretting what he'd said?

Her phone buzzed again. She almost ignored it, but something made her check.

It was from his number: *"I meant what I said. Every word. Sleep well, beautiful."*

She stared at the message for a long time, her thumb hovering over the reply button. She should ignore it. Should maintain the boundaries. Should protect herself from the inevitable disappointment.

Instead, she found herself typing: *"You too."*

It was simple. Non-committal. But as she hit send, she felt another crack form in those carefully constructed walls.

Sadie set her phone on the counter and headed to her bedroom. She needed sleep. Needed to reset and prepare for the week ahead. Needed to be Corporate Sadie again—focused, driven, in control.

But as she lay in her bed, in sheets that suddenly felt too cold and empty, she couldn't stop thinking about warm arms and whispered promises and the dangerous possibility that maybe—just maybe— Jarod could handle both versions of her.

That maybe he could be the one to finally merge her two worlds into something whole.

And that terrified her more than any risk she'd ever taken in her life.

Dawn was breaking when sleep finally claimed her. In her dreams, she stood at a crossroads—one path leading to the bright fluorescent lights of a boardroom, the other to the amber glow of the Velvet Room. And in the distance, at the point where both paths converged, stood a figure she couldn't quite make out.

But she knew, somehow, that it was waiting for her to choose.

The question was: which path would lead her there?

And more importantly—was she brave enough to find out?

CHAPTER 3
COMPARTMENTS

THE ALARM SHATTERED Sadie's dreams at 7 AM sharp. She slapped at her phone, groaning as sunlight streamed through the floor-to-ceiling windows she'd forgotten to cover with blackout shades. Three hours of sleep. Her body screamed for more, but Corporate Sadie didn't sleep in on Sundays. Corporate Sadie had a routine.

She dragged herself out of bed, every muscle reminding her of last night's activities. A dull, pleasant ache radiated through her thighs, and she felt the ghost of Jarod's fingers on her skin. She caught her reflection in the bathroom mirror—hair wild, mascara smudged beneath her eyes, a small mark on her collarbone where his mouth had been particularly insistent.

Evidence. All of it evidence of a life that wasn't supposed to bleed into this one.

Sadie turned on the shower—cold first, shocking her system awake—then gradually warming it until steam filled the bathroom. She stood under the spray and scrubbed away the night. The jasmine and sandalwood body wash from last night was replaced with an unscented exfoliating scrub. Practical. Professional.

She washed her hair twice, conditioning until it was sleek and manageable. The woman who'd walked into the Velvet Room with bedroom hair and fuck-me heels was circling the drain with the soap suds.

By the time she stepped out, wrapped in a plush white robe, she was already transforming back.

The gym bag was packed and waiting by the door—she'd learned long ago that preparation was everything. No makeup today, just moisturizer with SPF. Hair pulled back in a high ponytail. Black leggings and a sports bra under an oversized hoodie. White Nike sneakers that had never seen the inside of a nightclub.

This Sadie didn't turn heads. This Sadie blended in.

And that was exactly the point.

The gym was moderately crowded for a Sunday morning—the usual mix of fitness enthusiasts and people working off Saturday night's indulgences. Sadie claimed her favorite treadmill in the back corner, popped in her earbuds, and started her run.

Five miles. That was the rule. Five miles to clear her head and reset her brain.

Her playlist was pure motivation—Beyoncé, Megan Thee Stallion, a little Kendrick for good measure. Songs about power, control, being a boss. The Corporate Sadie soundtrack.

By mile three, her legs were burning, but she pushed through. Pain was good. Pain meant she was in control of her body, her choices, her life.

Her phone buzzed with a text. She glanced down without breaking stride.

LaKrecia: *"Brunch at Marcel's. 11 AM. Don't even think about canceling."*

Sadie smiled despite herself. LaKrecia Brooks had been her best friend since their sorority days at Spelman. They'd pledged together, graduated together, moved to the city together with big dreams and bigger ambition. LaKrecia knew her better than anyone—knew about the double life, the compartments, the careful balance Sadie maintained between her two worlds.

She was also the only person who told Sadie the truth, even when it hurt.

Sadie: *"I'll be there."*

LaKrecia: *"Damn right you will. And you're spilling ALL the tea about last night. I can feel the drama from across town."*

Sadie shook her head and pocketed her phone. LaKrecia's intuition was scary-accurate.

She finished her five miles, then moved to the weight section. Squats, lunges, deadlifts—building the body that made men stop and stare. But this wasn't for them. This was for her. Control. Discipline. Proof that she could push herself further than anyone expected.

An hour later, drenched in sweat and gloriously exhausted, she headed home to shower and change.

Marcel's was the kind of bougie brunch spot that served twenty-dollar mimosas and thirty-dollar avocado toast, but the ambiance was worth it. Exposed brick walls, hanging plants, natural light streaming through massive windows. The crowd was a mix of young professionals and influencer types—people who understood that brunch wasn't just a meal, it was a lifestyle.

Sadie arrived exactly at 11 AM, dressed in high-waisted jeans, a cream silk blouse, and tan ankle boots. Gold jewelry—simple but expensive. Hair loose and flowing. Minimal makeup. She looked like she'd just casually thrown together an outfit, when in reality she'd spent twenty minutes perfecting the "effortlessly chic" look.

LaKrecia was already seated at their usual corner table, looking stunning as always. She had rich, dark skin that glowed like she'd been dipped in honey, natural hair styled in an elegant twist-out that framed her face perfectly, and curves that she dressed to celebrate. Today she wore a burnt orange wrap dress that complemented her skin tone beautifully.

But it was her eyes—sharp, intelligent, missing nothing—that locked onto Sadie as she approached.

"Well, well, well." LaKrecia set down her mimosa and gave Sadie a thorough once-over. "Look who decided to grace me with her presence. How was your *evening*?"

Sadie slid into the seat across from her. "Can I at least order a drink first?"

"Server's already on it. I ordered you a Spicy Marg. You look like you need tequila." LaKrecia leaned forward, resting her chin on her hand. "So. Spill. Was it Jarod?"

The server appeared with Sadie's margarita—perfectly salted rim, jalapeño garnish. She took a long sip before answering. "When is it not Jarod?"

"Mmm-hmm." LaKrecia's perfectly arched eyebrow rose. "And?"

"And what?"

"Girl, don't play with me. I know that look. Something happened. Something different."

Sadie traced the rim of her glass, choosing her words carefully. "He asked about me. The real me. Wanted to know things—personal things."

LaKrecia's expression shifted from amused to concerned. "Like what kind of things?"

"My favorite color. What I do during the day. He said—" Sadie paused, remembering the weight of his words. "He said he wants more than just the physical. Wants to take me to dinner, get to know me, wake up next to me in a real bed."

"Damn." LaKrecia sat back, processing. "That's... not part of the arrangement."

"I know."

"What did you say?"

"I told him no. Told him he doesn't really want to know the real me. That he likes the fantasy, and the reality would disappoint him."

"Do you believe that?"

Sadie looked up, meeting her friend's eyes. "I don't know. Maybe. Probably."

LaKrecia was quiet for a moment, studying her. Then she reached across the table and took Sadie's hand. "Baby girl, we need to talk. Real talk. No bullshit."

"Krecia—"

"No, listen." Her grip tightened. "I love you. You know I do. You're brilliant, beautiful, successful—everything I aspire to be. But this thing you're doing? These compartments you've built? They're not sustainable."

Sadie pulled her hand back, defensive. "I'm fine. I've been doing this for two years, and it works."

"Does it? Because from where I'm sitting, you look exhausted. And not just 'stayed up too late getting your back blown out' exhausted. Soul-tired. Like you're running a marathon with no finish line."

"I'm just stressed from work—"

"Stop." LaKrecia's voice was firm but gentle. "Don't do that. Don't minimize this. I'm your best friend, Sadie. I see you. The real you. And I'm watching you split yourself into pieces—Corporate Sadie who commands boardrooms, and After Hours Sadie who commands bedrooms. But when do you just get to be... Sadie? Whole. Complete. Yourself."

The words hit harder than Sadie expected. She felt something crack in her chest—a hairline fracture in the armor she wore so carefully.

"I don't know how to be whole," she admitted quietly. "I don't know how to be both things at once. In the boardroom, I have to be ruthless, professional, untouchable. If they knew about my personal life—about the clubs, the men, the way I spend my nights—I'd be labeled. Written off. All my credibility gone."

"But what about with someone who cares about you? Someone who wants to know all of you, not just the parts you decide to show?" LaKrecia leaned forward again. "Sadie, I think Jarod might actually be serious. And I think that scares the shit out of you."

It did. God, it terrified her.

The server arrived with their food—LaKrecia's chicken and waffles, Sadie's salmon Benedict. They both ate in silence for a moment, the tension easing slightly.

"Tell me something," LaKrecia said after a while. "When you're with him—with Jarod—how do you feel?"

Sadie considered the question. Really considered it. "Powerful. Desired. In control. Like I can be exactly who I want to be without judgment."

"That's how you feel during sex. I asked how you feel when you're with *him*."

The distinction was subtle but significant. Sadie thought about lying in Jarod's arms, about the way he traced patterns on her skin, about the tenderness in his voice when he called her beautiful.

"Safe," she whispered. "I feel safe."

LaKrecia's smile was sad and knowing. "That's what you're running from, isn't it? Not intimacy. Not commitment. Safety. Being known. Being vulnerable."

Sadie's eyes stung. She blinked rapidly, refusing to let tears fall in the middle of a bougie brunch spot. "I can't afford to be vulnerable. Vulnerable women get hurt. Vulnerable women get overlooked, under-estimated, taken advantage of."

"Or," LaKrecia said gently, "vulnerable women get loved. Really, truly loved."

"I don't need love. I need success. Control. My own money, my own power, my own life."

"You can have all of that *and* someone who loves you. They're not mutually exclusive." LaKrecia speared a piece of chicken. "But you've convinced yourself they are. Why?"

Sadie was quiet for a long time. Then, finally, she started talking.

"My mother," she said softly. "You remember how she was."

LaKrecia nodded. She'd met Mrs. Monroe several times during college—a beautiful woman who'd given up her own career to support her husband's ambitions, only to be left high and dry when he traded her in for a younger model after thirty years of marriage.

"She loved him with everything she had," Sadie continued, her voice tight. "Put her dreams on hold, supported his career, made herself smaller so he could shine brighter. And when he didn't need her anymore? He threw her away like she was nothing. She had no career, no savings of her own, no identity outside of being his wife."

"Baby—"

"I promised myself I would never be her. Never be dependent on a man. Never let love make me weak or stupid or vulnerable. So I built these walls. Made these rules. If I keep everything compartmentalized, if I keep my heart separate from my body, then I can have the pleasure without the pain."

"But you're in pain anyway," LaKrecia pointed out. "Different pain, maybe. But pain nonetheless."

Sadie took a long drink of her margarita. "Better to hurt from loneliness than from betrayal."

"Is it though?" LaKrecia reached across the table again, and this time Sadie let her take her hand. "Sadie Monroe. Listen to me. You are not your mother. You're brilliant, successful, powerful in your own right. No man can take that from you unless you let him. And maybe—just maybe—Jarod isn't trying to take anything. Maybe he's trying to *add* to what you already have."

"Or maybe he just wants to conquer the fantasy. Men always want what they can't have."

"Have you considered that maybe he can't have you because you won't *let* him? That you're so busy protecting yourself that you're missing out on something real?"

Sadie pulled her hand away and sat back in her chair. "I can't think about this right now. I have a presentation Tuesday that could make or break my promotion to Senior VP. I need to focus."

"You always have something coming up that requires focus." LaKrecia's voice held a note of frustration. "There's always going to be another deal, another presentation, another reason to put your personal life on hold. When is it going to be enough? When are *you* going to be enough, just as you are?"

"When I'm sitting in the executive suite with my name on the door and a seven-figure salary. That's when."

LaKrecia sighed. "I hope it's worth it."

"It will be." But even as Sadie said it, she felt the hollowness of the words.

They finished their brunch with lighter conversation—office gossip, LaKrecia's latest dating disaster with a man who'd shown up to their date in Crocs, the new Issa Rae show they were both obsessed with. By the time they hugged goodbye on the sidewalk, the tension had eased, but Sadie could still feel LaKrecia's concerned gaze on her back as she walked away.

The rest of Sunday passed in its usual routine. Sadie went to the grocery store and bought ingredients for the week's meals—grilled chicken, salmon, vegetables, complex carbs. No processed foods, nothing that would make her sluggish or unfocused. She spent two hours in her kitchen, meal prepping and portioning everything into labeled containers.

Control. Discipline. Perfection.

By evening, she was reviewing her presentation for Tuesday's board meeting. The numbers were solid, her strategy was sound, her slides were impeccable. This was what she was good at—taking complex data and transforming it into a compelling narrative that made decision-makers open their wallets.

Her phone buzzed. Another text from Jarod's number.

"Been thinking about you all day. About what I said last night. I meant it, Sadie. Every word. When can I see you again?"

Her fingers hovered over the keyboard. She should shut this down. Should tell him they needed to take a break, re-establish boundaries, go back to the simple arrangement they'd had before things got complicated.

Instead, she found herself typing: *"Wednesday?"*

His response was immediate: *"I'll clear my schedule. Same place?"*

She should say yes. The Velvet Room was safe, familiar, part of the compartment where everything made sense.

But some reckless part of her—maybe the part that LaKrecia had awakened over brunch—made her type something different: *"Somewhere else. Somewhere we can talk."*

The three dots appeared and disappeared several times. Finally: *"There's a jazz club in the West End. Intimate, quiet. Good food. Would that work?"*

A jazz club. Public. Real. The kind of place where people went on actual dates, not just to fulfill physical needs.

"Send me the address," she typed before she could change her mind.

"It's a date."

The words on her screen felt weighted with significance. A date. Not an arrangement. Not a transaction. A date.

What the hell was she doing?

Sadie set down her phone and walked to her windows, looking out at the city as it transformed into its nighttime version. Lights flickered on in buildings across the skyline. The city that never slept, full of people living double lives, keeping secrets, building compartments.

She caught her reflection in the glass—somewhere between Corporate Sadie and After Hours Sadie. Neither fully one nor the other.

LaKrecia's words echoed in her head: *When do you just get to be... Sadie?*

She didn't have an answer. Didn't know if there even was an answer.

But Wednesday night, she'd show up at that jazz club. And maybe —just maybe—she'd let Jarod see a little bit more of the woman behind the fantasy.

Even if it scared her to death.

Her phone buzzed one more time. A text from LaKrecia: *"Proud of you for whatever you're about to do that's scaring you. That's where the growth happens. Love you, sis."*

Sadie smiled despite herself. Damn intuitive best friends and their ability to read minds across the city.

She typed back: *"Love you too. Even when you're annoyingly right about everything."*

"That's what best friends are for. Now go to bed and get some sleep. You look like hell."

"Thanks a lot."

"Anytime, boo."

Sadie did go to bed, though sleep was a long time coming. Her mind kept circling back to Wednesday night—to the jazz club, to Jarod, to the terrifying prospect of letting someone see behind the curtain.

When she finally drifted off, she dreamed of standing at that crossroads again. But this time, instead of two separate paths, they began to merge—slowly, tentatively, like two rivers flowing together into something new.

She didn't know if that was a dream or a nightmare.

She suspected she was about to find out.

CHAPTER 4
THE COLLISION BEGINS

MONDAY MORNING ARRIVED with the kind of crisp autumn air that made Sadie feel invincible. She'd slept surprisingly well after making the decision about Wednesday night, and woke with the clarity that came from good rest and strong coffee.

Corporate Sadie was in full effect.

She dressed in a charcoal gray power suit—Armani, tailored to perfection. The blazer nipped in at her waist before flaring slightly over her hips, and the trousers were cut to make her legs look impossibly long. Beneath the blazer, a silk camisole in deep emerald that brought out the golden undertones in her brown skin. Her hair was pulled back in a sleek low bun, not a strand out of place. Makeup was minimal but strategic—a bold lip in brick red, winged eyeliner that could cut glass.

She looked powerful. Untouchable. Exactly how she needed to look for the week ahead.

The morning passed in a blur of meetings and conference calls. Sadie was in her element—negotiating contracts, analyzing market trends, making decisions that would impact millions of dollars in revenue. This was her kingdom, and she ruled it with an iron fist wrapped in designer leather.

By lunchtime, her assistant Melissa appeared at her office door with a reminder. "Ms. Monroe, don't forget you have the Chamber of Commerce networking event tonight at six. The invitation is on your calendar."

Sadie glanced at her screen. Right. The quarterly networking mixer for young executives and entrepreneurs. She usually skipped these—they were more about schmoozing than substance—but her boss had specifically asked her to attend and "make connections." Translation: be visible, be impressive, remind everyone why she deserved that Senior VP position.

"Thanks, Melissa. I'll head straight there from the office."

"Should I have your dry cleaning delivered here so you can change?"

Sadie considered it, then shook her head. "No need. This suit will work fine."

Melissa's smile was knowing. "You could show up in a garbage bag and still be the most impressive person in the room."

"Flattery will get you everywhere. Speaking of which, how's that raise request coming along?"

"HR says they're reviewing it."

"Tell HR I said to approve it. You're the best assistant I've ever had, and I'm not losing you to another department because they won't pay you what you're worth."

Melissa's face lit up. "Thank you, Ms. Monroe. Really."

"Thank me by making sure I have coffee for this 2 PM meeting. The fancy kind from that place on Fifth."

"Already ordered. It'll be here in twenty minutes."

"See? Worth every penny." Sadie smiled as Melissa left, then turned back to her computer.

The afternoon flew by in a whirlwind of productivity. By 5:30, Sadie was shutting down her laptop and touching up her makeup in her office bathroom. She reapplied her lipstick, checked her teeth, made sure her bun was still sleek and perfect.

She looked good. Professional. Successful. Ready to network with the city's rising power players.

The event was being held at The Sterling—an upscale hotel with a rooftop lounge that offered stunning views of the city skyline. Sadie arrived fashionably late at 6:15, just as the crowd was reaching critical mass. She could hear the buzz of conversation and clinking glasses before she even stepped off the elevator.

The rooftop was transformed into an elegant networking space—high-top tables scattered throughout, a full bar at one end, a small stage where presumably someone would give a speech later. String lights were woven through the pergola overhead, giving everything a warm, inviting glow as the sun began its descent.

Sadie accepted a glass of champagne from a passing waiter and surveyed the crowd. The usual suspects—corporate climbers in expensive suits, entrepreneurs pitching their startups to anyone who would listen, a few politicians working the room for donations and endorsements.

She recognized several people from her industry and made her rounds, engaging in the kind of surface-level conversation that networking events required. Business cards were exchanged, LinkedIn connections were promised, vague mentions of "doing lunch sometime" were made with no real intention of follow-through.

It was exhausting and exhilarating in equal measure—this performance of success, this dance of ambition disguised as casual conversation.

Sadie was talking to a real estate developer about commercial properties when she felt it—that prickling awareness of being watched. She'd learned to trust that instinct over the years. In her nighttime world, knowing when eyes were on you was a survival skill.

She glanced around casually and locked eyes with a man standing near the bar.

He was tall—easily six-two—with warm brown skin and an athletic build that his navy suit couldn't quite hide. His hair was cut short with precision, and he had a neatly trimmed beard that framed a strong jawline. But it was his smile that caught her attention—genuine, reaching his eyes, the kind of smile that suggested he found something truly amusing rather than just performing politeness.

And he was looking directly at her.

Not the way men at the Velvet Room looked at her—that hungry, predatory gaze that said they wanted to consume her. This was different. Curious. Appreciative. Respectful.

Sadie felt something flutter in her chest. Something she hadn't felt in a long time when a man looked at her in a professional setting.

Interest.

She held his gaze for exactly three seconds before returning her attention to the real estate developer, who was still droning on about cap rates and ROI. But she was acutely aware of the man at the bar, could feel his presence like a magnetic pull.

"If you'll excuse me," she said smoothly to the developer, extracting herself from the conversation with practiced ease. "I need to refresh my drink."

She made her way toward the bar, her heels clicking against the rooftop deck. She didn't look directly at the man, but she knew he was watching her approach. She could feel the weight of his attention, and it sent a pleasant shiver down her spine.

Sadie reached the bar and ordered another champagne, letting herself settle into the moment. She'd learned long ago that the best way to intrigue someone was to not appear too eager.

"You're very good at that," a deep voice said beside her.

She turned slowly, letting a small smile play at her lips. Up close, he was even more attractive—warm brown eyes flecked with gold, a smile that transformed his entire face, and a presence that commanded space without demanding it.

"Good at what?" she asked, accepting her champagne from the bartender.

"The exit. You managed to extricate yourself from that conversation so smoothly he probably thinks it was his idea to let you go."

Sadie's smile widened. "Observation and flattery. Interesting opening gambit."

"Is that what this is? A gambit?" His eyes sparkled with amusement.

"Isn't it always, at these things? Everyone's playing chess, trying to make the right connections, say the right things, position themselves for the next opportunity."

"Cynical but accurate." He extended his hand. "TJ Morrison. And before you ask—yes, just the initials. My grandmother thought it sounded distinguished."

His hand was warm, his grip firm but not aggressive. Sadie noticed the calluses on his palm—this was someone who did more than push papers.

"Sadie Monroe. And my grandmother thought Sadie sounded 'sweet and approachable,' which is hilarious if you know me."

TJ's laugh was genuine and rich. "Something tells me you're a lot of things, but 'sweet and approachable' might not top the list."

"Is that your way of calling me intimidating?"

"It's my way of saying you look like someone who doesn't suffer fools gladly and has probably dismantled more than one ego in a boardroom."

"All accurate." Sadie took a sip of her champagne, studying him over the rim of her glass. "So what do you do, TJ Morrison? Besides observe people's networking tactics?"

"I'm in tech. Started a software company about five years ago—we develop security solutions for financial institutions. Boring stuff that keeps banks from getting hacked."

"Boring stuff that's probably very lucrative."

"It pays the bills." His smile was self-deprecating. "What about you?"

"Corporate finance. I'm at Meridian Capital—Senior Associate, gunning for Senior VP."

"Meridian? That's impressive. I've heard it's brutal there. Cutthroat."

"Only if you're not good at your job." Sadie's smile was sharp. "If you're excellent, it's paradise."

"And you're excellent."

It wasn't a question, but she answered anyway. "Always."

TJ studied her for a moment, and Sadie felt exposed in a way that was completely different from the Velvet Room. This wasn't sexual assessment—this was someone actually *seeing* her. Looking past the armor and trying to understand the person underneath.

"Can I ask you something?" he said.

"You can ask. I may not answer."

"Do you actually enjoy it? The corporate game, the ladder climbing, the constant competition?"

The question surprised her. Most people at these events talked about success like it was a given good, never questioning the cost or the why.

Sadie considered lying—giving him the polished answer about fulfillment and achievement. But something about the genuine curiosity in his eyes made her tell the truth.

"Sometimes," she said slowly. "I enjoy winning. Enjoy proving I'm the smartest person in the room, that I can outthink and outwork anyone. But the game itself?" She paused, surprised by her own honesty. "Sometimes it's exhausting. Performing excellence every single day, never letting your guard down, always having to be 'on.'"

"So why do it?"

"Because the alternative is being dependent on someone else. And I learned a long time ago that the only person you can truly rely on is yourself."

TJ nodded slowly. "That's both admirable and kind of sad."

"Sad?" Her defenses went up immediately.

"Not sad like pathetic. Sad like... lonely. Like you've built this fortress and made yourself queen, but there's no one inside the castle with you."

The observation hit too close to home. Sadie felt her walls slam into place, the friendly warmth she'd been feeling replaced by cool professionalism.

"That's quite an assumption to make about someone you just met."

"You're right. I apologize." TJ's expression shifted to genuine contrition. "That was presumptuous. I have a bad habit of trying to understand people too quickly. My ex-girlfriend used to say I analyzed everything to death."

"Ex-girlfriend?" Sadie raised an eyebrow. "Subtle way to let me know you're single?"

"Was it subtle? Damn. I thought I was being smooth." His self-deprecating smile was back, and despite herself, Sadie felt her walls lower slightly.

"Points for honesty, I suppose."

"How about points for buying you dinner?" TJ asked. "Not tonight —I can see you're working the room, and I don't want to interfere with your networking. But sometime this week? Somewhere we can actually talk without having to perform for a crowd?"

Sadie's mind raced. Wednesday she had plans with Jarod. Thursday she had a late meeting that would probably run past eight. Friday—

"Friday," she heard herself say. "Friday could work."

"Friday's perfect." TJ pulled out his phone. "Can I get your number? I'll text you some restaurant options and you can pick."

This was dangerous. This was blurring lines. This was exactly what she'd spent years avoiding—letting her professional life and personal life intersect.

But TJ wasn't asking her to the Velvet Room. He was asking her to dinner. A real dinner. The kind Corporate Sadie would go on, not After Hours Sadie.

She rattled off her number and watched him type it in.

"Got it. I'll text you tomorrow so you have mine." He slipped his phone back into his pocket. "I should let you get back to networking. But I'm really glad I talked to you, Sadie Monroe. You're... interesting."

"Interesting. That's a diplomatic word."

"It's an accurate word." His smile was warm. "Most people at these things are predictable. You're not. I like that."

He extended his hand again, and she shook it. But this time, his thumb brushed across her knuckles—a gesture so subtle it could have been accidental, but the look in his eyes said it wasn't.

"Until Friday," he said.

"Friday," she confirmed.

She watched him walk away, noting the confident set of his shoulders, the way he moved through the crowd with easy grace. Several people stopped him to talk, and he engaged with each one with what appeared to be genuine interest.

Sadie finished her champagne and ordered another, her mind spinning.

TJ Morrison was attractive, successful, intelligent, and seemed genuinely interested in her—the real her, not just the fantasy version. Under normal circumstances, that would be perfect.

But these weren't normal circumstances.

She had a date with Jarod on Wednesday. A date that was already pushing boundaries, already threatening to blur the careful lines she'd drawn between her two worlds.

And now she had a date with TJ on Friday. A man who existed firmly in her Corporate Sadie world, who knew nothing about the Velvet Room or the woman who walked through its doors seeking pleasure without complications.

"Girl, you better be careful." LaKrecia's voice echoed in her head. "This thing you're doing—these compartments—they're not sustainable."

Sadie felt the first tremor of unease. Like she was standing on a fault line, feeling the earth shift beneath her feet.

Her phone buzzed. A text from an unknown number: *"TJ here. Just making sure I typed your number right. Looking forward to Friday. - TJ"*

Before she could respond, another text came through. From Jarod: *"Counting down the hours until Wednesday. Can't stop thinking about you."*

Sadie stared at both messages on her screen. Two men. Two worlds. Two versions of herself.

And for the first time, she felt the walls between those worlds starting to crack.

She downed the rest of her champagne in one long swallow and dove back into the networking crowd, forcing a smile, making small talk, playing the game.

But in the back of her mind, a voice whispered a warning she couldn't quite ignore:

Something's about to break. And when it does, you won't be able to keep all the pieces separated anymore.

By the time Sadie left the event at 8:30, she'd collected fifteen business cards, made three potentially lucrative connections, and successfully avoided thinking too hard about Wednesday and Friday.

But as she drove home through the city streets, the reality of her situation settled over her like a weight.

She pulled into her parking garage and sat in her car for a long moment, engine off, staring at nothing.

Her phone buzzed again. LaKrecia: *"Lunch tomorrow? I have tea to spill about my latest disaster date."*

Sadie smiled despite herself and typed back: *"Can't tomorrow. Slammed with meetings. Wednesday?"*

"YOU have Wednesday plans. Remember? Jazz club?"

Damn. She'd forgotten she'd told LaKrecia about agreeing to meet Jarod somewhere public.

"Right. Thursday then?"

"Thursday works. And Sadie? Be careful. I love you."

"Love you too. And I'm always careful."

"That's what I'm worried about."

Sadie pocketed her phone and headed up to her apartment. Once inside, she kicked off her heels, poured herself a bourbon, and stood at her windows looking out at the city.

Somewhere out there, Jarod was probably thinking about Wednesday. And TJ was probably thinking about Friday.

And she was standing here, trying to figure out how to be two different people for two different men without losing herself in the process.

The bourbon burned going down, but not enough to quiet the voice in her head that kept asking the same question:

What happens when they find out about each other? What happens when your worlds collide?

Sadie didn't have an answer.

But she had a sinking feeling she was about to find out.

CHAPTER 5
DIFFERENT KIND OF CHEMISTRY

THE WEEK CRAWLED by with agonizing slowness. Tuesday's board presentation went flawlessly—Sadie had the executives eating out of her hand, and by the end of the meeting, her boss pulled her aside to tell her the Senior VP position was "looking very promising." She should have been elated. Instead, she felt oddly detached, like she was watching her own success from outside her body.

Wednesday arrived wrapped in anticipation and anxiety.

Sadie changed outfits three times before settling on something that walked the line between both her worlds—a deep plum wrap dress that hugged her curves but wasn't overtly sexy, paired with strappy heels and minimal jewelry. Her hair fell in soft waves past her shoulders. Makeup was natural but polished—she looked beautiful without looking like she was trying too hard.

She caught herself in the mirror and paused. Who was she dressing for? Corporate Sadie or After Hours Sadie?

The answer unsettled her: neither. She was trying to be... just Sadie.

Whatever that meant.

The jazz club—Mingus Room—was tucked away in the West End, the kind of place that didn't advertise because it didn't need to. Low lighting, intimate tables, a small stage where a quartet was playing something smoky and sensual. The crowd was an eclectic mix of artists, intellectuals, and lovers seeking ambiance.

Sadie arrived at 8 PM sharp and immediately spotted Jarod at a corner table. He stood when he saw her, and the smile that spread across his face made her stomach flip.

He looked different outside the Velvet Room. Still breathtaking and handsome in dark jeans and a charcoal button-down, but more... relaxed. Human. Real.

"You came," he said, and there was genuine relief in his voice.

"I said I would."

"I know. But part of me thought you might change your mind." He pulled out her chair, and she sat, hyper-aware of his proximity as he pushed it in behind her.

When he took his seat across from her, there was a moment of awkwardness—the strange limbo of two people who knew each other's bodies intimately but were navigating the unfamiliar territory of actual conversation.

"This place is beautiful," Sadie said, breaking the silence.

"I hoped you'd like it. My boy TJ turned me onto it. He's always finding these hidden gems around the city."

Sadie's heart stopped. "TJ?"

"Yeah, my best friend. We go way back—college roommates, started businesses around the same time, practically brothers. He's got impeccable taste in everything except women." Jarod laughed. "Man falls hard and fast for the wrong ones every time."

The room tilted slightly. Sadie reached for the water glass on the table, buying time to compose her face.

"What—" She cleared her throat. "What kind of business is he in?"

"Tech. Security software for financial institutions. Boring stuff that makes him stupid money." Jarod smiled with obvious affection. "He's good people though. Actually, he just met someone at some networking thing earlier this week. Been talking about her nonstop—says she's different from his usual type. More driven, ambitious. He's taking her to dinner Friday."

The water glass felt slippery in Sadie's hand. This couldn't be happening. The universe couldn't be this cruel.

"What's her name?" The question came out steadier than she felt.

"He didn't say. You know how TJ is—superstitious about jinxing things before the first date." Jarod reached across the table and took her hand, oblivious to the panic rising in her chest. "But enough about him. I want to talk about you. About us."

There is no us, Sadie wanted to scream. *There can't be, because your best friend is TJ Morrison, and I have a date with him in two days, and this is a disaster.*

But instead, she forced a smile. "What do you want to know?"

"Everything." His thumb traced circles on her palm—an unconsciously intimate gesture that would have melted her under different circumstances. "Start with the basics. What do you do during the day?"

She should lie. Should give him a vague answer. But the truth was already tangled enough without adding more deception.

"I work in corporate finance. Meridian Capital. I'm a Senior Associate."

His eyebrows rose. "Meridian? That's heavy. I've heard that place is brutal."

"It can be. But I'm good at what I do."

"I don't doubt that for a second." His smile was warm. "What else? What do you do when you're not crushing it at work or..." he lowered his voice, "meeting me at the Velvet Room?"

"I don't know. Work out. Meal prep. Read sometimes. Hang out with my best friend LaKrecia." It sounded boring when she said it out loud. Her life outside of work and the Velvet Room was essentially... maintenance. Preparing her body and mind for the next performance.

"What do you read?"

The question surprised her. "Mostly business books. Leadership theory, market analysis, that kind of thing."

"No fiction? No guilty pleasures?"

"I don't have time for guilty pleasures."

"Sadie." He squeezed her hand gently. "Everything you just described—work, working out, prepping for more work—that's not living. That's... existing in service of productivity."

"Says the man who runs his own business." But there was no heat in her words.

"True. But I also play basketball on Saturdays, go to concerts, travel when I can, spend time with people I care about. Life can't just be about climbing the ladder. At some point, you have to stop and ask what you're climbing toward."

The waiter arrived to take their drink orders—old fashioned for him, dirty martini for her—giving Sadie a moment to gather herself.

When the waiter left, Jarod leaned forward. "I'm not trying to criticize you. I just... I see this driven, brilliant, incredible woman, and I wonder if anyone's ever told her she's allowed to just... be. Without performing. Without proving anything."

"My mother told me that once," Sadie heard herself say. "Right before my father left her for his secretary. Told me to just 'be myself' and 'love would be enough.' Turned out love wasn't enough when yourself doesn't have a 401k or career prospects."

Jarod was quiet for a long moment. "I'm sorry that happened to her. To you. But not all men are your father, Sadie."

"Maybe not. But why take the risk?" She pulled her hand back, needing space. "I've built a good life. I'm successful, independent, in control. Why complicate it?"

"Because maybe control is overrated. Maybe the best things in life are the ones we don't plan for."

Their drinks arrived. Sadie took a long sip of her martini, the alcohol burning away some of the anxiety coiled in her chest.

The quartet on stage transitioned to a new song—something slow and sultry that wrapped around them like silk.

"Dance with me," Jarod said suddenly.

"What?"

"Dance with me. Here. Now." He stood and extended his hand. "No agenda. No expectations. Just two people moving to music."

Sadie glanced around. A few other couples were swaying together near the stage, lost in their own worlds. The lighting was low enough that they'd blend into the shadows.

Against her better judgment, she took his hand.

He led her to a quiet corner of the small dance floor and pulled her close—closer than was strictly appropriate for a first real date, but natural for two people who'd already learned every inch of each other's bodies.

His hand settled on the small of her back. Hers rested on his chest, feeling his heartbeat beneath her palm. They moved together slowly, finding a rhythm that had nothing to do with sex and everything to do with simply being present.

"You're tense," he murmured near her ear.

"I'm always tense."

"Even when I'm inside you, you're tense. Like you're waiting for something to go wrong."

The bluntness of his words in this intimate setting sent heat flooding through her. "Jarod—"

"I'm not trying to start something. I'm just making an observation." His hand pressed more firmly against her back, drawing her infinitesimally closer. "What would it take for you to relax? To trust?"

"I don't know." The honest answer. "I've been in control for so long, I don't know how to let go."

"But you do let go. I've watched you. I've felt you come apart in my arms."

"That's different. That's physical."

"Is it? Because from where I'm standing, letting someone pleasure you—really pleasure you—requires trust. Vulnerability. You let me see you at your most unguarded."

Sadie pulled back slightly to look at him. "That's not the same as emotional vulnerability."

"Isn't it though?" His eyes searched hers. "What's the difference? In both cases, you're giving someone the power to affect you. To make you feel things you can't control."

She didn't have an answer for that. The song shifted into something even slower, more intimate. Around them, other couples held each other close, lost in their own private worlds.

"I like you, Sadie," Jarod said quietly. "Not just your body, though that's... incredible. But *you*. The way your mind works. The walls you've built and the strength it took to build them. I want to know what's behind those walls."

"What if there's nothing there? What if the walls are all there is?"

"I don't believe that for a second."

They swayed in silence for a while longer. Sadie let herself relax into him—just a fraction, just enough to feel the solid warmth of his body against hers. To remember what it felt like to be held for reasons that had nothing to do with sex.

It felt dangerous. And wonderful. And terrifying.

When the song ended, they returned to their table. The waiter appeared to take their food orders—she got the salmon, he got the steak—and the conversation shifted to safer topics. He told her about his business, the ups and downs of entrepreneurship, his family scattered across the South. She found herself genuinely interested, asking questions, laughing at his stories.

"You have a beautiful laugh," he said at one point. "I've never heard it before. Not really."

"I laugh."

"You smile. You make sounds during sex that could raise the dead. But laugh? Like this—genuine, unguarded? First time."

She realized he was right. At the Velvet Room, everything was performance. Even her pleasure, as real as it was, existed within a carefully controlled framework. This—this conversation, this laughter, this easy back-and-forth—was different.

It was real.

And real was dangerous.

Their food arrived, and they ate while the quartet played on. The salmon was perfectly cooked, flaky and seasoned to perfection. Jarod insisted she try his steak, feeding her a bite from his fork with an intimacy that felt almost more personal than anything they'd done at the Velvet Room.

"So," he said, setting down his fork. "Level with me. How do you feel about tonight? About this—" he gestured between them, "—whatever this is becoming?"

Sadie took a long sip of her martini before answering. "Honestly? Terrified."

"Of me?"

"Of this. Of letting it be real. Of what happens when real gets complicated."

"What if it doesn't get complicated? What if it just... is?"

"Nothing is ever simple. Especially not when—" She stopped herself.

"When what?"

When your best friend is taking me to dinner Friday. When I'm living two completely separate lives. When everything is about to come crashing down around me.

"When people have expectations," she finished. "Once things become real, there are expectations. Demands. Obligations. I lose my freedom."

"Or maybe you gain something better than freedom." He reached across the table and took her hand again. "Partnership. Someone to share the weight. Someone who sees all of you—not just the parts you choose to show—and wants to stay anyway."

His words carved into her chest, finding all the soft places she'd tried to armor.

"I don't know how to do that," she whispered.

"Then let me teach you." His thumb brushed across her knuckles. "I'm not asking you to tear down all your walls overnight. Just... maybe let me peek over them once in a while. Let me see the woman you are when you're not performing for anyone."

Sadie felt tears prick her eyes and blinked them away furiously. She didn't cry. Crying was loss of control, and control was all she had.

"I have to tell you something," she heard herself say.

"Okay."

"I—" She stopped. What could she even say? *I'm going on a date with your best friend Friday. I met him at a networking event and he doesn't know about you or the Velvet Room or any of it. I'm living a double life and it's about to blow up in spectacular fashion.*

"It's okay," Jarod said gently. "Whatever it is, you can tell me."

But could she? Could she really?

Before she could answer, Jarod's phone buzzed on the table. He glanced at it and smiled. "Speaking of TJ—he's asking if I want to grab drinks after his dinner Friday. Man's already planning his post-date debrief." He looked up at Sadie. "You want to meet him sometime? I think you two would get along. You're both workaholics who need to learn how to relax."

The irony was so thick Sadie nearly choked on it.

"Maybe," she managed. "Sometime."

Jarod pocketed his phone and leaned back in his chair, studying her. "You got quiet. What's going on in that beautiful head of yours?"

Everything. Nothing. The walls are closing in and I don't know how to stop it.

"I'm just... processing. This—" she gestured around them, at the intimate table and the jazz and the realness of it all, "—this is different for me. I don't do dates. I don't do... this."

"I know. That's why it means so much that you're here." His smile was soft, genuine. "I'm not trying to rush you, Sadie. I just want you to know that I see you. All the pieces you're trying to hide. And I'm not going anywhere."

The words should have been comforting. Instead, they felt like a noose tightening around her neck.

They finished dinner with easier conversation—surface topics that didn't require vulnerability. By the time they left the jazz club at 11 PM, Sadie felt emotionally exhausted in a way that had nothing to do with physical exertion.

Jarod walked her to her car in the parking garage, his hand resting lightly on her lower back. When they reached her Mercedes, he turned her to face him.

"Thank you for tonight," he said. "For taking a chance. For letting me see more of you."

"I didn't really let you see much."

"You let me see enough." He cupped her face gently, his thumb brushing across her cheek. "Can I kiss you?"

The question shouldn't have surprised her—they'd done far more than kiss at the Velvet Room. But asking permission here, in this context, made it different. Made it mean something.

"Yes," she breathed.

He leaned in slowly, giving her time to change her mind. When his lips met hers, it was nothing like the passionate, desperate kisses they'd shared before. This was tender. Searching. A question instead of a demand.

Sadie felt herself melting into it, her hands coming up to rest on his chest. He kissed her like she was something precious, something to be savored rather than consumed.

When he finally pulled back, they were both breathing harder.

"I'll call you," he said.

"Okay."

"Sadie?" He waited until she met his eyes. "I meant what I said. I'm not going anywhere. Whatever you're afraid of—whatever walls you need to keep up for now—I can wait. I will wait."

The promise felt like both a blessing and a curse.

She watched him walk away, then sat in her car for a long moment before starting the engine.

Her phone buzzed. A text from TJ: *"Looking forward to Friday! I made reservations at Essence—8 PM. Hope that works for you."*

Essence. One of the most romantic restaurants in the city. The kind of place you took someone when you wanted to make an impression.

Sadie stared at the message, then at the club where Jarod had just treated her to one of the most intimate evenings of her life.

She was standing at the edge of a cliff, and she could feel herself starting to fall.

Thursday passed in a blur of meetings and conference calls. Sadie buried herself in work, trying not to think about Wednesday night or Friday dinner. But late Thursday evening, as she was preparing to leave the office, LaKrecia called.

"Lunch tomorrow," LaKrecia said without preamble. "And don't tell me you're busy. I'm invoking best friend emergency protocols."

"I have a dinner tomorrow night—"

"I know. That's why we're having lunch. You're about to walk into a minefield, and I need to make sure you're not completely self-destructing."

"I'm fine."

"Baby girl, you're many things, but fine ain't one of them right now. Lunch. Marcel's. Noon. Be there."

She hung up before Sadie could argue.

Friday morning, Sadie stood in front of her closet trying to decide what to wear to dinner with TJ. Everything felt wrong—too sexy, too corporate, too casual. Finally, she settled on a black midi dress with a modest neckline and long sleeves. Elegant. Sophisticated. The kind of dress Corporate Sadie would wear.

She paired it with simple gold jewelry and nude heels. Hair down in soft waves. Makeup natural and glowing. She looked beautiful in a completely different way than she did at the Velvet Room—polished rather than sultry, elegant rather than seductive.

LaKrecia took one look at her over lunch and shook her head.

"Girl, you look like you're going to a funeral, not a date."

"It's a conservative choice."

"It's a safe choice. Which means you're scared." LaKrecia set down her fork. "Talk to me. What's really going on?"

And Sadie found herself spilling everything—meeting TJ at the networking event, the date with Jarod Wednesday night, the horrifying realization that they were best friends, the impossibility of the situation she'd created.

When she finished, LaKrecia was quiet for a long moment.

"Well," she finally said. "You've really done it this time."

"I know."

"What are you going to do?"

"I don't know. Cancel on TJ? Tell Jarod the truth? Pretend it's not happening and hope the universe takes pity on me?"

"None of those are good options."

"I'm aware."

LaKrecia reached across the table and took Sadie's hand. "Baby, I love you. You know I do. But this—this is what happens when you try to live two separate lives. Eventually, they collide. And people get hurt."

"I never meant for this to happen."

"I know. But intention doesn't matter when the damage is done." She squeezed Sadie's hand. "You need to make a choice. Tonight. After your date with TJ, you need to figure out who you want to be and who you want to be with. Because you can't keep both men in separate boxes forever."

"What if I don't want either of them? What if I just want my life back—simple, compartmentalized, under control?"

"Is that really what you want? Or are you just scared of what happens when you let someone in?"

Sadie didn't answer. Couldn't answer.

LaKrecia sighed. "Go to dinner tonight. Be present. Be honest—at least with yourself. And then decide. But Sadie? Whatever you choose, own it. Don't be a coward about this. These men deserve better than that. And so do you."

Essence was everything its reputation promised—intimate lighting, floor-to-ceiling windows overlooking the river, tables spaced far enough apart to create privacy. The kind of restaurant where proposals happened, where anniversaries were celebrated, where serious conversations about the future took place.

Sadie arrived at exactly 8 PM, her stomach a knot of anxiety and anticipation. The hostess led her through the dining room, and she spotted TJ immediately. He stood when he saw her, and the smile that spread across his face was so genuine, so full of uncomplicated pleasure, that she felt a pang of guilt pierce through her chest.

He looked incredible in a tailored charcoal suit with a crisp white shirt, no tie. The top button was undone, giving him a relaxed elegance that suggested confidence without trying too hard.

"Sadie. Wow." His eyes traveled over her, appreciative but respectful. "You look absolutely stunning."

"Thank you. You clean up pretty well yourself." She let him pull out her chair, hyper-aware of his proximity as he pushed it in.

When he took his seat across from her, there was a moment where they just looked at each other. His smile was warm, open, and something in her chest twisted painfully.

He doesn't know. He has no idea who I really am.

"I'm really glad you said yes to this," TJ said. "I wasn't sure you would. You seemed... guarded at the networking event."

"I'm always guarded at those things. Everyone's performing, trying to present the best version of themselves."

"And now? Are you still performing?"

The question was gentle but direct. Sadie considered lying, then decided LaKrecia was right—she owed him at least honesty with herself.

"I'm trying not to be. But it's a hard habit to break."

"I appreciate that." The waiter appeared to pour their water and present wine menus. TJ glanced at her. "Red or white?"

"I trust your judgment."

He ordered a bottle of Pinot Noir—nothing too pretentious, but quality—and turned his attention back to her. "So. Sadie Monroe. I've been thinking about you all week."

"Have you?" She took a sip of water, trying to calm her nerves.

"Constantly. Which is unlike me, to be honest. I usually play it cool, wait a respectable amount of time before texting. But I found myself wanting to reach out every day. Had to physically restrain myself from coming across as desperate."

His self-deprecating honesty was disarming. "What stopped you?"

"My best friend Jarod. He told me I needed to chill, stop overthinking, and just let things develop naturally." TJ laughed. "He's usually the impulsive one, and I'm the overthinker. But something about you has me all twisted around."

Sadie's mouth went dry. She reached for her water again. "Tell me about Jarod. You mentioned you two go way back?"

"College roommates turned business partners turned brothers. We've been through everything together—failed startups, bad relationships, family drama. He's the one person who knows me completely and still chooses to deal with me."

"That's... rare. To have someone who really knows you."

"It is. Do you have someone like that?"

"My best friend LaKrecia. We've been tight since college. She's seen me at my worst and somehow still loves me."

"Then you understand. That kind of friendship is gold." TJ leaned forward slightly. "Actually, I was thinking—if this goes well, maybe we could all get together sometime. You, me, Jarod, LaKrecia. I think you'd really like him."

Sadie felt the walls closing in. "Maybe. Let's see how tonight goes first."

"Fair enough." The sommelier arrived with their wine, going through the tasting ritual with TJ. Once their glasses were poured and they were alone again, TJ raised his. "To new possibilities."

She clinked her glass against his, the crystal ringing clear in the intimate space. "To possibilities."

The wine was excellent—smooth with hints of cherry and oak. It warmed her from the inside, loosening some of the tension in her shoulders.

"So," TJ said, setting down his glass. "You said at the networking event that sometimes the corporate game is exhausting. If you could do anything—money and obligations aside—what would it be?"

No one had ever asked her that question. In her world, success was the goal. Period. The idea of wanting something different, something more, wasn't part of the equation.

"I don't know," she said slowly. "I've been focused on climbing the ladder for so long, I'm not sure I know what else there is."

"There's lots else. Travel, hobbies, passions that have nothing to do with profit margins and quarterly reports." He tilted his head, studying her. "When you were a kid, before the world told you what you should be, what did you want?"

Sadie felt something stir in her memory—a younger version of herself, unburdened by her parents' divorce and her mother's cautionary tale.

"I wanted to be a dancer," she heard herself say. "Ballet, specifically. I took classes from when I was five until I was sixteen. I was good, too. My teacher said I had real potential."

"What happened?"

"Reality happened. My father left, money got tight, and dance wasn't practical. So I focused on things that would guarantee financial security. Business school. Corporate America. Success."

"Do you ever miss it? Dancing?"

"Sometimes. Late at night, when I can't sleep, I'll put on music and just... move. Nothing choreographed. Just feeling the rhythm, letting my body remember what it used to know."

TJ's expression softened. "That's beautiful. And kind of heartbreaking."

"It's practical. Dancing doesn't pay bills or build retirement accounts."

"No, but it feeds the soul. And what good is financial security if your soul is starving?"

The question hit too close to home. Sadie looked away, out the window at the river flowing past, dark and endless.

"You're very philosophical for a tech guy."

"Tech is just what I do. It's not who I am." He reached across the table, his hand stopping just short of touching hers—offering but not demanding. "I build security systems, which is ironic because I'm constantly challenging myself to be more vulnerable, more open. Life's too short to just exist in the safe zones."

Sadie looked at his hand, so close to hers. She could feel the warmth radiating from his skin. Slowly, she closed the distance, letting her fingers brush against his.

His smile was brilliant.

The waiter arrived to take their orders. TJ ordered the duck breast; Sadie chose the seafood risotto. When they were alone again, he didn't let go of her hand.

"Tell me something else," he said. "Something real. Something you don't usually share."

Sadie thought about it. "I'm afraid of becoming my mother."

"How so?"

"She gave up everything for my father. Her career, her dreams, her identity. And when he left, she had nothing. No skills, no prospects, no sense of who she was outside of being his wife. I watched her fall apart, and I promised myself I'd never be that vulnerable. Never need someone so badly that losing them would destroy me."

TJ was quiet for a moment, his thumb tracing gentle circles on her palm. "I understand that fear. But Sadie—there's a difference between healthy independence and isolating yourself so completely that you can't let anyone in. One makes you strong. The other makes you lonely."

"LaKrecia says the same thing."

"Then LaKrecia is smart. Listen to her." He squeezed her hand gently. "I'm not asking you to give up your independence or your ambition. I'm just asking you to consider that maybe—just maybe—you can be successful *and* let someone care about you. They're not mutually exclusive."

"Everyone says that until caring turns into controlling. Until 'let me help' becomes 'let me decide for you.'"

"Is that what happened with your parents?"

Sadie nodded slowly. "My father made all the decisions. Where they lived, how money was spent, what my mother could or couldn't do. She thought it was love—him taking care of everything. But really, it was control. And when he was done with her, she didn't even know how to open her own bank account."

"That's not love. That's manipulation dressed up as care." TJ's voice was firm. "Real partnership means two whole people choosing to build something together. Not one person absorbing the other."

"How do you know the difference?"

"You ask questions. You pay attention. You notice if someone's trying to support your dreams or redirect them. If they celebrate your wins or feel threatened by them. If they want to know you or change you."

Their food arrived, beautifully plated and aromatic. They ate in comfortable silence for a few minutes, but Sadie's mind was spinning.

Everything TJ was saying made sense. He seemed genuine, thoughtful, emotionally intelligent. Under normal circumstances, he'd be exactly the kind of man she should want—successful but not arrogant, confident but not controlling, interested in her mind as much as her appearance.

But these weren't normal circumstances.

"Can I ask you something?" she said.

"Anything."

"Why me? You could probably date anyone. Why are you interested in someone who's admittedly guarded and emotionally unavailable?"

TJ set down his fork and met her eyes directly. "Because I see who you are underneath the armor. And she's fascinating. You're brilliant, driven, successful—all the surface stuff. But there's also this... hunger in you. Like you're searching for something you can't name. Something that all the boardroom victories and promotions won't satisfy."

"And you think you're what I'm searching for?" She didn't mean it to sound challenging, but it came out that way.

"No. I think *you* are what you're searching for. The real you. The whole person, not just the compartmentalized pieces." He leaned forward. "And I'd like to be there when you find her. If you'll let me."

Sadie felt tears prick her eyes again. Twice in one week—that had to be some kind of record.

"What if the real me disappoints you?"

"What if she doesn't?" He smiled. "What if she's even more incredible than the version you show the world?"

The conversation shifted to lighter topics—his family in Atlanta, her relationship with LaKrecia, favorite travel destinations, embarrassing stories from college. Sadie found herself laughing genuinely, relaxing into the conversation in a way she hadn't expected.

TJ was easy to talk to. He listened more than he spoke, asked thoughtful questions, seemed genuinely interested in her answers rather than just waiting for his turn to talk. And when he did share things about himself, they were real—not the polished networking version, but actual vulnerabilities and uncertainties.

By the time dessert arrived—chocolate lava cake they agreed to share—Sadie realized she was having a genuinely good time. Not performing. Not calculating her next move. Just... being.

It was terrifying and exhilarating in equal measure.

"I have to confess something," TJ said as they finished the last bites of dessert. "I googled you after the networking event."

"Oh God. What did you find?"

"Your LinkedIn profile, which is impressive as hell. A few mentions in business journals about deals you've closed. And exactly zero personal information, which I found intriguing. It's like you exist only in the professional sphere."

"I value my privacy."

"I respect that. But it also makes me wonder—who is Sadie when she's not closing deals and commanding boardrooms? What does she do for fun?"

She goes to exclusive clubs and has anonymous encounters with men who don't know her real name, Sadie thought. *She transforms into someone powerful and free and desired. She escapes into pleasure because it's the only place she doesn't have to think or plan or perform.*

"I work out," she said instead. "Spend time with LaKrecia. Read sometimes."

"That's still pretty productivity-focused. What about just... play? Doing something for no reason except that it's enjoyable?"

"I don't really know how to do that."

"Then maybe I can teach you." His smile was warm. "If you let me take you out again, I mean. No pressure—I just really enjoyed tonight and would love to see you again."

Sadie's heart hammered. She should say no. Should end this before it got more complicated. Should protect him from the inevitable hurt when everything came crashing down.

But looking at his open, hopeful expression, she found herself nodding. "I'd like that."

His smile could have lit up the entire restaurant. "Yeah?"

"Yeah. But TJ—I need you to understand something. I'm not easy. I have walls and issues and a tendency to self-sabotage when things get real. If you're looking for simple and uncomplicated, I'm not your girl."

"Lucky for you, I don't want simple. I want real. And real is always complicated." He signaled for the check. "Besides, anything worth having is worth working for. Right?"

The waiter brought the check, and despite Sadie's offer to split it, TJ insisted on paying. "Old-fashioned, I know. But this was my invitation. Next time, you can get it."

Next time. The words hung in the air between them, full of promise and possibility.

They left the restaurant and walked through the parking lot to her car. The night air was cool, and Sadie wrapped her arms around herself. TJ immediately shrugged out of his jacket and draped it over her shoulders.

"I'm fine—"

"Humor me," he said with a smile.

His jacket was warm from his body heat and smelled like his cologne—something clean and woodsy. Sadie found herself pulling it tighter around her shoulders.

When they reached her Mercedes, TJ turned her to face him. For a moment, they just stood there, the space between them charged with anticipation.

"I had a really great time tonight," he said.

"Me too. Surprisingly."

"Surprisingly?" He laughed. "I'm going to take that as a compliment."

"It is. I usually hate first dates. But this was... nice."

"Just nice? You're really good for my ego." But his eyes were dancing with humor.

"Fine. It was wonderful. You're easy to talk to, you listen, and you don't seem threatened by my success."

"Why would I be threatened? Your success is part of what makes you attractive. I want a partner, not a dependent."

The word "partner" made her stomach flip. It suggested future. Commitment. Things she'd spent years avoiding.

TJ seemed to sense her internal panic. "Too much too fast?"

"Maybe a little."

"Fair enough. Let me just say this: I really like you, Sadie Monroe. And I'd like to see where this goes. No pressure, no expectations—just two people getting to know each other and seeing what develops. Can you handle that?"

She wanted to say no. Wanted to tell him this was a mistake, that she wasn't who he thought she was, that she'd disappoint him eventually.

But looking at his warm brown eyes, full of hope and genuine interest, she found herself nodding. "I can handle that."

"Good." He leaned in slowly, giving her time to pull away. When she didn't, his lips met hers in a kiss that was gentle, questioning, sweet.

It was nothing like kissing Jarod—no desperation or hunger, no race toward physical release. This was exploratory, almost tentative. A first kiss that promised more without demanding it.

When he pulled back, they were both breathing a little harder.

"I'll call you," he said. "Maybe we can do something this weekend? Something fun and non-productive. Introduce you to the concept of play."

"I'll think about it."

"I'll take it." He opened her car door for her, waiting until she was settled before closing it. Then he leaned down to the window. "Drive safe. Text me when you get home so I know you made it okay."

"That's very—"

"Old-fashioned, I know. But humor me."

She found herself smiling. "Okay."

She watched him walk to his own car—a sleek BMW—before starting her engine. As she pulled out of the parking lot, she caught a glimpse of him in her rearview mirror, standing beside his car and watching her leave with that same warm smile.

Her phone buzzed before she'd even left the parking lot.

TJ: *Already missing you. Is that too much? That's probably too much. Sorry.*

Despite everything—the guilt, the anxiety, the tangled mess she'd created—Sadie found herself smiling.

Sadie: *It's a little much. But kind of sweet.*

TJ: *I can work with "kind of sweet." Drive safe, beautiful.*

She drove through the city streets on autopilot, her mind a whirlwind of conflicting emotions. The date had been wonderful. TJ was everything she should want—kind, successful, emotionally available, genuinely interested in knowing her.

But.

There was always a but.

Her phone buzzed again. This time, it was Jarod: *Hope you had a good Friday. Been thinking about Wednesday night. About you. When can I see you again?*

Sadie pulled over into an empty parking lot and stared at both messages on her screen.

Two men. Both incredible in completely different ways. Both interested in her. Both completely unaware of the other's existence in her life.

And both best friends.

The universe's sense of humor was cruel.

She thought about what LaKrecia had said at lunch: *You need to make a choice. These men deserve better. And so do you.*

But how could she choose when each man represented something different she needed? Jarod saw the passionate, free version of herself—the woman who embraced pleasure without apology. TJ saw the successful, driven version—the woman who could be vulnerable and still maintain her strength.

The problem was, neither saw the whole picture. Neither knew about the other. Neither understood that she was splitting herself into pieces, trying to give each of them the version they wanted while losing track of who she actually was.

Her phone rang. LaKrecia.

"How'd it go?" her friend asked without preamble.

"It was perfect. He was perfect. We had an amazing time."

"I hear a 'but' coming."

"But I don't know what I'm doing, Krecia. I really like him. And I really like Jarod. And they're best friends, and this is all going to explode, and—"

"Breathe," LaKrecia commanded. "Just breathe for a second."

Sadie inhaled deeply, then exhaled slowly.

"Better?"

"Marginally."

"Okay. Listen to me. You have two options here. One: you come clean to both of them right now, before this goes any further. Tell TJ about Jarod, tell Jarod about TJ, and let the chips fall where they may. Option two: you walk away from both of them and go back to your compartmentalized life."

"What if there's an option three?"

"There's not. You can't keep seeing both of them without them finding out. This is a small city, Sadie. They're best friends. Eventually—probably soon—they're going to figure it out. And when they do, you're going to lose both of them *and* look like a manipulative liar. Is that what you want?"

"No."

"Then choose. Tonight. Right now. Who do you want?"

Sadie closed her eyes. She thought about Wednesday night with Jarod—the intimacy, the vulnerability, the way he wanted to know her beyond the physical. She thought about tonight with TJ—the easy conversation, the gentle kiss, the promise of something real and uncomplicated.

"I don't know," she whispered.

"Then you're not ready for either of them." LaKrecia's voice was gentle but firm. "And baby, that's okay. But you need to tell them that. You need to be honest that you're not in a place to give anyone all of you right now."

"What if I never am? What if this is just who I am—compartmentalized and unavailable?"

"Then you need to own that and stop stringing people along. But Sadie? I don't think that's who you are. I think you're scared. And that's different."

They talked for another twenty minutes, LaKrecia alternating between tough love and gentle encouragement. By the time they hung up, Sadie felt marginally clearer, though no less anxious.

She drove home slowly, letting the city lights blur past. When she finally pulled into her parking garage, she sat in her car for a long moment before heading upstairs.

Once inside her apartment, she poured herself a bourbon and stood at her windows, looking out at the city that held all her secrets.

Her phone buzzed. A text from TJ: *Made it home safe. Already looking forward to seeing you again. Sweet dreams, Sadie.*

Then another from Jarod: *No pressure on when we see each other again. Just wanted you to know Wednesday night meant something to me. You mean something to me.*

Sadie stared at both messages, her chest tight.

She typed out three different responses to each of them, then deleted them all.

Finally, she turned off her phone and finished her bourbon in silence.

Monday, she would have to make a choice. Monday, she would have to figure out who she wanted to be and who she wanted to be with.

But tonight, she was just going to stand at her windows and let herself feel everything—the guilt, the desire, the fear, the longing. All the messy emotions she'd spent years compartmentalizing and controlling.

For once, she was just going to feel.

And tomorrow, she'd figure out what to do about it.

CHAPTER 6
THE UNRAVELING THREAD

MONDAY MORNING ARRIVED TOO QUICKLY, dragging Sadie from restless dreams into harsh reality. She'd barely slept, her mind replaying Friday night on an endless loop—TJ's gentle kiss, his warm smile, the promise of something real. And underneath it all, the memory of Wednesday with Jarod, the way he'd looked at her like she was the only woman in the world.

She went through her morning routine on autopilot—shower, coffee, the armor of a black Dolce & Gabbana suit that made her feel invincible even when she felt anything but. By the time she walked into Meridian Capital at 7:30 AM, Corporate Sadie was firmly in place.

The mask was perfect. No one could see the cracks.

Her assistant Melissa was already at her desk, looking far too cheerful for a Monday morning. "Ms. Monroe! You have fresh coffee waiting, and your 9 AM with Mr. Patterson got moved to 10. Also—" she lowered her voice conspiratorially, "—there's a delivery for you."

"A delivery?"

Melissa pointed to Sadie's office, her smile knowing.

Sadie pushed open her door and stopped short. On her desk sat a beautiful arrangement of purple flowers—deep violet irises mixed with lavender roses and darker purple calla lilies. The arrangement was stunning, sophisticated, and unmistakably deliberate in its color choice.

Her heart hammered as she approached the card.

"You said purple was your favorite. I've been thinking about everything you told me Wednesday night. About wanting to see more of the real you. These are a promise—I'm not going anywhere. - J"

Jarod. He'd remembered. A throwaway comment about her favorite color during their vulnerable conversation at the jazz club, and he'd remembered.

Sadie sank into her desk chair, staring at the flowers. They were gorgeous. Thoughtful. Exactly the kind of gesture that would make any woman feel seen and valued.

Her phone buzzed with a text.

TJ: *Good morning, beautiful. Hope you slept well. I keep replaying Friday night. When can I see you again?*

Sadie closed her eyes. This was unsustainable. LaKrecia was right—she needed to make a choice. But how could she when both men offered something different, something essential?

Before she could respond to TJ, another text came through from Jarod: *Did they arrive? Wanted to make sure they got there before you started your day.*

She stared at both messages, paralyzed by indecision.

Finally, she typed responses to both:

To Jarod: *They're beautiful. Thank you. You didn't have to do this.*

To TJ: *Good morning. Friday was wonderful. Can we talk later this week? Things are crazy at work right now.*

Jarod's response was immediate: *I wanted to. Been thinking about you constantly. Lunch today?*

TJ: *Of course. Take your time. I'm not going anywhere. Coffee this weekend maybe?*

She was juggling. Actively, deliberately juggling two men who had no idea the other existed in her life. The guilt was a physical weight in her chest.

Sadie: (to Jarod) *Can't do lunch. Slammed with meetings. But thank you again. Really.*

Sadie: (to TJ) *Coffee sounds perfect. Saturday?*

She set down her phone and forced herself to focus on work. She had the Patterson meeting at 10, followed by back-to-back conference calls, and a presentation to finalize for Wednesday's executive committee. Work was safe. Work was controllable. Work didn't make her feel like she was standing on the edge of a cliff.

The morning passed in a blur of spreadsheets and strategic planning. But every time her eyes drifted to the purple flowers on her desk, she felt that guilt twist tighter in her chest.

At noon, Melissa knocked on her door. "Ms. Monroe? There's a—um—there's someone here to see you. He doesn't have an appointment, but he said it's important."

"Who is it?"

"He said his name is Jarod."

Sadie's blood ran cold. "What?"

"Should I tell him you're busy?"

"No—I—" Sadie smoothed down her suit, buying time. "Give me two minutes, then send him in."

Melissa nodded and disappeared.

Sadie stood, her mind racing. What was he doing here? They'd never crossed this boundary before—never brought their personal connection into her professional space. The Velvet Room was one world, the jazz club was pushing boundaries, but here? This was dangerous.

She barely had time to compose herself before her office door opened and Jarod walked in.

He looked incredible in dark jeans and a fitted charcoal sweater that emphasized his athletic build. His smile was warm, easy, and completely oblivious to the panic coursing through her veins.

"Hey," he said, closing the door behind him. "I know you said you were busy, but I was in the neighborhood and thought I'd take a chance. Maybe steal you away for a quick lunch?"

"Jarod, I—" She glanced toward the glass wall of her office, acutely aware that anyone walking by could see them. "You can't just show up at my office."

His smile faltered slightly. "I'm sorry. I should have called first. I just—I got your text, and you seemed distant, and I wanted to see you. Make sure you were okay."

"I'm fine. I'm just busy. I told you that."

"Is this about the flowers? Did I overstep?" He moved closer, and Sadie instinctively stepped back, maintaining distance.

"The flowers were beautiful. Really. But Jarod, we need to talk about boundaries."

"Boundaries." The word came out flat. "Last Wednesday you were in my arms, telling me about your dreams and fears. Now you're talking about boundaries?"

"That was different. That was—" she lowered her voice, hyper-aware of the glass walls, "—that was private. This is my workplace. My professional life. They can't overlap."

Understanding dawned in his eyes, followed quickly by hurt. "I'm something you need to hide."

"That's not what I'm saying."

"That's exactly what you're saying." His voice was quiet but intense. "I get it now. Wednesday night, you let me see a little more of you, and it scared you. So now you're pulling back, rebuilding the walls, putting me back in my box."

"Jarod, please. Not here. Not now."

"Then when, Sadie? When are you going to stop compartmental-izing everything and everyone in your life? When are you going to let something be real?"

"I don't know!" The words came out sharper than she intended, and she immediately regretted raising her voice. She glanced at the glass again—Melissa was studiously not looking their direction, but others in the office might have noticed.

Sadie lowered her voice. "I don't know how to do this, okay? I don't know how to merge my worlds. I don't know how to be professional Sadie and personal Sadie at the same time. And I don't appreciate you showing up here unannounced and forcing the issue."

Jarod was quiet for a long moment, studying her. "You're right. I shouldn't have come without calling. That was presumptuous." He moved toward the door, then paused with his hand on the handle. "But Sadie? Eventually, you're going to have to figure out how to be just one person. A whole person. Because living in pieces like this—it's going to break you."

He left without another word, the door clicking shut behind him with a finality that felt ominous.

Sadie sank into her chair, her hands shaking. Through the glass wall, she watched him walk through the office and disappear into the elevator. Several of her colleagues had noticed—she could see them exchanging glances, no doubt wondering who the handsome stranger was and why their ice queen boss looked rattled.

Her phone buzzed.

LaKrecia: *Lunch? I'm sensing a disturbance in the force.*

Sadie: *You have no idea. Yes. The usual place. 1 PM.*

For the next hour, Sadie tried to focus on work, but her mind kept replaying Jarod's words: *Living in pieces like this—it's going to break you.*

He wasn't wrong.

LaKrecia took one look at Sadie's face when she arrived at Marcel's and ordered them both tequila shots before they even sat down.

"That bad?" LaKrecia asked.

"Worse." Sadie downed the shot, welcoming the burn. "Jarod showed up at my office today."

"Oh, shit."

"Yeah. He wanted to take me to lunch, and when I told him he couldn't just show up at my workplace, he accused me of keeping him in a box. Of living in pieces."

"I mean... he's not wrong."

"Whose side are you on?"

"Yours. Always. But baby, he's right. You *are* living in pieces. And it's not sustainable." LaKrecia signaled for two more shots. "What did you say?"

"I told him my professional and personal lives can't overlap. That I need boundaries."

"And?"

"And he looked at me like I'd broken his heart and left." Sadie accepted the second shot, considering it before drinking. "The worst part is, I could see it in his eyes—he thinks I'm ashamed of him. That I'm hiding him."

"Aren't you?"

"That's not—" Sadie stopped herself. "I'm not ashamed of him. I'm trying to protect my career. You know how it is. If people at Meridian found out about my personal life, about the Velvet Room, about any of it—I'd be done. All the credibility I've built, gone. I'd be 'that woman'—the one who sleeps around, who can't be taken seriously."

"But Jarod doesn't know about the Velvet Room. Neither does TJ. As far as they know, you're just dating. That's not scandalous."

"It feels scandalous when I'm dating both of them and they're best friends." Sadie finally downed the second shot. "How did my life become a soap opera?"

"You created the soap opera, baby. Now you have to deal with the plot twists." LaKrecia reached across the table and took her hand. "Real talk? You need to end it with one of them. Or both. But you can't keep stringing them along."

"I know. I just—" Sadie paused, trying to articulate what she was feeling. "They're so different. With Jarod, I feel... free. Powerful. Like I can be the sensual, passionate version of myself without judgment. But with TJ, I feel... safe. Understood. Like I can be vulnerable without it being weaponized against me."

"Those aren't mutually exclusive qualities, you know. You could find both in one person. Or you could—crazy thought—learn to be both versions of yourself with one person. Let someone see all of you."

"What if all of me is too much? Or not enough?"

"Then they weren't the right person." LaKrecia squeezed her hand. "But you'll never know if you don't try. And Sadie? Keeping yourself in pieces to fit what you think each man wants—that's not protection. That's self-sabotage."

The waiter arrived to take their order. Both ordered salads they wouldn't finish, too stressed to eat.

When they were alone again, Sadie leaned back in her chair. "TJ asked me to coffee on Saturday."

"And?"

"And I said yes. Which means I'm still juggling. Still splitting myself."

"What about Jarod? Where'd you leave things with him?"

"Badly. He left hurt and angry, and I haven't heard from him since." Sadie checked her phone—nothing. "Maybe that's for the best. Maybe he'll back off and make this decision easier."

"Or maybe you just pushed away someone who genuinely cares about you because you're too scared to let him in." LaKrecia's voice was gentle but firm. "I love you, Sadie. But sometimes you are your own worst enemy."

"I know."

"So what are you going to do?"

"I don't know. Go to coffee with TJ on Saturday. See what happens. Maybe the universe will give me a sign or something."

"The universe already gave you a sign, baby. It's practically screaming at you. You're just choosing not to listen."

The rest of the week passed in a tense blur. Jarod didn't text or call, and while part of Sadie was relieved, another part—the part she tried to ignore—felt his absence like a physical ache.

TJ, on the other hand, texted daily. Nothing demanding—just simple check-ins, funny memes, occasional compliments that made her smile despite herself. He was consistent, respectful of her boundaries, and patient in a way that both comforted and terrified her.

By Friday evening, Sadie was wound so tight she felt like she might snap. She'd closed two major deals, survived three executive meetings, and received preliminary confirmation that the Senior VP position was hers if she wanted it.

She should have been celebrating. Instead, she felt hollow.

She was sitting in her office at 7 PM, staring at the purple flowers that were starting to wilt, when her phone rang.

Jarod.

Her heart hammered as she answered. "Hello?"

"Hey." His voice was cautious, missing its usual warmth. "Can we talk?"

"Of course. What's going on?"

"Not on the phone. Can you meet me? Our usual place, 9 PM?"

The Velvet Room. Back to the beginning, back to the compartment where everything made sense.

"I'll be there."

"Thank you." He hung up before she could say anything else.

Sadie sat there for a long moment, staring at her phone. Then she texted LaKrecia: *Meeting Jarod tonight. Wish me luck.*

LaKrecia: *Be honest with him. And with yourself. Love you.*

At 8:30, Sadie left the office and went home to change. But this time, she didn't do the full transformation ritual. She kept her makeup simple, changed into jeans and a silk camisole, left her hair down. Not Corporate Sadie, not After Hours Sadie—just somewhere in between.

Just... Sadie.

The Velvet Room felt different tonight. Or maybe she felt different. The amber lighting that usually made everything feel warm and seductive now seemed harsh, exposing. The music that usually thrummed through her body now felt too loud, invasive.

Jarod was already at their usual booth when she arrived. He had a bottle of Hennessy on the table but hadn't touched it. His expression was unreadable as she approached.

"Thanks for coming," he said as she slid into the booth beside him —though this time, she left more space between them than usual.

"What did you want to talk about?"

He poured them both drinks, his movements precise and controlled. "I need to apologize for Monday. Showing up at your office —that was out of line. I overstepped, and I'm sorry."

"Jarod—"

"Let me finish." He finally looked at her, and the intensity in his eyes made her breath catch. "I'm sorry for pushing. But I'm not sorry for what I said. You do live in compartments, Sadie. And it's not just about protecting your career—it's about protecting yourself. Keeping everyone at arm's length so no one can really hurt you."

"That's not—"

"It is. And I get it. I understand why. Your mom, your fear of becoming dependent, all of it makes sense." He took a sip of his drink. "But here's the thing—I'm not your father. I don't want to control you or change you or make you dependent on me. I just want to know you. All of you. And I'm starting to realize you won't let me."

Sadie's throat felt tight. "I'm trying."

"Are you? Because from where I'm sitting, every time I get close, you pull back. Every time something gets real, you retreat behind your walls." He turned to face her fully. "I'm falling for you, Sadie. And it scares the hell out of me because I don't think you'll ever let yourself fall back."

The words hung in the air between them, heavy with meaning and expectation.

"I don't know how," she whispered. "I don't know how to fall without feeling like I'm losing myself."

"Then maybe I'm not the right person for you." His voice was sad but steady. "Because I can't do halfway. I can't be the man you see on Wednesday nights but pretend doesn't exist the rest of the week. I need more than that. I deserve more than that."

"You're right. You do." Tears pricked her eyes. "I'm sorry, Jarod. I never meant to hurt you."

"I know. But intention doesn't change impact." He reached out and tucked a strand of hair behind her ear—a gesture so tender it made her chest ache. "I care about you. More than I've cared about anyone in a long time. But I can't keep chasing someone who's running from connection. It's killing me."

"So what are you saying?"

"I'm saying I need you to make a choice. Either you're in this— really in it, willing to try to merge your worlds and let me be part of your whole life—or we end it now before someone gets hurt worse than they already are."

Sadie felt tears spill over, even as she tried to blink them back. "How long do I have?"

"That's up to you. But Sadie—don't take too long. Because every day I wait is another day I'm falling deeper for someone who might never catch me."

He stood, leaving the bottle of Hennessy on the table. "Think about it. Really think about what you want. Not what's safe, not what's controlled—what you actually want. And then let me know."

He pressed a kiss to the top of her head—chaste, almost brotherly— and walked away.

Sadie sat alone in the booth, tears streaming down her face, the

Velvet Room pulsing around her with life and pleasure and freedom she suddenly couldn't feel.

She'd come here for two years seeking escape. Seeking power. Seeking control.

And now, sitting alone with an untouched bottle of expensive cognac, she realized she'd been seeking the wrong things all along.

Her phone buzzed. A text from TJ: *Looking forward to tomorrow. Sleep well, beautiful.*

Sadie stared at the message through blurred vision.

Two men. Both wanting more than she knew how to give. Both deserving better than she could offer.

And somewhere in the middle—lost in the compartments and walls and carefully constructed armor—was just Sadie. Trying to figure out who she was and what she wanted.

She finished her drink alone, paid her tab, and left the Velvet Room.

As she drove home through the empty streets, she couldn't shake the feeling that something fundamental had shifted tonight. Some invisible line had been crossed, and there was no going back to the way things were.

Tomorrow she had coffee with TJ. And she still hadn't given Jarod an answer.

The universe wasn't giving her signs anymore. It was giving her ultimatums.

And time was running out.

CHAPTER 7
BEST FRIENDS

SATURDAY MORNING ARRIVED with the kind of crisp autumn clarity that made everything feel too bright, too sharp. Sadie woke at 6 AM after another restless night, Jarod's words echoing in her head: *I need you to make a choice.*

She went for a run—eight miles instead of her usual five—pushing her body until her lungs burned and her legs screamed. Physical pain was easier to manage than emotional turmoil. By the time she returned to her apartment, she'd made a decision.

She would tell TJ the truth today. Not all of it—not about the Velvet Room or the full extent of her relationship with Jarod—but enough. She'd tell him she was seeing someone else, that she needed to figure things out before moving forward with him. It was the right thing to do. The honest thing.

Even if it meant losing him before she'd really had him.

She showered and dressed carefully—high-waisted jeans, a cream cashmere sweater, cognac leather jacket. Hair loose and natural. Minimal makeup. She looked like weekend Sadie—the version that existed between Corporate and After Hours. The version that might actually be closest to the real her, if she could figure out who that was.

TJ had suggested a coffee shop in the arts district—Grounds, a cozy place known for its artisan roasts and homemade pastries. When Sadie arrived at 10 AM, he was already there, sitting at a corner table with two cups of coffee and a warm smile that made her stomach twist with guilt.

He stood when he saw her, and she noticed he'd dressed casually too—dark jeans, a navy henley that showed off his athletic build, and a leather jacket similar to hers. He looked relaxed, happy, completely unaware of the bomb she was about to drop.

"Hey, beautiful." He pulled her into a hug—brief but warm—and she let herself sink into it for just a moment before pulling back.

"Hi. Sorry if I'm late."

"You're right on time. I was just early. Excited to see you." He gestured to the table. "I got you a latte—oat milk, right? I remembered from dinner."

He'd remembered. Of course he had. Because TJ was thoughtful and attentive and exactly the kind of man any woman would be lucky to date.

"Thank you. That's perfect." She sat down across from him, wrapping her hands around the warm cup.

"How was your week? I know you said work was crazy."

"It was. But good. I think I'm getting the promotion I've been working toward."

"Sadie, that's amazing!" His smile was genuine, celebratory. "Senior VP, right? That's huge. We should celebrate properly. Dinner at whatever restaurant you want, my treat."

"TJ, I—" She took a breath, steeling herself. "I need to talk to you about something."

His smile faltered slightly, but he nodded. "Okay. That sounds serious."

"It is. And I should have said something sooner, but—" She looked down at her coffee, unable to meet his eyes. "I'm seeing someone else. Not seriously, but... it's complicated. And I don't think it's fair to you to keep seeing you without being honest about that."

The silence that followed felt endless. When she finally looked up, TJ's expression was carefully neutral—the kind of mask she recognized because she wore it herself so often.

"I see," he said quietly. "Can I ask... is it serious? With this other person?"

"I don't know. That's part of what makes it complicated. We've been seeing each other for a while, but we're not... we haven't defined what it is. And then I met you, and—" She struggled to find the right words. "You're incredible, TJ. You're everything I should want. But I can't move forward with you in good conscience when I haven't resolved things with him."

TJ was quiet for a long moment, his fingers drumming against his coffee cup. "I appreciate you being honest. That couldn't have been easy."

"It wasn't. But you deserve honesty."

"Does he know about me?" The question was careful, measured.

Sadie hesitated. "No. He doesn't."

"So you're keeping us both in separate boxes. Separate compartments." There was no judgment in his voice, just observation—which somehow made it worse.

"I know how that sounds."

"It sounds like you're protecting yourself. Which I understand. But Sadie—" He leaned forward, his expression earnest. "You can't build something real if you're constantly hiding pieces of yourself. Eventually, all those separate compartments collapse."

The words were so similar to what Jarod had said, to what LaKrecia kept telling her, that Sadie felt something crack inside her chest.

"I know. That's why I'm telling you now. Before this goes any further. Before anyone gets hurt worse."

"Too late for that," TJ said with a sad smile. "I'm already invested. Already thinking about future dates and introducing you to my friends and what you'd look like at my family's Christmas dinner. So yeah, this hurts. But I respect you for being honest."

"I'm sorry."

"Don't be. You didn't do anything wrong. Well—" he paused, "—maybe you should have told me before our dinner date, but I get why you didn't. These things are complicated."

"So where does this leave us?"

TJ took a long sip of his coffee, considering. "That's up to you. I'm still interested in getting to know you, if you're willing. But I can't do halfway, Sadie. I can't be the guy you see on weekends while you figure things out with someone else. That's not fair to anyone."

"You're right. It's not."

"So here's what I'm thinking—you take time to figure out what you want. Who you want. And if you decide it's me, you call me. If it's him, I'll respect that and move on. But I'm not going to sit around hoping while you keep one foot in each world."

The ultimatum was gentler than Jarod's but no less final. Two men, two choices, two versions of the future—and she had to pick one.

"That's fair," Sadie said quietly. "More than fair, actually."

They sat in uncomfortable silence for a moment. Then TJ reached across the table and took her hand. "For what it's worth? I think you're incredible. And I think whoever ends up with you—whether it's me or this other guy—is lucky as hell. I just hope you pick someone who sees all of you and loves all of you. Not just the pieces you choose to show."

Tears pricked Sadie's eyes. "You're making this really hard."

"Good. If I'm going down, I'm going down swinging." His smile was sad but genuine. "Can I ask you one thing?"

"Anything."

"The other guy—does he make you happy?"

Sadie thought about Jarod. About the way he looked at her like she was a goddess, about the way he touched her like she was precious, about the way he challenged her to be more than just her armor.

"Yes," she said honestly. "He does. But he also scares me."

"Because he makes you feel things you can't control?"

"How did you—?"

"Because that's how I feel about you." TJ squeezed her hand gently. "That's how you know it's real. When someone gets past all your defenses and makes you feel vulnerable and terrified and alive all at once."

"When did you get so wise?"

"Trial and error. Lots of error." He released her hand and sat back. "I've been the guy who played it safe before. Dated women who were easy and uncomplicated and never challenged me. And you know what? I was bored out of my mind. You're the first person in years who makes me actually *feel* something."

"TJ—"

"But if you don't feel the same way, that's okay. I'd rather know now than six months from now when I'm completely in love with you and you're still keeping me at arm's length."

The words "in love with you" hung in the air, shocking in their honesty.

"You barely know me."

"I know enough. I know you're brilliant and driven and scared to death of being vulnerable. I know you laugh at my terrible jokes and you pretend to hate my optimism but secretly find it endearing. I know you have walls that would make Fort Knox jealous, but underneath them is someone who just wants to be seen and accepted for who she really is." He paused. "Am I wrong?"

"No," she whispered. "You're not wrong."

"Then give me a chance. Give *us* a chance. Once you figure things out with the other guy. That's all I'm asking."

Before Sadie could respond, the door to the coffee shop opened and a familiar laugh made her blood run cold.

She looked up and felt the world tilt sideways.

Jarod walked in, accompanied by another man. They were laughing about something, completely at ease with each other. Jarod looked relaxed in ways she rarely saw him—no intensity, no hunger, just genuine happiness.

And then Jarod saw her.

His smile froze. His eyes went wide. And then he saw who she was sitting with, and his expression transformed into something between confusion and dawning horror.

"TJ?" Jarod's voice cut through the coffee shop ambiance.

TJ turned in his seat, and his face lit up. "Rod! Hey, man! What are you doing here?"

Sadie felt like she was watching a car crash in slow motion—seeing the disaster unfold but powerless to stop it.

"Just grabbing coffee before—" Jarod's eyes locked on Sadie again, and she watched him piece it together. The woman TJ had been talking about all week. The dinner date Friday night. The coffee today.

It was her.

TJ stood, completely oblivious to the tension crackling in the air. "Perfect timing. I want you to meet someone." He gestured to Sadie with pride and affection that made her want to sink through the floor. "This is Sadie Monroe. The woman I was telling you about. Sadie, this is my best friend Jarod."

The silence that followed was deafening. Sadie couldn't move, couldn't breathe, couldn't do anything but watch Jarod's face cycle through shock, hurt, betrayal, and finally—understanding.

"We've met," Jarod said, his voice carefully neutral. "Haven't we, Sadie?"

TJ looked between them, confused. "You have? How? When?"

"A few times, actually." Jarod's eyes never left Sadie's face, and she could see the calculation happening behind them. Watching him put together the timeline—her distance after Wednesday night, her strange behavior, all the pieces falling into place. "Small world, isn't it?"

"That's crazy!" TJ laughed, still completely unaware. "Where'd you guys meet?"

"Through work," Sadie heard herself say, the lie automatic. "Brief interactions. Nothing major."

"Hmm." Jarod's smile didn't reach his eyes. "I wouldn't call it nothing. But sure. Work."

The man with Jarod—tall, handsome, clearly confused by the weird energy—cleared his throat. "I'm gonna grab our coffees. Be right back."

As he walked away, TJ gestured to Jarod. "Sit with us! We can all catch up. This is perfect—you guys can get to know each other better."

"Actually—" Jarod's jaw was tight, "—we need to head out. Got that thing, remember?" He looked at his friend, who nodded despite clearly having no idea what "thing" Jarod was referring to.

"Oh, come on. Just for a few minutes?" TJ was practically beaming, thrilled at the coincidence. "Sadie and I were just talking about—well, actually it was kind of personal. But now that you're both here—"

"TJ." Jarod's voice was sharp enough to make his friend stop mid-sentence. "We really need to go."

TJ's smile faltered. "Is everything okay?"

"Fine. Everything's fine." But Jarod's eyes were still on Sadie, and the hurt in them was like a physical blow. "Just remembered we have somewhere to be. But hey—" his voice took on an edge, "—you two kids have fun. Get to know each other. Really get to know each other."

"Rod, what's going on with you?" TJ stood, concerned. "You're being weird."

"Am I?" Jarod finally looked at his friend, and Sadie saw the internal war playing out on his face. The urge to tell TJ everything fighting against years of friendship and loyalty. "Maybe ask Sadie. She seems to know a lot about weird behavior lately."

"What does that mean?"

"Nothing. Forget it." Jarod backed toward the door. "I'll call you later, brother. Enjoy your coffee date."

He was gone before TJ could respond, his friend hurrying after him with their drinks.

TJ turned back to Sadie, bewildered. "What the hell was that about?"

Sadie's hands were shaking. She gripped her coffee cup to hide it. "I don't know. Maybe he's having a bad day?"

"That wasn't just a bad day. That was—" TJ studied her face, and she watched awareness dawn. "Sadie. The guy you've been seeing. The one you're trying to figure things out with. It's not—"

"TJ—"

"Oh my God." He sat down heavily, the color draining from his face. "It's Jarod. You're seeing Jarod."

There was no point in lying anymore. The truth was written all over her face, in Jarod's behavior, in the impossible coincidence that had just blown up her entire world.

"Yes," she whispered.

TJ stared at her like he'd never seen her before. "How long?"

"A few months. We met at—" She stopped. Couldn't tell him about the Velvet Room. "We met through friends. It was casual at first. Then it got complicated."

"Complicated." TJ laughed, but there was no humor in it. "That's one word for it. Does he know about me?"

"No. Not until just now, I guess."

"So you've been seeing both of us. Best friends. And neither of us knew about the other." He ran his hands over his face. "Jesus Christ, Sadie."

"I didn't know you two were friends. Not at first. By the time I found out, it was too late. I didn't know how to—"

"How about telling the truth?" His voice was sharp now, anger replacing shock. "How about being honest instead of juggling us like we're interchangeable?"

"You're not interchangeable. That's the problem. You're both—" She struggled to articulate it. "You're both incredible in different ways. I didn't plan this. I never meant to hurt either of you."

"But you did." TJ stood abruptly. "You hurt both of us. And you damaged a friendship that's been solid for over a decade."

"I'm sorry."

"Sorry doesn't fix this." He grabbed his jacket. "I need to go talk to Jarod. Try to salvage what's left of my friendship before you completely destroy it."

"TJ, please—"

"What, Sadie? What could you possibly say right now that would make this better?" He looked at her with something close to pity. "You told me you were scared of being vulnerable. Scared of letting people in. But you know what I think? I think you're so busy protecting yourself that you can't see the damage you're doing to everyone around you."

The words hit like physical blows. "That's not fair."

"Fair? You want to talk about fair?" TJ shook his head. "Forget it. I'm done. We're done. Whatever this was—" he gestured between them, "—it's over. And if Jarod has any sense, he'll run as far from you as possible."

He walked out without looking back, leaving Sadie alone at the table with two cooling cups of coffee and the wreckage of her carefully compartmentalized life scattered around her.

For a long moment, she just sat there, unable to process what had just happened. Other coffee shop patrons were staring—they'd clearly witnessed at least part of the drama—but Sadie couldn't bring herself to care.

Her phone buzzed. A text from Jarod: *I need to see you. Tonight. 8 PM. The jazz club. Come alone. We need to talk.*

Then another from TJ: *Don't contact me again. I mean it.*

And finally, LaKrecia: *Whatever just happened, I can feel it from here. Call me when you're ready. I love you.*

Sadie stared at the three messages, her chest tight with something that felt like panic and grief and a strange sense of inevitability.

She'd known this was coming. Had felt it building like a storm on the horizon. All her careful compartmentalization, all her walls and rules and boundaries—they'd finally collapsed under the weight of her own deception.

And now she was sitting in the rubble, trying to figure out if anything was salvageable.

Her hands still shaking, she picked up her phone and called LaKrecia.

"Baby girl?" LaKrecia's voice was soft, concerned. "What happened?"

"Everything," Sadie whispered. "Everything just fell apart."

"I'm coming to you. Where are you?"

"Grounds. The coffee shop in the arts district."

"Stay there. I'll be there in fifteen minutes."

"Krecia?"

"Yeah?"

"You were right. About all of it. And now I've lost both of them."

"Oh, honey. We'll figure this out. Just hang tight, okay? I'm on my way."

LaKrecia hung up, and Sadie sat alone with the ruins of her double life, waiting for her best friend to arrive and help her make sense of the senseless.

Outside, the autumn sun shone bright and indifferent. People walked by with their coffee and their plans and their uncomplicated lives. And inside, Sadie Monroe—successful, driven, controlled— finally let herself cry.

Not the careful, contained tears she allowed herself in private. But the raw, ugly sobbing of someone who'd just watched everything she'd been building come crashing down around her.

The barista approached cautiously. "Miss? Are you okay? Do you need anything?"

Sadie looked up at her—young, concerned, probably wondering what kind of drama she'd just witnessed.

"I need," Sadie said through her tears, "to figure out how to be just one person instead of pieces. But I have no idea where to start."

The barista looked confused. "Um... would you like another coffee?"

Despite everything, Sadie laughed—a broken, desperate sound. "Sure. Why not. Make it a double shot. I have a feeling it's going to be a very long day."

CHAPTER 8
THE CONFESSION

LAKRECIA FOUND Sadie exactly where she'd said she'd be—still sitting at the corner table, now on her third double-shot latte, mascara streaked down her face. The concerned barista had brought over a box of tissues at some point, and Sadie had gone through half of it.

LaKrecia slid into the chair TJ had vacated and took one look at her best friend's face before reaching across the table to grip both her hands.

"Tell me everything."

And Sadie did. The words spilled out in a torrent—meeting TJ at the networking event, the date with Jarod at the jazz club, Friday night with TJ, Jarod showing up at the Velvet Room demanding she choose, and finally, the catastrophic collision at this very coffee shop just an hour ago.

When she finished, LaKrecia was quiet for a long moment.

"Well," she finally said. "You really went and did it."

"I know."

"Like, spectacularly. Epically. This is going to be talked about for years."

"I know!"

"And now you have to face Jarod tonight at the jazz club."

"I know." Sadie's voice cracked. "Krecia, what am I going to do? TJ told me never to contact him again. Jarod looked at me like I'd betrayed him. Which I did. I betrayed both of them."

"Yes, you did." LaKrecia's voice was firm but not unkind. "But you didn't do it maliciously. You did it because you were scared and compartmentalized and trying to protect yourself. It was still wrong, but at least understand why you did it."

"Understanding why doesn't fix it."

"No, it doesn't. But it's a starting point." LaKrecia squeezed her hands. "Tonight, when you meet Jarod, you need to be completely honest. No more half-truths, no more compartments, no more walls. Tell him everything—about the Velvet Room, about why you kept things separate, about what you were afraid of. All of it."

"What if he hates me?"

"He might. But Sadie, he already feels betrayed. Being honest now can't make it worse. And maybe—just maybe—if he understands where you were coming from, there's a chance to salvage something."

"What about TJ?"

LaKrecia shook her head slowly. "TJ is done, baby. You heard him. And honestly? I don't blame him. Finding out your girlfriend has been seeing your best friend behind your back? That's a double betrayal. He needs time and space. Lots of both."

"So I've lost him."

"Probably. At least for now. Maybe forever." LaKrecia's expression softened. "But here's the thing—you were never fully with either of them. You were always holding back, always keeping pieces of yourself locked away. So what you really lost is the potential of what could have been. And that hurts, but it's not the same as losing something real."

Sadie wiped her eyes with another tissue. "How are you so wise?"

"Because I've been watching you self-destruct for two years, and I knew eventually it would come to this." LaKrecia stood and pulled Sadie to her feet. "Come on. We're going back to your place. You need to shower, pull yourself together, and prepare for tonight. Whatever happens with Jarod, you need to walk in there with dignity and honesty. No more running."

"I don't know if I can do this."

"You can. You're Sadie fucking Monroe. You've closed million-dollar deals and commanded boardrooms full of men who wanted to see you fail. You can have one honest conversation with a man you care about."

"This is different. Those men didn't matter. Jarod—" Sadie's voice broke. "Jarod matters."

"I know, baby. That's why you have to do this right."

The rest of the day passed in a fog. LaKrecia took Sadie home and basically supervised her like a child—made her eat, made her hydrate, made her take a shower and wash away the tear-streaked makeup.

By 6 PM, Sadie was dressed in dark jeans and a simple black sweater. No armor, no performance. Just simple and honest, like she was trying to be.

LaKrecia had left an hour earlier, but not before making Sadie promise to call her after the meeting with Jarod, no matter what time it was.

Now, at 7:30, Sadie sat in her living room watching the sun set over the city, trying to find the courage to face what she'd done.

Her phone had been silent all day except for two messages—one from her mother (which she ignored) and one from work (which she'd respond to Monday). Nothing from TJ. Nothing more from Jarod after his initial text.

The silence was deafening.

At 7:45, Sadie grabbed her keys and headed out. The drive to Mingus Room felt both too long and too short. Her heart hammered the entire way, and by the time she pulled into the parking garage, she felt like she might be sick.

You can do this. You have to do this.

She walked into the jazz club at exactly 8 PM. The quartet was playing something slow and mournful—appropriate for the occasion. The Saturday night crowd was thicker than Wednesday had been, couples tucked into intimate corners, the amber lighting making every-thing look warm and romantic.

Jarod sat at the same table they'd occupied Wednesday night. But this time, there was no warmth in his posture, no anticipation in his eyes. He looked... guarded. Hurt. Like someone preparing for battle.

Sadie's stomach twisted as she approached. When she reached the table, he didn't stand, didn't smile. Just gestured to the seat across from him—not beside him, across. The distance felt intentional. Painful.

"Thank you for coming," he said, his voice carefully neutral.

"Of course." She sat down, her hands folded in her lap to keep them from shaking. "Jarod, I—"

"Let me go first." He poured himself a drink from the bottle of Hennessy on the table—their usual—but didn't offer her one. "I've spent the last eight hours trying to make sense of this. Trying to figure out how I missed it. And you want to know what I keep coming back to?"

Sadie waited, her throat tight.

"Every time I asked about your life, you deflected. Every time I tried to get close, you pulled back. You told me you worked in corporate finance, but you never mentioned Meridian specifically. You said you were busy with work, but you never gave details. You compartmentalized everything so carefully that I never even thought to question it." His laugh was bitter. "And then today, seeing you with TJ—my brother, the person I trust most in the world—it all clicked. You weren't just compartmentalizing your work life and personal life. You were compartmentalizing me and him."

"I didn't know you were best friends," Sadie said quietly. "Not at first. When I met TJ at the networking event, I had no idea he was your TJ. It wasn't until Wednesday night, when you mentioned his name, that I realized."

"And then you said nothing." The hurt in his voice was palpable. "You realized your two worlds were colliding, and instead of being honest with either of us, you just... kept going. Kept seeing both of us like we were interchangeable."

"You weren't interchangeable. That was the problem." Sadie forced herself to meet his eyes. "You were both... important. In different ways. And I didn't know how to choose."

"So you chose neither. And lied to both." Jarod leaned back in his chair, studying her. "Here's what I can't figure out—did you even like me? Or was I just the exciting secret, the passion you could turn on and off when convenient?"

"Of course I liked you. Like you. Jarod, what we had—have—it wasn't fake."

"Wasn't it though? Because I was falling for Sadie—the woman who told me about wanting to be a dancer, about her favorite color, about her fears and dreams. But that woman doesn't exist, does she? She's just another performance. Another compartment."

The words cut deep because they were true. At least partially.

"No," Sadie said, her voice stronger than she felt. "That woman is real. She's just... buried under a lot of protection and fear."

"Then help me understand." Jarod leaned forward, and she could see the genuine confusion and pain in his eyes. "Make me understand why you did this. Because right now, all I can see is that you were so scared of being vulnerable with one person that you split yourself between two. And in the process, you hurt the two people who cared about you most."

Sadie took a deep breath. This was it—the moment LaKrecia had told her about. Complete honesty, no matter how painful.

"You're right. About all of it. I did split myself. I kept you and TJ in separate boxes because it felt safer that way. Because..." She paused, gathering courage. "Because you each saw a different part of me, and I was terrified of anyone seeing the whole picture."

"Why?"

"Because I didn't think I could be both women at once. With you, I could be passionate, sensual, free. Someone who embraced pleasure without apology. With TJ, I could be professional, driven, successful—but also vulnerable in a way I hadn't let myself be in years. Both versions felt real. But I didn't know how to integrate them."

"So you kept us separate. Let us each have our piece of you while keeping the full picture hidden."

"Yes."

Jarod was quiet for a moment, processing. "Did you ever consider just... being all of yourself with one person? Letting someone see both sides?"

"No," Sadie admitted. "Because I've spent years building these compartments. They're how I survive. Corporate Sadie is ruthless and controlled because that's what it takes to succeed in my world. After

Hours Sadie is free and powerful because that's the only place I get to escape the pressure. And the real Sadie—the one who's scared and scarred and just trying to figure out who she is—she's buried so deep I'm not sure I even know her anymore."

"After Hours Sadie?" Jarod caught the phrase. "What does that mean?"

This was it. The final wall coming down.

"There's something you don't know about me. About how we met." Sadie's hands were shaking now, so she gripped the edge of the table. "The Velvet Room—that's not just a place I go sometimes. It's... it's my escape. Has been for two years. I go there to be someone different. Someone powerful and desired and free from all the pressure and expectations."

Understanding dawned slowly in Jarod's eyes. "The other men. The way you moved through that space like you owned it. This isn't new for you."

"No. It's not." Sadie forced herself to maintain eye contact, even as shame burned through her. "I've had... arrangements before. Physical connections without emotional complications. That's what I thought we were at first. Just another arrangement."

"But we became more than that."

"Yes. And that terrified me. Because emotional connections mean vulnerability, and vulnerability means risk. Means someone can hurt you. Control you. Leave you with nothing, like what happened to my mother."

Jarod was quiet for a long time, his expression unreadable. The quartet transitioned to a new song—something even more melancholy than the last.

"Thank you for being honest," he finally said. "I know that couldn't have been easy."

"It wasn't. But you deserve the truth. Both you and TJ deserve it, even if it's too late."

"It is too late. For TJ at least." Jarod's voice was heavy. "I talked to him after I left the coffee shop. He's devastated. Feels betrayed by both of us—you for deceiving him, me for... existing in your life without him knowing. Our friendship—" His voice cracked slightly. "Our friendship might not survive this."

The guilt crashed over Sadie like a wave. "I'm so sorry. I never wanted to damage your friendship. Never wanted to hurt either of you."

"But you did. Intentions don't change impact, Sadie. We've established that." He poured himself another drink, and this time he poured one for her too. Slid it across the table. "Here's what I need to know. And I need you to be completely honest. Can you do that?"

"Yes."

"If you had to choose—if you could go back and only pursue one of us—who would it be?"

The question hung in the air between them, impossible and essential.

Sadie looked at the drink in front of her, at the amber liquid that represented so much of what had brought them together. She thought about Jarod—the passion, the intensity, the way he made her feel alive and free. Then she thought about TJ—the gentleness, the safety, the way he made her feel like vulnerability was strength.

"I don't know," she said honestly. "And I think that's the problem. You both offered something I needed. Something essential. But I was so busy trying to keep both of you that I couldn't fully commit to either. And now I've lost both."

"Maybe that's for the best."

The words hurt, even though she'd known they were coming.

"You deserve better than me," Sadie said quietly. "You deserve someone who's whole. Someone who doesn't need to split themselves into pieces to feel safe."

"I wanted to be the person who helped you become whole." Jarod's voice was soft, sad. "That's what kills me. I saw all those walls, all that fear, and I thought—stupidly—that if I was patient enough, gentle enough, if I showed you that being vulnerable didn't mean being weak, you'd let me in. Let me see all of you."

"I wanted to. God, Jarod, I really wanted to. But I didn't know how."

"Did you love him?" The question was quiet but sharp. "TJ. Did you love him?"

Sadie thought about it—really thought about it. "I don't know. I think I could have. He was... easy to be with. Easy to talk to. Being with him felt like coming home after a long day. Safe."

"And me? What did I feel like?"

"Like jumping off a cliff. Terrifying and exhilarating and free. Like I could be anyone, do anything, feel everything."

"So I was the thrill, and he was the comfort." Jarod nodded slowly, like pieces were finally falling into place. "You know what's funny? TJ and I used to joke about finding women who could be both. The adventure and the stability. The passion and the peace. Turns out we found her. We just had to share her without knowing it."

"I'm sorry."

"Stop apologizing." Jarod's voice was firm. "What's done is done. Apologies don't change it. What matters now is what you do next."

"What do you mean?"

"I mean—" He leaned forward, his eyes intense. "—are you going to keep living in compartments? Keep splitting yourself into acceptable pieces for different people? Or are you going to do the hard work of figuring out who Sadie Monroe really is when all the walls come down?"

"I don't know how to do that."

"Therapy might be a good start. Real therapy, not just performance reviews with a corporate coach." His smile was sad. "You're brilliant, Sadie. Successful, beautiful, driven—all the surface stuff. But underneath all that armor, you're still that scared girl watching her mother fall apart. And until you deal with that, until you learn that vulnerability isn't weakness and depending on someone doesn't make you your mother, you're going to keep sabotaging anything real."

Tears spilled down Sadie's cheeks. "When did you get so wise?"

"Therapy. Two years of it after my last relationship imploded. Best decision I ever made." He reached across the table and wiped away a tear with his thumb—a gesture so tender it made her chest ache. "I care about you, Sadie. Even after all this, even knowing what I know now, I still care. But I can't be with you. Not like this. Not when you're still this broken and scared."

"I understand."

"Do you?" His hand dropped away. "Because I need you to really understand. What you did—keeping TJ and me separate, lying by omission, playing us both—that destroyed something. Not just my trust in you, but TJ's trust in me. He thinks I knew. Thinks I was in on it somehow. Our friendship—a friendship that's been solid for over a decade—is damaged. Maybe permanently. And that's on you."

The words were harsh but fair. Sadie absorbed them, let them sink in.

"I'll talk to him," she said. "I'll tell him you knew nothing. That you're innocent in all of this."

"He won't believe you. Not right now. Maybe not ever." Jarod drained his glass. "But you should try anyway. You owe him that much."

"I owe you both so much more than that."

"Yeah. You do." He stood, and Sadie realized this was goodbye. Final. Irrevocable. "I'm going to go now. I can't sit here with you and pretend we can just go back to the way things were. Too much has happened."

"Jarod—" Sadie stood too, desperate for something—closure, forgiveness, one more chance. "Is there any possibility—any at all— that someday we could try again? Once I've done the work, figured myself out?"

He considered the question for a long moment. "Maybe. Someday. If you really do the work. If you become the whole person you're capable of being. If you learn that being vulnerable doesn't make you weak." He paused at the edge of the table. "But Sadie? Don't wait for me. Don't do the work because you think it'll get me back, or TJ back, or anyone back. Do it for yourself. Because you deserve to be whole. You deserve to know who you really are under all those walls and compartments."

"I will. I promise."

"Good." He started to walk away, then turned back one last time. "For what it's worth? I think when you finally figure out who you really are, when you finally let all those pieces come together, you're going to be extraordinary. Even more than you already are. I just wish I could be there to see it."

And then he was gone, disappearing into the crowd, leaving Sadie alone at the table with two empty glasses and a bottle of Hennessy that tasted like regret.

She sat down slowly, her legs suddenly unsteady. Around her, the jazz club pulsed with life—couples holding hands, people laughing, the music washing over everyone like a blessing. But Sadie felt removed from it all, like she was watching life happen from behind glass.

Her phone buzzed. A text from LaKrecia: *How did it go?*

Sadie stared at the message for a long time before responding: *It went exactly as it should have. It's over. Both of them. I lost both of them.*

LaKrecia: *I'm so sorry, baby. Are you okay?*

Sadie looked at the question. Was she okay? No. She was devastated. Ashamed. Regretful. But underneath all that was something else —something that felt almost like relief.

The compartments had collapsed. The walls had come down. All her careful control and protection had failed spectacularly. And now she was sitting in the rubble, forced to face herself without the armor.

It was terrifying.

It was also, strangely, freeing.

Sadie: *I will be. Eventually. Right now I'm just... sitting with it. Feeling it. All of it.*

LaKrecia: *That's good. That's growth, baby. I'm proud of you.*

Sadie: *Even though I destroyed everything?*

LaKrecia: *You didn't destroy everything. You destroyed the walls you were hiding behind. There's a difference. What's underneath might be messy and scared and broken, but at least it's real. And real is where healing begins.*

Sadie finished the drink Jarod had poured for her, paid her tab, and left the jazz club. As she walked to her car, she felt the cool autumn air on her face and realized she was crying again. But this time, the tears felt different. Not desperate or panicked. Just... honest. Raw. Real.

She sat in her car for a long time before starting the engine. Then she pulled out her phone and did something she hadn't done in years.

She googled therapists in her area.

Not corporate coaches. Not career counselors. Real therapists who specialized in trauma and attachment and learning to be vulnerable.

She made a list of five, promising herself she'd call them Monday morning. This was the work Jarod had talked about. The work she needed to do for herself, not for any man or any relationship, but because he was right—she deserved to be whole.

As she drove home through the empty streets, Sadie thought about everything she'd lost—Jarod's intensity, TJ's gentleness, the possibility of what could have been with either of them. The grief was real and heavy.

But underneath the grief was something else. Something that felt almost like hope.

Maybe this was rock bottom. Maybe this was what it took to finally stop running, stop compartmentalizing, stop splitting herself into acceptable pieces.

Maybe this was where the real work began.

When she got home, she changed into pajamas, poured herself one final bourbon, and stood at her floor-to-ceiling windows looking out at the city.

Corporate Sadie was exhausted. After Hours Sadie felt hollow. But somewhere underneath both of them was just Sadie—scared and scarred and searching.

And for the first time in years, she was ready to let that woman emerge. Even if it hurt. Even if it was terrifying. Even if it meant sitting with all the messy, complicated emotions she'd spent years avoiding.

She was ready to be whole.

Even if she had to do it alone.

CHAPTER 9
THE MORAL MAZE

MONDAY MORNING FELT like walking through a dream—or more accurately, a nightmare. Sadie went through her routine mechanically: shower, coffee, the black Armani suit that usually made her feel invincible. But today, the armor felt hollow. She was going through the motions of being Corporate Sadie while feeling completely untethered from that identity.

The weekend had been a blur of isolation and introspection. She'd ignored calls from her mother, responded to LaKrecia's check-ins with brief texts, and spent hours sitting at her windows, staring at the city and trying to make sense of who she was without the compartments.

Saturday night, she'd resisted every urge to go to the Velvet Room. Sunday, she'd canceled her usual gym session and meal prep routine. Instead, she'd done something she hadn't done in years—she'd put on music and danced. Just moved. No audience, no performance, just her body remembering what it used to know.

It had felt both liberating and heartbreaking.

Now, sitting in her office at 7:45 AM with coffee she couldn't taste, Sadie stared at the list of therapists on her phone. She'd promised herself she'd call today. Make appointments. Start the work.

But first, she had to get through a normal workday. Had to pretend everything was fine, even though her entire personal life had imploded spectacularly.

Melissa knocked on her door at 8:00 sharp. "Morning, Ms. Monroe. You have the executive committee meeting at nine, followed by—" She stopped, studying Sadie's face. "Are you okay? You look... tired."

"Rough weekend. I'm fine."

"The purple flowers from last week are wilting. Should I have them removed?"

Sadie looked at the arrangement on her desk—the irises and roses and calla lilies that Jarod had sent. They were brown now, dying, a perfect metaphor for what had happened between them.

"Yes. Please. Thank you, Melissa."

As Melissa carefully removed the vase, Sadie felt a pang in her chest. Another piece of Jarod disappearing from her life.

Her phone buzzed with a text. For a split second, her heart leapt—maybe it was Jarod, or even TJ, reaching out. But it was just her boss: *Good luck with the committee meeting. Knock 'em dead.*

The Senior VP position. She'd almost forgotten. Today's meeting would essentially seal the deal—final approval from the executive committee, pending board ratification next month.

Six months ago, this would have been the most important moment of her career. Now, it felt strangely empty. What was the point of climbing to the top if you were completely alone when you got there?

Stop it, she told herself firmly. *This is what you worked for. What you sacrificed for. Don't let heartbreak diminish your achievements.*

She gathered her presentation materials, checked her appearance one last time, and headed to the conference room with her head high and her mask firmly in place.

The meeting went exactly as expected—she presented her strategic vision for the next fiscal year, fielded questions with practiced ease, and watched the executives nod approvingly at her projections and proposals.

"Excellent work, Ms. Monroe," the CEO said when she finished. "Your promotion to Senior VP is approved, pending final board approval next month. But between you and me?" He smiled. "That's just a formality. Welcome to the executive leadership team."

Handshakes all around. Congratulations. Pats on the back. Everything she'd worked toward for years, finally within reach.

She should have been elated. Instead, she felt numb.

Back in her office, Sadie sat at her desk and stared at her phone. The list of therapists was still there, waiting. She'd promised herself. Promised Jarod, in a way, that she'd do the work.

Before she could second-guess herself, she clicked on the first name —Dr. Patricia Chen, specialized in trauma, attachment disorders, and relationship patterns. The website showed a woman in her fifties with kind eyes and a warm smile. Her bio mentioned working with high-achieving women dealing with vulnerability and intimacy issues.

Perfect. Too perfect. Like the universe was pointing a giant arrow at exactly what Sadie needed.

She dialed the number before fear could stop her.

"Dr. Chen's office, this is Marie speaking."

"Hi. I'd like to schedule an initial consultation."

"Wonderful. Dr. Chen has an opening this Wednesday at 6 PM, or next Monday at 4 PM. Which works better for you?"

Wednesday. Three days away. Soon enough that she couldn't back out, far enough that she could mentally prepare.

"Wednesday at six works."

"Perfect. Can I get your name and contact information?"

After providing her details, Sadie hung up feeling something she hadn't felt in days—a tiny spark of hope mixed with absolute terror.

She'd just made an appointment to talk to someone about her deepest fears, her trauma, the walls she'd spent years building. There was no performance in therapy, no compartments. Just raw, honest truth.

The thought made her want to throw up and also felt strangely like relief.

Her phone buzzed. LaKrecia: *Lunch? I'm worried about you.*

Sadie hesitated, then agreed. She needed to tell someone what she'd just done. Needed someone to hold her accountable so she didn't cancel the appointment out of fear.

They met at a small café near Sadie's office—nowhere fancy, just sandwiches and coffee and honest conversation.

LaKrecia took one look at Sadie's face and reached across the table to grip her hand. "How are you holding up?"

"I got the promotion. Senior VP. Official as of next month."

"That's amazing! We should celebrate—" LaKrecia stopped, reading Sadie's expression. "But you're not happy about it."

"I am. I think. It just feels... hollow. Like I finally got everything I thought I wanted, but it doesn't mean what I thought it would."

"Because you're realizing success isn't the same as fulfillment?"

"Maybe. Or because I'm realizing that being at the top is lonely as hell when you've systematically pushed away everyone who tried to get close."

"Have you heard from either of them? Jarod or TJ?"

"No. Nothing. And I don't expect to." Sadie took a sip of her coffee. "But I did something today. Something big."

"What?"

"I made an appointment with a therapist. Dr. Patricia Chen. Wednesday at six."

LaKrecia's eyes filled with tears. "Sadie. I'm so proud of you."

"Don't be proud yet. I haven't actually gone. I might cancel."

"You won't. Because you know you need this. And because I'm going to text you every day until Wednesday to make sure you go." LaKrecia squeezed her hand tighter. "This is huge, baby. This is the first step toward actually healing instead of just surviving."

"I'm terrified."

"Of course you are. Therapy means being vulnerable. Being honest. Looking at all the shit you've been running from. It's scary as hell."

"What if I can't do it? What if I sit in that office and just... freeze? Can't talk, can't open up?"

"Then you sit in silence for fifty minutes and try again next week. There's no failure in therapy except not showing up." LaKrecia released her hand and sat back. "But Sadie? I think you're going to surprise yourself. I think once you start talking—really talking, without the walls and performance—it's going to pour out of you."

"That's what I'm afraid of."

They ate in comfortable silence for a few minutes. Then LaKrecia asked gently, "Have you thought about reaching out to TJ? To apologize, even if he doesn't want to hear it?"

"Every day. But Jarod said TJ thinks he was in on it somehow. That our friendship is damaged because of me. What could I possibly say that would make that better?"

"The truth. That Jarod knew nothing. That this was all you, your compartmentalization, your fear. Take full responsibility without making excuses."

"He told me not to contact him again."

"He did. But that was Saturday, in the heat of the moment. It's Monday now. He's had time to process. Maybe he's ready to hear you out. Or maybe he's not. But you owe him the attempt."

Sadie knew LaKrecia was right. She did owe TJ the attempt. Owed it to him and to Jarod, to try to salvage their friendship even if she couldn't salvage anything with either of them personally.

"I'll think about it."

"Don't think. Do. Tonight. Send him a message. Short, honest, taking full responsibility. Give him the option to respond or not, but at least try."

"What do I even say?"

LaKrecia pulled out her phone and started typing. "Something like this: 'TJ, I know you asked me not to contact you, and I'll respect that after this message. But I need you to know that Jarod knew nothing about us seeing each other. He was completely innocent in all of this. What I did—keeping you both separate, deceiving you both—that was entirely my choice and my failure. I destroyed something beautiful between you two, and I'm sorrier than I can express. You don't need to respond. I just needed you to know the truth. Jarod deserves his best friend back, and you deserve to know he never betrayed you. I did.'"

Sadie stared at the message. "That's perfect. Too perfect. He'll know you helped me write it."

"So? The point isn't to seem authentic. The point is to tell the truth. Who cares if I helped you find the words?"

"You're right." Sadie copied the message into her notes. "I'll send it tonight. After work. When I'm home and can handle whatever response comes—or doesn't come."

"Good." LaKrecia smiled. "Look at you, taking responsibility, going to therapy, trying to make amends. Growth looks good on you, even if it hurts like hell."

"It does hurt. Everything hurts right now."

"That's how you know it's real. Real emotions hurt. The compartmentalized, controlled version you've been living—that's numb. Comfortable maybe, but numb. This pain? This is you actually feeling. And feeling is the first step toward healing."

The rest of the workday crawled by. Sadie went through the motions—conference calls, emails, a meeting with her team to discuss Q4 targets. Everyone congratulated her on the promotion news that had already leaked through the office grapevine. She smiled and thanked them and felt like a fraud the entire time.

At 6 PM, she finally left the office. But instead of going straight home, she found herself driving aimlessly through the city. Past the Velvet Room—she slowed down as she passed the building, remembering the woman she'd been when she walked through those doors. That woman felt like a stranger now.

Past the jazz club where she'd had her first real date with Jarod. The building looked different in daylight—ordinary, not magical.

Past Essence, the restaurant where TJ had taken her and looked at her like she was something precious.

Every location was a ghost of her former life, haunting her with what could have been if she'd just been brave enough to be whole.

When she finally made it home, it was nearly 8 PM. She changed into comfortable clothes, poured herself a bourbon—her nightly ritual—and stood at her windows looking out at the city.

Her phone sat on the counter, the message to TJ still in her notes, waiting to be sent.

Just do it. Rip off the band-aid.

She opened her messages, found TJ's contact—his last message to her still read "Don't contact me again. I mean it."—and pasted in the message LaKrecia had helped her write.

Her finger hovered over the send button.

This was it. The last communication. The final attempt to make things right, even if she couldn't fix anything.

She hit send before she could change her mind.

The message showed as delivered immediately. Then, agonizing seconds later, "Read."

He'd seen it. Was he going to respond? Block her? Forward it to Jarod?

Three dots appeared. Disappeared. Appeared again.

Sadie's heart hammered. She gripped her bourbon glass so tightly she thought it might shatter.

Finally, a response came through: *I believe you. About Jarod not knowing. I talked to him yesterday, and he was too hurt and confused for it to have been an act. You really did play us both without either of us knowing.*

Another message: *I'm not ready to forgive you. Maybe I never will be. But I appreciate you telling me the truth about Jarod. He's been my brother for over a decade. I can't lose him because of your mess.*

And then: *I hope you figure yourself out, Sadie. Because you're right—you destroyed something. Not just with me and you, or you and Jarod, but potentially between me and him. And I hope whatever you were running from was worth it.*

The messages felt like knives, each one precise and crushing, but they also felt deserved.

Sadie typed back: *It wasn't worth it. Nothing was worth hurting you both. I know that now. I'm sorry doesn't fix anything, but I am. Deeply, truly sorry.*

The three dots appeared again, then disappeared. No response came.

After ten minutes, Sadie realized that was it. The conversation was over. Maybe forever.

She forwarded the exchange to LaKrecia with a simple message: *Done. He believes me about Jarod at least.*

LaKrecia: *That's something. Not everything, but something. How do you feel?*

Sadie considered the question. How did she feel?

Sad. Guilty. But also... lighter? Like I've been carrying this weight and now at least some of it is shared. He knows the truth. That has to count for something.

LaKrecia: *It counts for everything. You told the truth even when it hurt. That's growth, baby. I'm proud of you.*

Sadie finished her bourbon and poured another—smaller this time. She needed to feel tonight, not numb it away, but a little liquid courage couldn't hurt.

Her phone buzzed again. This time, a message from an unknown number: *This is Jarod. TJ forwarded me your conversation with him. Thank you for telling him the truth. He and I are talking again. Slowly. It's going to take time to rebuild what was broken, but at least there's a chance now. I don't know if you and I will ever have that chance, but I wanted you to know—what you did tonight mattered. It helped. So thank you.*

Sadie read the message three times, tears streaming down her face.

She typed and deleted five different responses before settling on: *I'm glad you two are talking. Your friendship is more important than anything that happened between us. I meant what I said at the jazz club—I'm going to do the work. Figure myself out. Become whole. Not for you, not for TJ, but for me. Thank you for pushing me toward that.*

The response came quickly: *That's all I ever wanted for you. Good luck, Sadie. I mean that.*

And then, nothing. The conversation was over. Both of them—TJ and Jarod—had said their pieces. Given her what closure they could. And now it was up to her to actually do the work she'd promised.

Sadie saved Jarod's new number in her phone, even though she knew she wouldn't use it. Couldn't use it. This was goodbye, at least for now. Maybe forever.

She walked to her bedroom and opened the drawer where she kept mementos—ticket stubs, photos, little pieces of her life. She pulled out a notebook she'd bought years ago but never used, one of those fancy journals with thick paper and a leather cover.

She opened to the first page and wrote:

Day One of being just Sadie.

I don't know who that is yet. I've been Corporate Sadie and After Hours Sadie for so long that the real me—whoever she is—got buried underneath. Today I lost two incredible men because I was too afraid to let either of them see all of me. Today I started the process of figuring out who I am when I'm not performing for anyone.

Wednesday I have my first therapy appointment. I'm terrified. I'm also hopeful. Maybe that's progress.

Things I know about myself: - I love purple, the color of twilight - I wanted to be a dancer before life got in the way - I'm afraid of becoming my mother - I'm afraid of being vulnerable - I'm afraid of losing control - I'm afraid of being alone - But I'm more afraid of living in pieces forever

Today hurt. Tomorrow will probably hurt too. But I'm going to keep showing up. Keep feeling. Keep being honest, even when it's terrifying.

That's all I can promise right now.

She closed the journal and set it on her nightstand. A physical representation of the work ahead.

Her phone buzzed one last time. LaKrecia: *Get some sleep. Tomorrow is a new day. Love you, sis.*

Sadie: *Love you too. Thank you for not giving up on me.*

LaKrecia: *Never. That's what best friends are for.*

Sadie got ready for bed, going through her routine mechanically. But when she climbed under the covers, instead of immediately reaching for her phone to scroll mindlessly, she just lay there in the dark.

Feeling everything. The grief. The guilt. The fear. The tiny spark of hope that maybe—just maybe—she could become someone whole.

Someone who didn't need compartments to feel safe.

Someone who could be vulnerable without breaking.

Someone who could love and be loved without losing herself.

She didn't know if that person was possible. Didn't know if the work ahead would be enough to heal years of self-protection and trauma.

But for the first time in her life, she was willing to find out.

Even if it hurt.

Even if it took years.

Even if she had to do it completely alone.

Because LaKrecia was right—she deserved to be whole. And that journey started now.

CHAPTER 10
DINNER WITH THE DEVIL

THE REST of Monday and all of Tuesday passed in a strange fog. Sadie threw herself into work with an intensity that bordered on obsessive—staying late, taking on extra projects, volunteering for assignments that weren't even in her purview. If she kept moving, kept her mind occupied, she didn't have to think about the wreckage of her personal life.

LaKrecia texted daily check-ins: *How are you holding up? Remember therapy Wednesday at 6. Don't you dare cancel.*

Sadie wouldn't cancel. She'd made a promise to herself, and despite everything, she was a woman who kept her commitments. Even the terrifying ones.

Wednesday morning arrived with unseasonable warmth—one of those autumn days that felt like summer's last gasp before winter settled in for good. Sadie dressed in a charcoal pantsuit with a silk blouse the color of champagne. Professional armor, but softer somehow. She'd stopped wearing the severe blacks and sharp lines that screamed "don't touch me." Baby steps toward being more approachable, more human.

She was reviewing contracts in her office when Melissa knocked at 11:30.

"Ms. Monroe? You have a visitor. He says it's urgent."

Sadie's heart jumped. "Who is it?"

"He said his name is TJ Morrison. Should I tell him you're in a meeting?"

TJ. Here. At her office.

The last place she expected him to show up after everything that had happened.

"No. Send him in." Her hands were already shaking as she stood, smoothing down her suit jacket.

The door opened and TJ walked in, looking nothing like the warm, open man she'd had dinner with at Essence. He wore a dark suit that emphasized his broad shoulders, his expression unreadable. Professional. Distant. Like they were strangers about to negotiate a business deal.

"TJ. I—I didn't expect to see you."

"I know. But we need to talk, and I figured neutral territory would be best. Your office is public enough that we'll both stay civil." He closed the door behind him but didn't sit. "Do you have a few minutes?"

"Of course. Please, sit."

He took the chair across from her desk—the same position he'd been in at the coffee shop before everything exploded. The symmetry was painful.

"I got your message Monday," he started. "And Jarod confirmed everything. That he didn't know about me, that you kept us completely separate."

"That's true. He was innocent in all of this."

"I know. We've been talking. Trying to repair the damage." TJ's jaw tightened. "It's going to take time. A friendship doesn't just bounce back from something like this. But at least we're talking."

"I'm glad. Really. Your friendship is—"

"Don't." His voice was sharp. "Don't tell me what my friendship is worth. You destroyed it, Sadie. Maybe we'll rebuild it, maybe we won't. But you don't get to comment on its value."

The words stung, but she deserved them. "You're right. I'm sorry."

"I didn't come here for apologies." He leaned forward slightly. "I came to tell you something. Something you need to hear before you hear it from someone else."

Sadie's stomach dropped. "What?"

"Jarod and I are meeting for dinner tonight. At Ember—that new steakhouse downtown. We're trying to get back to normal, do the things we used to do before... this. Before you."

"That's good. That's what you should be doing."

"We both have dates." He paused, letting that sink in. "I'm bringing someone I've been talking to—Sarah, a woman I met through work. And Jarod is bringing someone he reconnected with recently. We're doing a double date. Moving forward. Putting all of this behind us."

The news hit Sadie like a physical blow. Of course they were moving on. Why wouldn't they? She'd betrayed them both, destroyed their trust. Moving on was the healthy thing to do.

But knowing it intellectually and hearing it out loud were two different things.

"I'm happy for you both," she managed, her voice remarkably steady. "You deserve to move forward."

"Do you mean that?" TJ studied her face. "Because you look like I just punched you in the stomach."

"I mean it. What I feel about it doesn't matter. You and Jarod both deserve happiness. Deserve relationships with women who can be fully present and honest. I couldn't give you that."

"No. You couldn't." He stood. "I didn't tell you this to hurt you, Sadie. I told you because Ember is a popular spot, and there's a chance you could be there or someone you know could be there. I didn't want you blindsided. Didn't want you seeing us out with other women and thinking we did it to send you a message."

"I appreciate that. Truly."

"Also—" He moved toward the door, then paused. "Jarod asked me not to tell you. Said it was none of your business what we do now. But I thought you deserved to know. One last courtesy before we completely close this chapter."

"Thank you. For the courtesy. And for letting me know about Jarod —that you two are talking again."

TJ's expression softened slightly. "For what it's worth, I hope you actually do the work you talked about. Hope you figure yourself out. Because Sadie, you're brilliant and driven and could be amazing. You're just... broken. And broken people break other people."

He left before she could respond, the door clicking shut with a finality that echoed through her chest.

Sadie sank into her chair, her hands trembling. Both of them. Moving on. With other women. Tonight.

She should be happy for them. Should want them to find happiness after what she'd put them through.

And she did want that. In theory.

But the reality of it—imagining Jarod's intense gaze focused on someone else, imagining TJ's warm smile directed at another woman—felt like someone was carving out her insides with a dull knife.

This was what she'd chosen, though. This was the consequence of keeping them in separate boxes, of being too afraid to be vulnerable with either of them.

Her phone buzzed. LaKrecia: *Lunch?*

Sadie: *Can't. Swamped with work.*

LaKrecia: *Liar. What happened?*

Of course LaKrecia could tell something was wrong. Best friend radar.

Sadie: *TJ came to my office. He and Jarod are going on a double date tonight. Both bringing other women. Moving on.*

The response was immediate: *Oh honey. I'm sorry. Are you okay?*

Sadie stared at the question. Was she okay?

No. She was devastated. Jealous. Filled with regret so thick she could barely breathe.

But she was also... something else. Something that felt almost like acceptance.

Sadie: *I will be. This is what should happen. They should move on. I just wish it didn't hurt so much to watch.*

LaKrecia: *That's normal. You had feelings for both of them, even if you couldn't fully express them. Seeing them move on hurts. Let yourself feel it.*

Sadie: *I'm trying. It's exhausting.*

LaKrecia: *That's growth, baby. Feeling instead of numbing. I'm proud of *you. And remember—therapy tonight at 6. Don't cancel just because you're hurting.*

Sadie: *I won't. I promise.*

She set down her phone and tried to focus on work, but her mind kept drifting to Ember. To the image of Jarod and TJ with other women, laughing and moving forward while she sat alone with the consequences of her choices.

A dark, self-destructive part of her whispered: *You could go. Show up at Ember. See them. Make them remember what they're missing.*

But that was old Sadie talking. Compartmentalized Sadie who thought she could control situations and people with her presence and sexuality.

New Sadie—whole Sadie, or at least Sadie trying to become whole—knew that showing up would be selfish and destructive. Would hurt them more and accomplish nothing except feeding her own ego.

So she wouldn't go.

She'd go to therapy instead. Start doing the actual work of healing instead of the performance of it.

Even if it killed her to imagine them happy with someone else.

The afternoon crawled by with agonizing slowness. Every time Sadie checked the clock, barely any time had passed. By 4 PM, she was ready to climb out of her skin.

She left the office at 5:30—earlier than usual but late enough not to seem like she was fleeing. The therapy office was only fifteen minutes away, in a professional building near the medical district. She'd googled it obsessively the last few days, memorizing the route, reading reviews, preparing herself mentally.

But nothing could actually prepare her for walking into that office.

The waiting room was soothing—soft lighting, comfortable chairs, abstract art on the walls that probably cost more than most people's cars. Instrumental music played quietly from hidden speakers. Everything designed to make you feel calm and safe.

Sadie felt anything but calm.

She checked in with the receptionist—a kind-looking older woman named Marie who'd scheduled her appointment—and sat down to wait. Her hands were shaking. Her heart was racing. Every instinct screamed at her to leave, to run, to protect herself from whatever was about to happen.

You can do this. You promised yourself. You promised Jarod, in a way. You promised LaKrecia. You can do this.

At exactly 6 PM, a door opened and a woman appeared. Dr. Patricia Chen looked exactly like her website photo—late fifties, kind eyes behind stylish glasses, wearing professional but approachable clothing. She smiled warmly at Sadie.

"Sadie Monroe?"

"Yes." Sadie stood, her legs unsteady.

"I'm Dr. Chen. Please, come in."

The office was even more soothing than the waiting room—a comfortable couch, Dr. Chen's chair positioned at an angle that felt conversational rather than confrontational, more abstract art, a small fountain in the corner providing gentle white noise.

"Have a seat wherever you're comfortable," Dr. Chen said, closing the door. "This first session is really just about getting to know each other, seeing if we're a good fit. There's no pressure to dive into anything deep unless you want to."

Sadie perched on the edge of the couch, her posture rigid. "Okay."

Dr. Chen settled into her chair with the ease of someone who'd done this thousands of times. "So. What brings you to therapy, Sadie?"

The question was simple, but the answer felt impossibly complex. Where did she even start? The compartmentalization? The double life? The two men she'd hurt? Her mother's cautionary tale? Her fear of vulnerability?

"I—" Sadie's voice cracked. She cleared her throat and tried again. "I've been living in pieces. Separate compartments. Different versions of myself for different situations. And recently, those compartments collided and... everything fell apart. I hurt people. Good people who didn't deserve it. And I realized I don't actually know who I am under all the performance and protection."

Dr. Chen nodded, her expression open and nonjudgmental. "That must be exhausting. Living in pieces."

The simple validation made Sadie's eyes sting with tears. "It is. It's so exhausting. But I didn't know any other way to be."

"Can you tell me about these compartments? What were the different versions?"

Sadie took a breath and started talking. About Corporate Sadie—ruthless, driven, controlled, climbing the ladder at any cost. About After Hours Sadie—sensual, free, powerful, seeking pleasure without emotional risk. About the real Sadie—buried so deep she wasn't sure she existed anymore.

Dr. Chen listened without interrupting, occasionally jotting notes but mostly just present, attentive.

When Sadie paused, Dr. Chen asked gently, "What do you think made you need these compartments? When did you start building them?"

And suddenly, Sadie was talking about her parents' divorce. Her father leaving. Her mother falling apart—losing her identity, her confidence, her sense of self because she'd built her entire life around a man who decided she wasn't enough anymore.

"I watched her become nothing," Sadie said, tears streaming down her face now. "She gave up everything for him—her career, her dreams, her independence. And when he left, she had nothing. She was nothing. Just this broken woman who didn't know how to exist without him."

"And you decided that would never be you."

"Never. I would never need anyone that badly. Would never be that vulnerable. I'd build my own success, my own money, my own power. No one could take that from me."

"But that meant keeping everyone at a distance. Never letting anyone close enough to hurt you the way your father hurt your mother."

"Yes." The admission felt like a release. "I thought if I kept things compartmentalized—if I kept my professional life separate from my personal life, if I kept physical pleasure separate from emotional connection—then I'd be safe. In control. Protected."

"And were you? Safe?"

Sadie laughed bitterly. "No. I was lonely as hell. And when I finally met people who wanted more than just one piece of me, I panicked. Tried to keep them in separate boxes. And ended up losing them both."

Dr. Chen was quiet for a moment, then asked, "Do you think your mother was weak for loving your father?"

The question caught Sadie off guard. "I... yes? She gave up everything for him. That's weakness."

"Is it? Or was she making choices based on what she valued at the time? Maybe she loved him. Maybe she wanted to support his dreams. Maybe she believed that's what love looked like—sacrifice and support."

"But look where it got her!"

"It got her hurt when the relationship ended. But Sadie, every relationship that ends causes hurt. That's the risk we take when we love someone. The question isn't how to avoid hurt—that's impossible. The question is whether the love and connection are worth the risk of potential hurt."

Sadie sat with that, the words settling over her like a blanket.

"Your mother's mistake wasn't loving your father," Dr. Chen continued. "It was losing herself in the process. Making him her entire identity instead of maintaining her own. But you can love someone—be vulnerable with someone—without losing who you are. The two aren't mutually exclusive."

"I don't know how to do that."

"That's why you're here. To learn." Dr. Chen smiled gently. "Sadie, what you're describing—this compartmentalization, this fear of vulnerability—it's a trauma response. Your brain developed a protection mechanism based on what you witnessed with your mother. It kept you safe for a long time. But now it's keeping you from the very thing you actually want—real connection."

"What if I'm not capable of real connection? What if I'm too broken?"

"You're not broken. You're self-protected. There's a difference." Dr. Chen leaned forward slightly. "And I can see already that you're capable of connection. You cared about these two men—Jarod and TJ. You cared enough that losing them hurts. That's not broken. That's human."

Sadie wiped her eyes with the tissue box Dr. Chen had quietly pushed toward her. "They're moving on. Both of them. They're on a double date right now, actually. With other women."

"How does that make you feel?"

"Devastated. Jealous. Regretful." Sadie paused. "But also... like it's what should happen. They deserve to be happy. Deserve women who can be fully present and honest. I couldn't be that for them."

"Not yet," Dr. Chen corrected. "You couldn't be that for them yet. But that doesn't mean you'll never be able to. Growth is possible, Sadie. Change is possible. If you're willing to do the work."

"I am. I think. It's just so scary."

"Of course it is. You're dismantling protection mechanisms you've spent years building. That's terrifying. But you know what I think?" Dr. Chen's smile was warm. "I think you're braver than you give yourself credit for. You're here. You showed up. You're doing the work, even though it scares you. That takes incredible courage."

The session continued for another twenty minutes—Dr. Chen explaining what therapy would look like going forward, discussing frequency (weekly to start), and answering Sadie's questions about the process.

When their time was up, Sadie felt wrung out but also strangely lighter. Like she'd been carrying a weight she didn't realize was there, and someone had finally helped her set it down—at least partially.

"Same time next week?" Dr. Chen asked as Sadie stood to leave.

"Yes. Definitely yes."

"Good. And Sadie? Be gentle with yourself this week. You did something really brave today. Let yourself acknowledge that."

Sadie nodded, not trusting herself to speak without crying again.

She sat in her car in the parking lot for a long time, processing everything. It was 7:15 PM. The double date at Ember was probably in full swing—appetizers ordered, drinks flowing, laughter and connection and the promise of moving forward.

Part of her wanted to drive there. See them. Torture herself with visual confirmation of what she'd lost.

But a bigger part—the part that was trying to grow, trying to be whole—knew that was self-destructive.

Instead, she drove to LaKrecia's apartment. Texted from the parking lot: *I'm here. Can I come up? I need my best friend.*

LaKrecia: *Door's unlocked. I've got wine and ice cream. Come.*

When Sadie walked into LaKrecia's apartment, her best friend took one look at her face and pulled her into a fierce hug.

"I went to therapy," Sadie said against LaKrecia's shoulder.

"I'm so proud of you."

"And they're out right now. With other women. Moving on like I never existed."

"I know, baby. I know it hurts."

They sat on LaKrecia's couch with wine and ice cream, and Sadie told her everything—the therapy session, the things Dr. Chen had said about trauma responses and protection mechanisms, the realization that she wasn't broken, just self-protected.

"She sounds amazing," LaKrecia said. "Like exactly what you need."

"She is. But Krecia, it hurt so much. Talking about my mom, about why I built these walls. I cried for like half the session."

"That's good. That's healing." LaKrecia squeezed her hand. "You've been holding all of that in for years. It needs to come out."

"I keep thinking about them. Jarod and TJ. Wondering if they're having a good time. If their dates are going well. If they're thinking about me at all or if I'm just... gone. Erased."

"They're thinking about you. Trust me. You don't spend months with someone and then just forget them because you're on a date with someone new. But Sadie? Even if they are moving on, even if they do forget—you need to move on too. Not to someone else, but to yourself. To becoming whole."

"I know. I just... I miss them. Both of them. In different ways."

"Of course you do. You had real feelings for both of them, even if you couldn't fully express them. It's okay to grieve what could have been."

They sat in comfortable silence for a while, the kind that only exists between people who've known each other forever. Then LaKrecia asked, "What are you going to do now?"

"Keep going to therapy. Keep working on myself. Keep trying to figure out who Sadie Monroe is when she's not performing for anyone."

"That's all you can do. One day at a time."

"Dr. Chen said something that stuck with me. She said my mother's mistake wasn't loving my father—it was losing herself in the process. That I can love someone without losing who I am."

"She's right."

"But I don't know how to do that. I've spent so long equating vulnerability with weakness, equating love with loss of self. How do I unlearn that?"

"By practicing. By starting small. By being vulnerable in safe spaces —like therapy, like with me—and learning that it doesn't destroy you. That you can be open and honest and still be yourself." LaKrecia refilled their wine glasses. "It's not going to happen overnight. But it will happen. If you keep showing up, keep doing the work, keep being brave—it will happen."

Sadie wanted to believe her. Wanted to believe that she could become someone who didn't need compartments to feel safe. Someone who could be fully present with another person without fear.

But right now, sitting on her best friend's couch with wine and tears and the ghost of what could have been haunting her—she just felt lost.

Lost and trying to find her way home to herself.

And maybe that was enough for today.

At 10 PM, Sadie finally left LaKrecia's apartment and drove home. The city was alive with nightlife—people heading to bars and clubs, starting their Thursday night early, seeking connection and pleasure and escape.

She used to be one of them. Used to put on her armor and head to the Velvet Room, seeking that temporary high of being desired and powerful and free.

Now the thought of it made her feel empty.

When she got home, she changed into pajamas, poured herself a small bourbon—just one, to take the edge off—and opened her journal.

Day Three of being just Sadie, she wrote.

Today TJ came to my office to tell me he and Jarod are moving on. Dating other women. It hurt more than I expected. More than I had any right for it to hurt.

But I also went to therapy. My first real session. Dr. Chen helped me understand that I'm not broken—just self-protected. That I built compartments as a trauma response to watching my mother fall apart. That loving someone doesn't mean losing myself.

I don't know if I believe that yet. But I want to.

Jarod and TJ are out there right now, on dates with women who can probably give them what I couldn't—presence, honesty, wholeness. Part of me is jealous. Part of me hopes they find happiness.

Both parts are true. I'm learning that I can hold contradictory feelings at once. That's growth, I guess.

Tomorrow I go back to work. Back to being Corporate Sadie, but maybe a little less compartmentalized. A little more integrated.

Small steps. One day at a time.

That's all I can promise.

She closed the journal and got into bed, her body exhausted from the emotional weight of the day. As she lay there in the dark, she thought about Jarod and TJ.

Were they still at dinner? Had they gone somewhere else—maybe back to one of their places for drinks and conversation? Were they laughing, telling stories, introducing their dates to each other?

Were they happy?

God, she hoped they were happy. Even if it hurt to imagine.

Because that's what love was, she was starting to realize. Not possession or control. Not keeping someone in a compartment where they couldn't hurt you.

Love was wanting someone to be happy, even if that happiness didn't include you.

And maybe—just maybe—learning to love like that, to be vulnerable like that, was the first step toward becoming whole.

Sadie closed her eyes and let herself feel everything—the grief, the regret, the tiny spark of hope that someday, somehow, she'd figure this out.

And tomorrow, she'd wake up and try again.

One day at a time.
One step toward wholeness.
Even if she had to walk that path alone.

CHAPTER 11
THE SLIP

THE NEXT TWO weeks passed in a strange rhythm. Sadie went to work, attended meetings, closed deals, and accepted congratulations on her impending promotion. She went to therapy every Wednesday, slowly peeling back layers of protection and fear with Dr. Chen's gentle guidance. She had dinner with LaKrecia twice a week, maintaining the one relationship in her life that felt solid and real.

And she stayed away from the Velvet Room.

That part was harder than she'd expected. Not because she missed the sex—though she did, in an abstract way—but because she missed the escape. The transformation. The feeling of being powerful and desired and free from all the pressure of being Corporate Sadie.

Without that outlet, she was forced to just... be. To sit with her feelings instead of numbing them. To process her grief and regret instead of burying it under physical pleasure.

It was exhausting. And necessary.

Dr. Chen had given her homework—to notice when she felt the urge to compartmentalize, to escape, to perform. To sit with those urges instead of acting on them. To ask herself what she was really trying to avoid feeling.

Most of the time, the answer was: everything.

By the second Friday after her first therapy session, Sadie was feeling cautiously optimistic. She'd made it through two weeks without self-destructing. Two weeks of feeling instead of numbing. Two weeks of trying to be integrated instead of compartmentalized.

She was exhausted, but she was doing it.

LaKrecia texted her Friday morning: *Girls' night tonight? Wine, pizza, terrible reality TV?*

Sadie: *Perfect. My place or yours?*

LaKrecia: *Yours. I want to lie on that obscenely comfortable couch you have.*

Sadie: *Done. 7 PM?*

LaKrecia: *See you then. Proud of you for making it two weeks, by the way. That's huge.*

Sadie smiled at her phone. Two weeks did feel huge. Two weeks of not running to the Velvet Room every time things got hard. Two weeks of not numbing herself with bourbon and anonymous pleasure. Two weeks of actually doing the work.

The day passed quickly—meetings, emails, a lunch presentation to potential clients that went exceptionally well. By 5 PM, Sadie was wrapping up for the weekend, looking forward to a quiet night with her best friend.

She was packing her laptop when Melissa knocked on her door.

"Ms. Monroe? There's someone here to see you. He doesn't have an appointment, but he said it's important."

Sadie's stomach dropped. Another unannounced visitor. The last time that happened, it had been TJ delivering news about the double date.

"Who is it?"

"He said his name is Jarod."

The world tilted slightly. Jarod. Here. Two weeks after their last conversation at the jazz club. Two weeks of silence.

"Should I tell him you're in a meeting?" Melissa asked, reading Sadie's expression.

"No. Send him in." She needed to face this. Whatever this was.

Melissa disappeared, and a moment later, Jarod walked through her door.

He looked different than the last time she'd seen him—tired, maybe. Or just worn down by everything that had happened. He wore dark jeans and a gray henley, casual but put-together. His expression was carefully neutral, but his eyes—those intense dark eyes—held something she couldn't quite read.

"Hi," he said, closing the door behind him.

"Hi." Sadie remained standing behind her desk, needing the barrier. "I'm surprised to see you."

"I'm surprised to be here." He shoved his hands in his pockets. "Can we talk? Just for a few minutes?"

"Of course. Sit, please."

He took the chair across from her desk, and the déjà vu was overwhelming. How many times had they sat across from each other—at the Velvet Room, at the jazz club, in charged moments filled with desire and possibility?

This felt different. More tentative. Like they were strangers trying to remember how to be around each other.

"How have you been?" he asked.

"Surviving. Working. Going to therapy." She sat down, folding her hands on her desk. "You?"

"Same. Working a lot. Therapy twice a week, actually. TJ and I are doing joint sessions to work through... everything."

"That's good. I'm glad you're both getting help."

"It's brutal," he admitted with a sad smile. "Sitting there talking about how we both fell for the same woman, how we both got played, how our friendship almost imploded because of it. But it's helping. Slowly."

The word "played" stung, but Sadie didn't argue. That's what it must have felt like to them.

"How's TJ?" She couldn't help asking.

"He's good. Dating that woman Sarah. It's early, but he seems happy. Lighter than he's been in weeks." Jarod paused. "She's uncomplicated. Honest. Everything you weren't."

"I deserve that."

"I didn't say it to hurt you. Just stating facts." He leaned forward slightly. "I came here because I need to tell you something. And I thought doing it in person was better than a text."

Sadie's heart hammered. "Okay."

"I've been seeing someone. Nothing serious yet, just dating. But it's going well, and I wanted you to hear it from me. In case we run into each other around the city or something."

The news hit harder than she'd expected, even though she'd known it was coming. Had known since TJ told her about the double date two weeks ago. But knowing intellectually and hearing it directly were different things.

"That's great," Sadie managed, her voice steady even as something cracked inside her chest. "You deserve happiness. Deserve someone who can be present and honest."

"Her name is Maya. She's a yoga instructor. We met at a coffee shop —she literally spilled her latte on me and was so mortified that I asked her to dinner to make up for it." His smile was genuine, warm. "She's easy to be with. No walls, no compartments. Just... present."

"She sounds wonderful."

"She is." He studied Sadie's face. "Are you okay? Really?"

"I'm—" She paused, considering. Dr. Chen had been working with her on honesty, on expressing feelings instead of hiding behind polished responses. "I'm hurt. Jealous. But I'm also happy for you. Both things can be true, right?"

"Yeah. Both things can be true." His expression softened. "For what it's worth, Sadie, I didn't come here to hurt you. I came because I thought you deserved to know. Because despite everything, I still care about you. Just... not in the same way."

"I know. I understand."

"Do you?" He leaned back in his chair. "Because I need you to really understand. What we had—whatever it was—it's over. I'm moving forward with Maya. TJ's moving forward with Sarah. We're both healing and trying to rebuild. And that means you can't be part of our lives anymore."

The finality of it was like a door slamming shut.

"I get it. Really. You both need clean breaks to heal."

"We do. But I also wanted to tell you—" He paused, choosing his words carefully. "TJ and I have been talking about you in therapy. About what happened. And we both realized something. You weren't the villain in this story, Sadie. You were just scared. Traumatized. Trying to protect yourself the only way you knew how."

Tears pricked Sadie's eyes. "That doesn't excuse what I did."

"No, it doesn't. But it helps us understand why you did it. And understanding makes it easier to forgive. Eventually." He stood. "We're not there yet. Maybe we won't ever fully get there. But we're trying. And I hope you're trying too. To heal. To become the person you talked about at the jazz club—whole, integrated, brave enough to be vulnerable."

"I am. Every day. It's hard, but I'm trying."

"Good." He moved toward the door, then paused. "One more thing. The woman you're becoming—the one who goes to therapy, who's honest about her feelings, who's doing the work—she's going to be incredible. And someday, some man is going to be lucky enough to meet her. The real her. All of her."

"Just not you."

"No. Not me. I'm sorry, Sadie. But I need someone I can trust completely. And I don't know if I'll ever be able to trust you again. That's not your fault—it's just the consequence of what happened."

"I understand. Thank you for being honest."

He nodded, his hand on the door handle. "Take care of yourself, Sadie. Really take care. Not the performative kind, but the real kind."

"You too, Jarod."

And then he was gone, the door closing softly behind him, taking with him any remaining possibility of what could have been.

Sadie sat at her desk for a long time, staring at the closed door. She should feel devastated. Should be falling apart.

Instead, she felt... clear. Sad, yes. But also clear.

Both of them had officially moved on. Both were dating other women. Both were healing and rebuilding their friendship without her.

This was closure. Real, final closure.

She pulled out her journal and wrote:

Jarod came to my office today. He's seeing someone named Maya. TJ is seeing someone named Sarah. They're both moving on, healing, building lives that don't include me.

It hurts. But it also feels right. They deserve happiness. Deserve women who can be fully present.

I'm not that woman yet. But I'm becoming her. One therapy session at a time. One honest conversation at a time. One day at a time.

This is closure. It hurts, but it's necessary. The door is closed. Now I can stop looking back and start looking forward.

She closed the journal and checked the time. 5:45 PM. LaKrecia would be at her apartment in an hour and fifteen minutes.

Sadie packed up her things and headed home, driving on autopilot. When she got to her apartment, she changed into comfortable clothes —leggings and an oversized sweater—and ordered pizza. Opened a bottle of wine.

And waited for her best friend to arrive so she could fall apart in safe arms.

LaKrecia showed up at exactly 7 PM with a second bottle of wine and a bag of candy.

"Emergency provisions," she announced, setting them on the counter. Then she took one look at Sadie's face. "What happened?"

"Jarod came to my office."

"Oh, honey." LaKrecia pulled her into a hug. "Tell me everything."

They settled on Sadie's obscenely comfortable couch with wine and pizza, and Sadie recounted the conversation—Jarod's new girlfriend Maya, TJ's girlfriend Sarah, the closure, the finality of it all.

"How do you feel?" LaKrecia asked when she finished.

"Sad. But also... relieved? Like I've been waiting for the other shoe to drop, and it finally did. Now I can stop waiting and start actually moving forward."

"That's really mature, Sadie. I'm impressed."

"Don't be too impressed. I'm barely holding it together." Sadie took a long drink of wine. "But I'm holding it together. That's something, right?"

"That's everything." LaKrecia squeezed her hand. "Two weeks ago, this news would have sent you spiraling. Would have sent you to the Velvet Room or to a bottle of bourbon. But you're here, processing your feelings, talking about it. That's huge growth."

"It doesn't feel huge. It feels exhausting."

"Growth is exhausting. But it's worth it." LaKrecia refilled their wine glasses. "So what now? What's next for Sadie Monroe?"

"More therapy. More work. More figuring out who I am when I'm not performing." Sadie paused. "Dr. Chen suggested I might try dating eventually. Not seriously, just... practice being present and honest with someone. Getting comfortable with vulnerability in small doses."

"How do you feel about that?"

"Terrified. I don't know how to date. Everything with Jarod and TJ started physical and maybe got emotional. I've never done the normal thing—coffee, conversation, getting to know someone slowly."

"But you could learn. If you wanted to."

"Maybe. Eventually. Right now, I just need to focus on myself. On becoming whole before I try to share that wholeness with anyone else."

They ate pizza and drank wine and watched terrible reality TV— some show about people getting engaged sight unseen. The ridiculousness of it was exactly what Sadie needed—something light and mindless to take her brain off her own drama.

Around 10 PM, LaKrecia's phone buzzed. She glanced at it, then smiled.

"What?" Sadie asked.

"Nothing. Just a guy I've been talking to. Xavier. He wants to grab drinks tomorrow."

"Xavier? You're holding out on me! Details, please."

LaKrecia laughed. "There's not much to tell yet. We matched on an app, had coffee last week, good conversation. He's funny, has a real job, doesn't live with his mother. The bar is low, but he clears it."

"I'm happy for you. You deserve someone good."

"So do you, babe. When you're ready." LaKrecia set down her wine glass. "Can I say something that might be hard to hear?"

"Always."

"I'm proud of you. For how you're handling this. For going to therapy, for doing the work, for not self-destructing. Two months ago, I was worried you were going to implode completely. But look at you now—sad, yes, but surviving. Healing. That takes incredible strength."

"I don't feel strong. I feel like I'm barely keeping my head above water."

"That's what strength looks like sometimes. Not dramatic gestures or perfect composure. Just showing up. Doing the work. Surviving the hard days." LaKrecia reached over and hugged her. "You're going to be okay, Sadie. Better than okay. You're going to be extraordinary once you figure out who you really are."

"That's what Jarod said. That the woman I'm becoming is going to be incredible."

"He's right. And someday, you'll meet someone who gets to know that woman from the start. No compartments, no walls. Just you. Whole and honest and brave."

"I hope so. Right now, I just want to make it through tonight without falling apart."

"You're doing great. And I'm not going anywhere." LaKrecia settled back into the couch. "Now, let's watch these ridiculous people make terrible decisions and feel better about our own lives."

They watched TV until midnight, when LaKrecia finally Ubered home. Sadie cleaned up the pizza boxes and wine bottles, went through her nighttime routine, and climbed into bed.

But sleep didn't come easily.

She lay in the dark, thinking about Jarod with Maya. About TJ with Sarah. About how quickly they'd moved on, found new people, started building new possibilities.

And she was happy for them. Really, truly happy.

But she was also achingly lonely.

Not for them specifically—though she missed them both in different ways. But for connection. For intimacy. For someone who knew her and chose to stay anyway.

Her phone sat on the nightstand, dark and silent. No texts from Jarod. No messages from TJ. The silence felt heavier than usual tonight.

Before she could stop herself, she picked up the phone and opened her contacts. Scrolled through until she found a number she hadn't called in months.

A regular from the Velvet Room. Someone who'd been disappointed when she'd stopped showing up.

Her thumb hovered over the call button.

One phone call. One text. She could be back in that world in an hour. Could feel powerful and desired and free again, if only for a night. Could escape all this painful growth and just... feel good.

This is a test, she realized. *The universe is testing me.*

Dr. Chen's voice echoed in her head: "Notice when you feel the urge to escape. To numb. To go back to old patterns. Sit with the urge instead of acting on it. Ask yourself what you're really trying to avoid feeling."

What was she trying to avoid?

The loneliness. The grief. The fear that she'd be alone forever because she'd destroyed her chance with two incredible men.

She set down the phone without calling.

Picked up her journal instead.

Almost slipped tonight, she wrote. *Almost called someone from my old life. Almost went back to the Velvet Room mentality—escape through pleasure, numb the pain, avoid the feelings.*

But I didn't.

I sat with the urge. Felt the loneliness and grief and fear. And then I chose differently.

This is progress. Even when it doesn't feel like progress. Even when it hurts.

Jarod has Maya. TJ has Sarah. And I have myself. And maybe that's enough for now.

Maybe learning to be enough for myself is the whole point.

She closed the journal, set it on her nightstand, and turned off the light.

In the darkness, she let herself cry—for what she'd lost, for what could have been, for the loneliness that came with choosing growth over comfort.

But she also felt something else underneath the tears. Something that felt almost like pride.

She'd faced a trigger and hadn't self-destructed. Had felt the urge to escape and chose to stay present instead.

It was a small victory. But Dr. Chen said healing happened in small victories, accumulated over time.

So Sadie lay in the dark and let herself feel everything—the pain and the pride, the grief and the growth, the loneliness and the tiny spark of hope that maybe, just maybe, she was becoming someone worth knowing.

Someone whole.

Someone brave enough to be vulnerable.

Someone who didn't need compartments to feel safe.

It would take time. Months, probably. Maybe years.

But tonight, she'd made it through without running. Without escaping. Without going back to old patterns.

And tomorrow, she'd wake up and try again.

One day at a time.

One choice at a time.

One step toward wholeness, even when every instinct screamed at her to run.

That was enough.

For tonight, that was more than enough.

CHAPTER 12
ADDICTION

SATURDAY MORNING ARRIVED with autumn rain—the kind of steady, gray drizzle that made the city look washed out and tired. Sadie woke at 8 AM feeling wrung out from the emotional weight of the previous day, but also strangely proud of herself for making it through without self-destructing.

She went for a run despite the rain, letting the water soak through her clothes as she pounded the pavement. The physical discomfort was grounding, keeping her present in her body instead of lost in her head.

By the time she returned to her apartment, soaked and exhausted, she felt marginally more centered. She showered, made coffee, and settled on her couch with her laptop to catch up on work emails.

The day passed quietly. She meal prepped for the week, responded to a few work messages, watched a documentary LaKrecia had recommended. Normal, boring, healthy activities that didn't involve numbing or escaping or compartmentalizing.

By 6 PM, she was restless. The apartment felt too quiet, too empty. The rain had stopped, and the city was emerging into a cool, clear evening. People would be heading to restaurants, bars, clubs. Starting their Saturday nights with possibility and promise.

Sadie's phone sat on the counter, tempting.

She'd successfully resisted calling anyone from the Velvet Room last night. But the urge hadn't gone away—it had just been postponed.

Just one night, the voice in her head whispered. *Just to prove you can. To feel powerful again. You don't have to tell Dr. Chen. It doesn't have to mean anything.*

But it would mean something. It would mean she was running again. Escaping again. Choosing comfort over growth.

She was pulling out her journal to write through the urge when someone knocked on her door.

Sadie froze. She wasn't expecting anyone. LaKrecia had texted earlier that she had her date with Xavier tonight. No one else had a reason to show up unannounced at her apartment.

She checked the peephole and her heart stopped.

Jarod.

What the hell was he doing here? He'd just come to her office yesterday to tell her he was moving on, that they couldn't be part of each other's lives anymore. Why was he at her apartment on a Saturday night?

Sadie opened the door slowly, and the look on his face made her stomach drop.

He looked wrecked. Hair disheveled like he'd been running his hands through it. Eyes slightly wild. Still in the same clothes from yesterday—jeans and the gray henley—like he hadn't gone home, hadn't slept.

"Jarod? What are you doing here?"

"I need to come in." His voice was rough, strained. "Please. I can't—I need to talk to you."

Every instinct told her this was a bad idea. That whatever was happening, letting him into her apartment would complicate everything. But he looked so lost, so desperate, that she stepped aside.

"Come in."

He walked past her, bringing with him the scent of cologne and rain and something else—desperation. He paced to her windows, stared out at the city, then turned back to face her.

"I lied yesterday," he said abruptly. "When I came to your office. About being okay. About moving on. About Maya."

Sadie's heart hammered. "What do you mean?"

"Maya is real. The dates happened. But I'm not okay. I'm not moving on." He ran his hands through his hair again, a gesture she recognized as stress. "I went home yesterday after seeing you, and Maya called to ask about getting together tonight. And I couldn't. I couldn't pretend I was present, couldn't pretend I was interested, couldn't pretend you aren't still under my skin like a fucking addiction I can't shake."

"Jarod—"

"I broke it off with her. Told her I wasn't ready, which is true. But the real truth is—" He crossed the room in three long strides, stopping just inches from her. "The real truth is I can't stop thinking about you. Can't stop replaying everything we had, everything we could have had if you'd just been brave enough to choose me."

"This isn't fair," Sadie whispered, even as her body responded to his proximity, her heart racing. "You came to my office yesterday and closed the door. Gave me closure. You can't just show up now and—"

"And what? Tell you the truth? That I've been miserable for three weeks? That every woman I try to date feels wrong because she's not you?" His hands came up to frame her face, and the touch was electric. "That I dream about you every night? That I wake up hard thinking about your body, your voice, the way you looked at me at the jazz club when you let your walls down?"

"Stop." But she didn't pull away. Couldn't pull away. Her body remembered his touch, craved it.

"I tried to move on. Tried to do the healthy thing. But Sadie—" His forehead dropped to hers, and she could feel his breath against her lips. "I'm not over you. I don't know if I ever will be."

"This is a bad idea. We both know it's a bad idea." But even as she said it, her hands came up to rest on his chest, feeling his heart pounding as hard as hers.

"The worst idea," he agreed. "But I can't stay away anymore. Can't keep pretending I don't want you."

"What about TJ? What about your friendship?"

"TJ's with Sarah tonight. He's moving on. He'll be fine." Jarod's hands slid from her face down her neck, her shoulders, leaving heat in their wake. "But I'm not fine. I'm fucking miserable. And I know you are too. I can see it in your eyes."

He was right. She was miserable. Had been for three weeks, maybe longer. And having him here, touching her, looking at her like she was oxygen and he was drowning—it was breaking down every wall she'd tried to rebuild.

"We can't do this," she tried one more time. "We'll just hurt each other again."

"Then let's hurt each other. Let's be broken together. Just for tonight." His lips hovered over hers, not quite touching. "Tell me you don't want this. Tell me you don't miss this. And I'll leave. I'll walk out that door and never come back."

Sadie knew she should say it. Should tell him to leave. Should protect both of them from the inevitable fallout of giving in to this.

But she was so tired of being strong. So tired of doing the right thing. So tired of sitting alone in her apartment feeling everything while everyone else moved on and found happiness.

And God, she missed him. Missed his intensity, his passion, the way he made her feel alive and free.

"I can't," she whispered. "I can't tell you I don't want this. Because I do. I want you so badly it's killing me."

The words were barely out of her mouth before his lips crashed into hers.

The kiss was nothing like their first kiss at the Velvet Room—exploratory and seductive. This was desperate. Hungry. Three weeks of longing and regret and unfinished business poured into one kiss.

His hands tangled in her hair, angling her head to deepen the kiss. She gripped his henley, pulling him closer, needing to eliminate any space between them. Their tongues met and tangled, tasting, claiming, remembering.

"I missed you," he breathed against her lips. "Missed this. Missed the way you taste."

"Jarod—" She tried to form a coherent thought, but his mouth moved to her neck, finding that spot below her ear that made her knees weak. "We shouldn't—"

"I know." But his hands were already sliding under her sweater, fingertips trailing fire across her skin. "We should stop. We should talk. We should—"

"Fuck talking," Sadie pulled his mouth back to hers. "I don't want to talk. I don't want to think. I just want to feel."

And God, did she want to feel.

She pulled his henley over his head, revealing the body she'd memorized with her hands and mouth. Smooth dark skin over defined muscles. She pressed her lips to his chest, right over his racing heart, and heard his sharp intake of breath.

"Bedroom," he growled, but she shook her head.

"Here. Now. I can't wait."

He lifted her effortlessly, her legs wrapping around his waist as he carried her to the couch. He set her down and immediately pulled her sweater over her head, revealing the simple black bra underneath.

"You're so fucking beautiful," he murmured, his hands cupping her breasts through the fabric. "I thought I'd imagined how perfect you are. But reality is better."

He unhooked her bra with practiced ease, and then his mouth was on her, tongue circling her nipple until it peaked. Sadie's head fell back, a moan escaping as pleasure shot straight through her core.

His hands moved to her leggings, pulling them down along with her underwear in one smooth motion. And then she was naked on her couch, and he was kneeling between her legs, looking at her like she was a feast laid out just for him.

"I'm going to make you come so hard you forget your own name," he promised, his voice dark with intent.

"Big talk," she managed, even as her body trembled with anticipation.

"Let me show you."

His mouth descended on her, and Sadie's world narrowed to sensation. His tongue moved with skillful precision, remembering exactly what she liked, exactly how to drive her crazy. He slid two fingers inside her, curling them just right while his mouth worked her clit.

"Jarod—oh God—" Her hands fisted in his hair, holding him there, not that he showed any signs of stopping.

The orgasm built quickly, pleasure coiling tighter and tighter in her belly. She was already so wound up from weeks of wanting him, weeks of denying herself, that it didn't take long before she was right on the edge.

"Come for me," he commanded against her. "Let me hear you."

And she did. The orgasm crashed over her, pulling a cry from deep in her chest. Her body arched off the couch, pleasure pulsing through her in waves that seemed endless.

When she finally came back to herself, he was kissing his way up her body—her stomach, between her breasts, her collarbone, her neck—until his mouth found hers again.

She could taste herself on his lips, and it was incredibly erotic.

"Your turn," she breathed, reaching for his jeans.

But he caught her hands, stopping her. "Not yet. I'm not done with you."

"Jarod, I need you inside me. Now."

"Soon." He released her hands and stood, stripping off his jeans and boxer briefs in one smooth motion.

He was already hard, impressively so, and Sadie's mouth literally watered at the sight. She'd missed this. Missed him. Missed the way his body fit with hers like they were made for each other.

He grabbed a condom from his wallet—of course he'd brought one, they both knew why he'd really come here—and rolled it on with shaking hands.

Then he was positioning himself between her thighs, the head of him pressing against her entrance.

"Look at me," he commanded. "I want to see your eyes when I'm inside you."

She met his gaze, and the intensity there took her breath away. This wasn't just physical for him. It never had been, even when they'd both pretended it was.

He entered her slowly, giving her time to adjust, and Sadie's eyes fluttered closed at the sensation of being filled, stretched, completed.

"Eyes," he reminded her, and she forced them open.

He began to move—slow, deep strokes that hit every nerve ending.

One hand gripped her hip, the other braced beside her head, holding his weight off her.

"I've thought about this every day," he confessed, his rhythm increasing. "Every night. The way you feel around me. The sounds you make. The way you look when you come."

"Jarod—" His name was a plea, a prayer.

"I know, baby. I know." He adjusted his angle slightly, and suddenly he was hitting that perfect spot inside her that made stars burst behind her eyelids.

"Right there—don't stop—please don't stop—"

"Never." His hand slid between them, fingers finding her clit, circling with just the right pressure. "Come with me this time. I want to feel you."

The combination of sensations was overwhelming. Him inside her, filling her completely. His fingers working her clit. The intensity of his gaze. The emotion pouring off both of them in waves.

"I'm close—" she gasped. "So close—"

"Let go," he commanded. "I've got you."

And she did. The second orgasm was even more powerful than the first, ripping through her entire body. She cried out his name, her inner walls clenching around him.

She felt him follow her over the edge, his body tensing as he found his release, her name on his lips like a benediction.

He collapsed beside her on the couch, both of them breathing hard, skin slick with sweat. For a long moment, neither of them spoke. The only sound was their gradually slowing breathing and the distant hum of the city outside.

Finally, Jarod turned his head to look at her. "I should regret that."

"But you don't."

"No. I don't." He reached out and tucked a strand of hair behind her ear—such a tender gesture after what they'd just done. "Do you?"

Sadie considered the question honestly. Should she regret it? Probably. They'd both acknowledged this was a bad idea before they'd done it anyway. This complicated everything—his healing, her growth, the closure they'd supposedly found.

But lying there next to him, her body still humming with pleasure, she couldn't bring herself to regret it.

"No," she admitted. "I don't regret it. Even though I probably should."

"We're a disaster, you and me."

"The worst kind of disaster."

He pulled her close, and she let herself curl into his side, her head on his chest. His heart was still racing, gradually slowing to normal.

"What are we doing, Sadie?" His voice was quiet, vulnerable.

"I don't know. Making a mistake? Giving in to addiction? Self-sabotaging?"

"All of the above, probably." His fingers traced patterns on her shoulder. "I came here tonight planning to tell you I couldn't stay away. That I wanted to try again. To give us a real shot."

Her heart jumped. "And now?"

"Now I'm lying here realizing nothing's changed. I still don't trust you. Still don't know if you're capable of being fully present with me. Still scared you'll compartmentalize me again the moment things get real." He pressed a kiss to the top of her head. "But I want you anyway. That's the problem. I want you even though I know it's probably going to destroy me."

Sadie's chest felt tight. "I don't want to destroy you. I never wanted that."

"I know. But intent doesn't change impact." He shifted slightly so he could look at her. "Here's what I'm thinking. And you can tell me if I'm crazy."

"Okay."

"What if we tried this? Really tried. Not the compartmentalized version where you keep me separate from the rest of your life. A real relationship. You let me into all your worlds—work, personal, every-thing. I meet LaKrecia. You tell people about me. We do the scary, vulnerable thing of actually building something together."

Hope and terror warred in Sadie's chest. "And if I can't? If I panic and pull away again?"

"Then we're done. For real this time. No more second chances." His eyes were serious. "I can't keep doing this—the back and forth, the maybe-we-will-maybe-we-won't. It's killing me. So either we're all in, or we're all out."

"That's terrifying."

"Love is terrifying. That's how you know it's real."

The word "love" hung between them, shocking in its casual delivery.

"Did you just say love?" Sadie's voice was barely a whisper.

"Yeah. I did." He cupped her face gently. "I'm falling in love with you, Sadie. Maybe I already have. And that scares the shit out of me because I don't know if you'll ever let yourself fall back. But I'm willing to risk it. If you are."

Tears pricked Sadie's eyes. This was everything she'd been afraid of—someone seeing all of her, loving all of her, asking her to be vulnerable and present and whole.

"I don't know how," she admitted. "I don't know how to do this without running."

"Then we figure it out together. You go to therapy. I go to therapy. We communicate. We're honest, even when it's hard. We take it slow and build something real instead of something based on intensity and physical chemistry."

"What about TJ? What about your friendship?"

Jarod's expression darkened slightly. "TJ's going to be pissed. Probably feel betrayed all over again. But that's on me to manage. Our friendship is strong enough to survive this. Eventually."

"Are you sure?"

"No. But I'm willing to risk it. For you. For us." He kissed her forehead. "The question is—are you?"

Sadie's mind raced. Every logical part of her screamed this was a bad idea. That she wasn't ready. That she'd just hurt him again. That she should protect them both by saying no.

But another part—the part Dr. Chen had been slowly uncovering in therapy—wanted this desperately. Wanted to try. Wanted to believe she could be the kind of person who loved someone without losing herself.

"I'm terrified," she said honestly.

"Me too."

"What if I mess this up again?"

"Then we deal with it. Together." He sat up, pulling her with him. "But Sadie, I need you to really commit. No more compartments. No more hiding me from parts of your life. If we do this, we do it right. Full transparency. Full honesty. Even when it's scary."

"Even when it's scary," she repeated, trying to make herself believe it was possible.

"So?" He looked at her expectantly. "Are you in? Really in?"

This was it. The moment where she chose. Safety and solitude, or risk and connection. The comfortable numbness of compartmentalization, or the terrifying aliveness of vulnerability.

Dr. Chen's voice echoed in her head: *Growth happens when we choose courage over comfort.*

"Yes," Sadie heard herself say. "I'm in. Terrified, but in."

The smile that spread across Jarod's face was brilliant. He pulled her into a kiss that was different from the desperate ones earlier—this was tender, promising, full of possibility.

When they finally pulled apart, he rested his forehead against hers. "We're really doing this."

"We're really doing this." Sadie's heart hammered with equal parts terror and hope. "When do we start?"

"Now. Right now." He stood and pulled her to her feet. "Get dressed. We're going to dinner. A real dinner, at a real restaurant, where we sit and talk and get to know each other like normal people. Not at the Velvet Room. Not in secret. Out in the open."

"Tonight? It's already 7:30."

"So? I'll make a reservation somewhere. We'll go out, be seen together, start building this thing the right way." He started gathering his clothes. "Unless you're not ready for that?"

It was a test, Sadie realized. A small one, but a test nonetheless. Was she really willing to be seen with him publicly? To start integrating her worlds?

"Give me twenty minutes to get ready," she said.

His smile said everything. She'd passed the first test.

While he used the bathroom to freshen up, Sadie went to her

bedroom and stared at her closet. What did you wear on a first real date with someone you'd already slept with multiple times? Someone who'd seen you at your most vulnerable and still wanted to try?

She settled on dark jeans, a silk blouse in deep burgundy, and heeled boots. Hair down and loose. Makeup minimal but polished. She looked like herself—not Corporate Sadie, not After Hours Sadie. Just Sadie.

When she emerged, Jarod was sitting on her couch, dressed and scrolling through his phone.

"Got us a reservation at Harvest—that farm-to-table place everyone's talking about. 8:30. That work?"

"Perfect."

He stood and looked at her, really looked at her, and something in his expression made her chest tight.

"What?" she asked.

"Nothing. You just look... real. Not performing. Just you." He crossed to her and took her hand. "I like you like this. Natural. Present."

"I like me like this too. I'm just not sure I know how to be her consistently."

"Then we practice. Every day. Until it becomes natural." He laced his fingers through hers. "Ready?"

"As I'll ever be."

They took his car—a sleek BMW that smelled like leather and his cologne. As he drove through the city, Sadie stared out the window and tried to process what had just happened.

An hour ago, she'd been restless and lonely, contemplating falling back into old patterns. Now she was in a car with Jarod, heading to dinner, having agreed to try an actual relationship. With full transparency and vulnerability and all the scary things she'd spent years avoiding.

"You're quiet," Jarod observed. "Second thoughts?"

"Constant second thoughts. But I'm still here."

"That's all I'm asking. Just keep showing up, even when it's scary."

They arrived at Harvest and were seated at a cozy corner table. The restaurant was beautiful—exposed brick, hanging Edison bulbs, an open kitchen where you could watch the chefs at work. The kind of place you took someone you were trying to impress.

The kind of place you took someone on a real date.

Over dinner—pan-seared salmon for her, ribeye for him—they talked. Really talked. Not about sex or intensity or physical chemistry. About life. About dreams. About fears.

Jarod told her about growing up in Atlanta, about his family—two sisters who drove him crazy, parents who'd been married forty years and still held hands. About starting his business and nearly losing everything in the first year. About his first heartbreak at twenty-three that had made him wary of commitment for years.

Sadie told him about watching her mother fall apart, about her drive to never be that vulnerable. About her friendship with LaKrecia, who'd been her anchor through everything. About her upcoming promotion and how empty it felt without anyone to celebrate with.

"You can celebrate with me," Jarod said. "And with LaKrecia. And with yourself. Success doesn't need an audience to be real."

"I'm starting to realize that."

They shared a dessert—chocolate lava cake that was sinfully good —and Sadie felt something she hadn't felt in weeks. Maybe months.

Peace.

She was sitting across from a man who'd seen her at her worst, who knew about her compartmentalization and fear, and who still wanted to try. Still believed she could be the whole person she was working toward becoming.

It was terrifying and wonderful in equal measure.

"What are you thinking?" Jarod asked, his eyes warm in the candlelight.

"That this is nice. Normal. The kind of date I've never let myself have because it felt too vulnerable."

"And how does it feel? The vulnerability?"

"Scary. But also... kind of good?" She smiled. "I'm still waiting for the other shoe to drop. For you to realize this is a mistake. But right now, in this moment, it feels... right."

"It does feel right." He reached across the table and took her hand.

"And when the scary moments come—because they will—we talk about them. We don't run. We work through them."

"Together."

"Together."

They left the restaurant around 10:30, both of them full and relaxed. The night air was cool and crisp, perfect autumn weather. As they walked to his car, Jarod kept his hand at the small of her back—a subtle, possessive gesture that felt both comforting and thrilling.

"Your place or mine?" he asked as they got in the car.

The question held weight. Going to either place meant continuing what they'd started. Meant spending the night together, waking up together, starting to build routines and familiarity.

It meant moving forward instead of retreating into safety.

"Yours," Sadie decided. "I want to see where you live. How you exist in your own space."

His smile was approving. "Another test passed."

"How many tests are there?"

"As many as it takes for us both to trust this. To trust each other." He started the car. "But Sadie? You're doing great. I know it doesn't feel like it, but you are."

As they drove to his place—a loft in the arts district, all exposed brick and industrial chic—Sadie thought about Dr. Chen. About her next therapy session Wednesday. About how she'd explain this to her therapist.

I slept with Jarod. Then agreed to try an actual relationship with him. Then went on a real date. Then agreed to spend the night at his place. Am I self-sabotaging or growing? Am I running toward something or away from something?

She didn't have the answers yet.

But as Jarod pulled into his building's parking garage and came around to open her door—such a small, gentlemanly gesture that made her heart flutter—Sadie decided the answers could wait.

Tonight, she was just going to be present. Be honest. Be vulnerable.

Be just Sadie, trying her best to build something real.

Even if it terrified her.

Even if she didn't know if she could sustain it.

Even if every instinct screamed at her to protect herself.

She was choosing courage over comfort.

One moment at a time.

One choice at a time.

One step toward wholeness, even when the path was uncertain.

And for tonight, that was enough.

CHAPTER 13
THE PROPOSAL

SADIE WOKE SLOWLY, awareness filtering in through layers of warmth and contentment. For a moment, she couldn't place where she was—the room was unfamiliar, the sheets a different thread count than her own, the light coming through the windows at the wrong angle.

Then she felt the arm draped across her waist, the solid warmth of a body behind hers, and memory flooded back.

Jarod's loft. His bed. The night they'd spent together—not just the sex (though there'd been plenty of that), but the talking afterward. The vulnerability. The slow exploration of what it meant to actually be with someone instead of just sleeping with them.

She shifted slightly, and the arm tightened around her waist.

"Don't even think about sneaking out," Jarod's voice rumbled against her neck, thick with sleep. "We're doing this different, remember?"

"I wasn't going to sneak out."

"You were thinking about it. I can tell." He pressed a kiss to her shoulder. "Your body got all tense, like you were calculating the fastest escape route."

He wasn't wrong. The urge to flee—to retreat to the safety of her own space before things got too real—was strong. But she'd made a promise last night. To try. To stay. To be present even when it was uncomfortable.

"Old habits," she admitted. "But I'm staying."

"Good." He pulled her closer, molding his body to hers. "Because I'm making you breakfast, and my pancakes are legendary. You'd be missing out."

Despite her anxiety, Sadie smiled. "Legendary pancakes? That's quite a claim."

"I'm a man of many talents." His hand slid under her shirt—his shirt, actually, that she'd borrowed last night—fingers splaying possessively across her stomach. "As I believe I demonstrated thoroughly last night."

Heat flooded through her at the memory. "No complaints on that front."

"Just on the staying-over front?"

She turned in his arms so she could face him. In the morning light streaming through the massive loft windows, he looked softer somehow. Hair mussed from sleep, eyes still slightly heavy-lidded, the intensity that usually radiated from him dialed down to something gentler.

"Not complaints. Just... unfamiliarity. I don't do this. The morning after. The domestic intimacy. The—" she gestured around them, "—whatever this is."

"This is called a relationship, baby. People do it all the time."

"Other people. Not me."

"Not you yet," he corrected. "But you're learning." He brushed a strand of hair from her face. "How do you feel? Really?"

Sadie considered the question honestly. "Terrified. Vulnerable. Like I'm standing at the edge of a cliff and you're asking me to jump."

"But?"

"But also... kind of good? Like maybe jumping off the cliff won't kill me. Maybe I'll actually fly."

"That's my girl." He kissed her forehead. "Come on. Let me feed you. Everything's less scary on a full stomach."

They got up—Sadie in his t-shirt and her underwear from last night, Jarod in pajama pants that hung low on his hips—and moved to the kitchen area of his loft. The space was beautiful in daylight—high ceilings, exposed brick walls, industrial metal accents mixed with warm wood. Masculine but not cold. Lived-in but not messy.

It felt like him. Confident and intense but with an underlying warmth that most people didn't get to see.

Jarod moved around the kitchen with easy competence, pulling out ingredients while Sadie sat at the breakfast bar and watched. There was something intimate about this—watching him make pancakes in his own space, seeing him comfortable and unguarded.

"Coffee?" he asked, and she nodded gratefully.

He poured her a cup—black, no sugar, exactly how she took it—and she realized he'd remembered from their nights at the Velvet Room. Small details that added up to being seen.

"So," he said as he mixed pancake batter, "we need to talk about logistics."

"Logistics?"

"Yeah. Like, when do we tell TJ? Because that's happening. Probably soon. Before he hears it from someone else."

The mention of TJ sent a spike of anxiety through Sadie's chest. "Does he have to know? Right away, I mean?"

Jarod paused, giving her a look. "Sadie. We agreed. No more compartments. No more hiding. That includes telling my best friend that I'm dating the woman who played us both three weeks ago."

"When you put it like that, it sounds even worse."

"It is worse. Which is why we need to handle it head-on. Together." He poured batter onto the griddle. "I'm thinking I tell him first. Just me. Let him process, get angry, whatever he needs to do. Then, when he's ready, we all sit down together. You apologize again, explain that we're trying to do this right, and we move forward."

"What if he's not ready? What if he never is?"

"Then that's his choice. But I have to try. He's my brother, Sadie. I can't build something with you while destroying my relationship with him." He flipped the pancakes with practiced ease. "But I also can't live my life based on what TJ might feel. I have to do what's right for me. And what's right for me is giving us a real shot."

The words should have been comforting. Instead, they made Sadie feel the weight of what she'd done—the damage she'd caused not just to her relationships with both men, but to their relationship with each other.

"I'm sorry," she said quietly. "For all of it. For putting you in this position."

"I know. And I forgive you. But Sadie—" He plated the pancakes and set them in front of her, then came around the counter to stand beside her. "You have to forgive yourself too. You keep carrying this guilt like a shield, and it's going to poison what we're trying to build."

"How do I forgive myself when I hurt people I care about?"

"By doing better. By being better. By showing up and being present and honest, even when it's hard. That's how you make amends—not by drowning in guilt, but by changing your behavior." He tilted her chin up to look at him. "You're doing the work. Therapy, self-reflection, trying to be vulnerable. That's huge. Give yourself credit for that."

Tears pricked Sadie's eyes. "You're being too nice to me. I don't deserve it."

"Stop deciding what you deserve. I'm choosing to be with you. To give this a shot. Let me make my own choices about what I can handle."

She nodded, not trusting herself to speak.

They ate breakfast in comfortable silence, the pancakes living up to their legendary reputation. When they were done, Jarod loaded the dishwasher while Sadie checked her phone.

Several texts from LaKrecia: *How was girls' night? You went quiet early.*

Then: *Wait. Are you with someone? Please tell me you didn't go to the Velvet Room.*

Then: *SADIE MONROE answer your phone right now.*

Sadie winced. She'd forgotten to update LaKrecia last night. Her best friend was probably losing her mind with worry.

She typed quickly: *I'm okay. Not at the Velvet Room. Will call you later. I'm... with Jarod.*

The response was immediate: *WHAT. Call me RIGHT NOW. I need details.*

Sadie: *Later. I promise. Still processing.*

LaKrecia: *Fine. But we're having lunch TODAY. No excuses.*

"LaKrecia?" Jarod asked, reading her expression.

"Yeah. She's freaking out that I'm with you."

"Good. She should know. That's what full transparency looks like—telling the people who matter what's happening in your life." He dried his hands on a towel. "Why don't you invite her to lunch? The three of us. Let me meet her properly."

"You want to meet my best friend? Today?"

"Why wait? You said she's the most important person in your life. I should know her. And she should be able to look me in the eye and decide if I'm good enough for her girl." He smiled. "Plus, it's another test. Are you willing to integrate me into your life, or are you going to keep me separate from LaKrecia?"

He was right. This was exactly the kind of thing she would have avoided before—introducing someone she was seeing to her best friend, blending her worlds. But she'd committed to doing this differently.

"Okay," she said. "I'll text her."

Sadie: *Change of plans. Lunch at 1 PM. Bringing Jarod. He wants to meet you.*

LaKrecia: *Oh shit. This is serious. Okay. Where?*

Sadie: *Your pick.*

LaKrecia: *Marcel's. Where this all started. And Sadie? I'm proud of you. Scared for you, but proud.*

Sadie showed Jarod the exchange, and he grinned. "I like her already. Anyone who's both proud and scared is being realistic."

"She's protective. Fair warning—she's going to grill you."

"Good. I'd be worried if she didn't." He glanced at the clock. "It's 10:30 now. That gives us a few hours. What do you want to do?"

The old Sadie would have said she needed to go home, shower, change, prepare. Would have used the time to rebuild her walls and armor before facing the vulnerability of introducing Jarod to her best friend.

The new Sadie—the one she was trying to become—took a breath and chose differently.

"Stay here. With you. Maybe watch a movie or just... be together. Get used to this. Whatever this is."

The smile that spread across Jarod's face was worth the discomfort of staying when every instinct told her to flee.

"Whatever this is," he repeated. "I like that. Come on—I've got a ridiculous collection of movies, and my couch is perfect for lazy Sunday mornings."

They spent the next two hours exactly like that—curled up on his couch watching an action movie neither of them paid much attention to, talking during the boring parts, comfortable in a way that felt both foreign and right.

Jarod told her about TJ—how they'd met freshman year of college, both assigned to the same dorm room. How they'd bonded over being the only two business majors who also loved basketball. How they'd supported each other through failures and successes, bad relationships and good ones.

"He's going to hate this," Jarod said quietly. "Us. He's going to feel betrayed all over again."

"Then maybe we shouldn't—"

"No." His arm tightened around her. "I'm not giving this up because TJ might be uncomfortable. But I am going to handle it carefully. Tell him myself. Give him space to process. And hope that eventually, he'll understand."

"What if he doesn't?"

"Then I'll deal with it. But Sadie, I can't live my life trying to make everyone else comfortable. I tried that before—played it safe, dated women who were easy and uncomplicated, never rocked the boat. And I was miserable. You make me feel alive. Challenged. Like I'm actually living instead of just existing. I'm not giving that up."

The words made her chest tight with emotion she couldn't quite name. "You make me feel that way too. Terrified, but alive."

"Then we're doing something right."

At 12:30, Sadie reluctantly got dressed in her clothes from the night before. Jarod offered to drive her home to change, but she shook her head.

"No. LaKrecia needs to see me like this—slightly rumpled, obviously having spent the night somewhere. It's part of being honest. Part of not hiding."

"Look at you, being all transparent and integrated."

"Don't get too excited. I'm still one panic attack away from running."

"I know. But you're here. That's what matters."

They drove to Marcel's in Jarod's car, and Sadie felt her anxiety ratchet up with every mile. This was real now. She was introducing Jarod to LaKrecia as her... what? Boyfriend? Partner? The man she was trying to build something with?

All of it felt impossibly vulnerable.

LaKrecia was already seated at their usual table when they arrived, looking stunning in a burnt orange dress that complemented her skin beautifully. Her expression was carefully neutral as they approached, but Sadie could see the protective concern in her eyes.

"Krecia, this is Jarod. Jarod, my best friend LaKrecia."

Jarod extended his hand with a genuine smile. "It's good to finally meet you properly. Sadie talks about you constantly."

LaKrecia shook his hand, her grip firm. "I wish I could say the same, but until three weeks ago, I didn't know you existed. Sadie was pretty good at compartmentalizing."

"Fair point." Jarod didn't flinch at the subtle accusation. "But she's working on that. We both are."

They sat down, and there was a moment of awkward silence before LaKrecia leaned forward, her eyes on Jarod.

"Okay. Let's cut through the bullshit. You and TJ both got played by my best friend. It was messy and hurtful and damaged all of you. So why are you here? Why are you trying again with someone who lied to you and broke your trust?"

Sadie winced, but Jarod remained calm. "Because I understand why she did it. Because I've spent two years in therapy learning about trauma responses and protection mechanisms, and I recognize them in her. Because despite everything, I care about her. And because I think she's capable of being the whole, integrated person she's working toward becoming."

"That's a lot of faith to put in someone who already hurt you once."

"It is. But I'm not going in blind this time. We've talked about boundaries and expectations. About full transparency and honesty. About what happens if she compartmentalizes again—which is that we're done, for real. I'm taking a risk, but it's a calculated one."

LaKrecia studied him for a long moment, then turned to Sadie. "And you? Are you really ready for this? For a real relationship with someone who's going to expect all of you, not just the pieces you choose to show?"

"I don't know," Sadie admitted. "I'm terrified. But I'm trying. Going to therapy, doing the work, practicing being vulnerable. Jarod is patient with me, but he also holds me accountable. That's what I need."

"And TJ? How does he factor into this?"

"We're telling him," Jarod said. "Soon. Probably tomorrow. I'll talk to him first, let him process, then we'll all sit down if he's willing."

"He's going to be pissed."

"I know. But I'm hoping he'll understand eventually. He's my brother. I can't lose him. But I also can't let fear of his reaction keep me from pursuing something real with Sadie."

The waiter arrived to take their orders, giving everyone a moment to breathe. When he left, LaKrecia's expression had softened slightly.

"I'm not going to lie—I'm worried. Worried about Sadie, worried about this situation, worried that everyone's going to end up hurt again. But—" she reached across the table and took Sadie's hand, "—I'm also proud of you. For trying. For being honest. For not running back to the Velvet Room when things got hard."

"That was a close call Friday night," Sadie admitted. "I almost called someone. Almost fell back into old patterns. But I didn't."

"Because you're stronger than you think." LaKrecia squeezed her hand, then released it. "Okay, Jarod. I'm going to ask you some questions, and I need you to be brutally honest."

"Shoot."

"What happens when Sadie panics and pulls away? Because she will. It's what she does when things get too real."

"We talk about it. I don't let her retreat into old patterns. I call her on it, and we work through it together. Or we don't, and we end things. But I'm not enabling her compartmentalization. That helps no one."

"What happens if TJ never forgives either of you? If your friendship ends because of this?"

Jarod's expression darkened. "That would devastate me. TJ is my brother. But I can't live my life based on what might make him comfortable. I have to make choices for myself. And I'm choosing to try with Sadie. If TJ can't accept that, I'll have to find a way to live with it."

"What are your intentions with my best friend?"

"To build something real. To see if we can be together without all the deception and compartmentalization. To support her growth while also expecting her to show up for me. To be honest and vulnerable and see where this goes."

LaKrecia looked at Sadie. "And you believe him?"

"I want to. God, I want to. But Krecia, I'm so scared. Scared I'll mess this up again. Scared I'm not capable of what he's asking for. Scared that I'll hurt him worse the second time around."

"Those are valid fears. But they're also reasons to try, not reasons to run." LaKrecia sat back as their food arrived. "Here's what I'm going to say. I'm cautiously optimistic. Jarod seems genuine, and you seem committed to doing the work. But Sadie—" her voice turned firm, "—if you pull the same shit again, I'm done defending you. You'll lose him, you'll lose TJ's respect permanently, and you'll prove that you're not ready for a real relationship. This is your shot. Don't blow it."

"No pressure," Sadie said weakly.

"There should be pressure. This matters. He matters. You matter. So show up. Be present. Be honest. And when it gets scary—because it will—don't run. Talk to him. Talk to me. Talk to Dr. Chen. But don't run."

They ate lunch with lighter conversation after that—LaKrecia telling stories about Sadie in college, Jarod sharing embarrassing moments from his business ventures, all of them laughing and gradually relaxing into something that felt almost normal.

By the time they finished, Sadie felt cautiously hopeful. LaKrecia had given her conditional approval. Jarod had handled her best friend's interrogation with grace and honesty. They were doing this—really doing this.

As they walked out of the restaurant, LaKrecia pulled Sadie aside while Jarod went to get the car.

"He's good for you," she said quietly. "He challenges you without trying to change you. That's rare. Don't fuck it up."

"I'm trying not to."

"I know, baby. I know." She hugged her fiercely. "Call me after he talks to TJ tomorrow. I want to make sure you're okay."

"I will. And Krecia? Thank you. For always having my back, even when I don't deserve it."

"That's what best friends are for. Now go. Be with your man. Practice being present and vulnerable. And remember—growth is uncomfortable. That's how you know it's working."

Jarod pulled up, and Sadie got in the car. As they drove away, she looked back to see LaKrecia watching them, concern and hope warring on her face.

"She's intense," Jarod observed. "But I like her. She cares about you fiercely."

"She does. And she's right to be worried. I have a track record of self-destructing."

"Had a track record. Past tense." He reached over and took her hand. "You're writing a new story now. We both are."

They spent the rest of Sunday at Sadie's apartment—she needed to shower and change, and it felt important to have him in her space too. To let him see where she lived, how she existed in her own environment.

He wandered around while she showered, looking at her books, her carefully curated decor, the view from her windows.

"This is very you," he said when she emerged. "Beautiful, controlled, expensive. But also kind of cold. Like you're afraid to make it too personal."

He wasn't wrong. Her apartment looked like a showroom—perfect and untouchable. No photos, no mementos, no evidence of a life actually lived.

"I never saw the point in making it homey," she admitted. "It was just a place to sleep between work and... other activities."

"Maybe we change that. Add some warmth. Some personality. Make it feel like a home instead of a hotel."

The casual "we" made her stomach flip. He was already thinking long-term. Already imagining a future where they did things together, made changes together, built a life together.

It was terrifying and wonderful.

They ordered Thai food for dinner and ate it on her couch, watching a documentary about something Sadie forgot the moment it ended. All she could focus on was Jarod's presence in her space—solid, comfortable, real.

Around 9 PM, he stood reluctantly. "I should go. Let you get some rest. Big week ahead—I'm talking to TJ tomorrow."

"Do you want me there? When you tell him?"

"No. That's something I need to do alone. But I'll call you after. Let you know how it goes."

"What if he's so angry he doesn't want to see me? Doesn't want us to explain?"

"Then we give him time. As much as he needs. But Sadie—" He pulled her to her feet and wrapped his arms around her. "No matter what happens with TJ, we're solid. Okay? This is between us. We don't let his reaction—however justified—derail what we're building."

"Okay," she whispered against his chest.

He tilted her chin up and kissed her—slow and deep and promising. "I'll text you tomorrow. After I talk to him. Try not to spiral."

"No promises."

He laughed and kissed her again. "Fair enough. Goodnight, baby."

"Goodnight."

She walked him to the door and stood there long after he'd left, processing everything that had happened in the last twenty-four hours.

Yesterday at this time, she'd been restless and lonely. Now she was in a relationship. Had introduced her boyfriend (boyfriend!) to her best friend. Was preparing for the fallout of that relationship to hit TJ.

It was a lot.

She pulled out her journal and wrote:

I'm with Jarod. Actually with him. In a real relationship with transparency and vulnerability and all the scary things I've avoided for years.

We told LaKrecia. She's cautiously supportive. Tomorrow he tells TJ. That's going to be brutal.

I'm terrified. Terrified I'll mess this up. Terrified I'm not capable of what he's asking for. Terrified that TJ will hate us both and Jarod will resent me for damaging his friendship.

But I'm also... hopeful? For the first time in weeks, I feel like maybe I can do this. Maybe I can be the whole person Jarod believes I can be.

Dr. Chen is going to have a field day with this in our session Wednesday.

One day at a time. One choice at a time. One step toward being someone who can love and be loved without losing herself.

That's all I can promise. To keep trying.

She closed the journal and got ready for bed, her body exhausted from the emotional rollercoaster of the weekend. As she lay in the dark, her phone buzzed.

Jarod: *Thank you for today. For meeting me halfway. For being brave. Sleep well, beautiful.*

Sadie: *Thank you for being patient with me. For seeing potential in someone who's still figuring out how to be whole.*

Jarod: *I see you, Sadie. All of you. And I'm not going anywhere.*

The words should have been comforting. They were comforting.

But they also felt like a weight—the weight of expectation, of possibility, of someone believing in her more than she believed in herself.

She hoped she could live up to it.

Hoped she could be the woman he thought she could be.

Hoped that tomorrow, when he told TJ, their tentative new beginning wouldn't come crashing down before it even really started.

But hope was something. After weeks of despair and regret, hope was everything.

So Sadie held onto it—fragile and tentative but real—and let herself drift off to sleep.

Tomorrow would bring whatever it would bring.

Tonight, she was choosing to believe that maybe, just maybe, she could do this.

She could be whole.
She could be loved.
She could be brave enough to try.
And that was enough.
For tonight, that was more than enough.

CHAPTER 14
CRACKS IN THE FOUNDATION

MONDAY MORNING ARRIVED TOO QUICKLY. Sadie woke with a knot of anxiety in her stomach that no amount of coffee or deep breathing could ease. Today, Jarod was telling TJ about them. About their relationship. About the fact that he'd chosen to try again with the woman who'd played them both.

She went through her morning routine on autopilot—shower, power suit (navy today, with a silk blouse the color of cream), hair sleek and professional. Corporate Sadie armor firmly in place, even though the woman underneath felt anything but armored.

Her phone buzzed as she was finishing her makeup.

Jarod: *Morning, beautiful. Meeting TJ for lunch at 1 PM. Wish me luck.*

Sadie: *Good luck. Let me know how it goes. I'll be thinking about you.*

Jarod: *Try not to spiral. Whatever happens, we're solid. Remember that.*

Sadie: *I'll try.*

She pocketed her phone and stared at herself in the mirror. The woman looking back appeared calm, controlled, successful. No one would guess that underneath the polished exterior, she was barely holding it together.

Fake it till you make it, she told herself. *That's what you do best.*

The morning at work passed in a blur of meetings and conference calls. Sadie threw herself into tasks with an intensity that bordered on manic, anything to keep her mind off what was happening between Jarod and TJ.

At 12:45, her phone buzzed. LaKrecia: *How are you holding up?*

Sadie: *Barely. Jarod's telling TJ at 1 PM.*

LaKrecia: *Want me to come sit with you? I can take a long lunch.*

Sadie: *No. I need to get through this on my own. But thank you.*

LaKrecia: *Call me if you need me. Anytime. I mean it.*

Sadie set down her phone and tried to focus on the contract in front of her, but the words blurred together. All she could think about was Jarod and TJ sitting across from each other at some restaurant, having the conversation that would either salvage their friendship or destroy it completely.

And it would be her fault. All of it.

At 1:15, she gave up pretending to work and just stared out her office window at the city below. People moved through their lives— heading to lunch, running errands, existing in their own dramas and complications. From up here, they looked so small. So insignificant.

She felt small too. Like all her careful planning and control and compartmentalization had been for nothing, because here she was— vulnerable and exposed and waiting for news that could shatter the fragile new thing she was trying to build with Jarod.

Her phone rang at 2:30, and she nearly jumped out of her skin.

Jarod's name on the screen.

She answered on the second ring, her heart hammering. "How did it go?"

"Can you get away from the office? I need to see you."

His voice was carefully neutral, which told her nothing and everything.

"I can leave. Where do you want to meet?"

"That park near your building. The one with the fountain. Twenty minutes?"

"I'll be there."

She hung up and grabbed her coat, telling Melissa she was stepping out for a bit. The elevator ride down felt endless, and the walk to the park even longer.

Jarod was already there when she arrived, sitting on a bench near the fountain, staring at nothing. He looked tired—not just physically, but emotionally. Like the conversation with TJ had drained something essential from him.

Sadie sat down beside him, leaving a few inches of space between them. "Tell me."

He took a deep breath. "It went about as well as could be expected. Which is to say, not well at all."

"Is he angry?"

"Furious. Hurt. Feels betrayed all over again—by you for playing us both, by me for choosing to try again with you." Jarod rubbed his hands over his face. "He said some things. Called you manipulative. Said I was thinking with my dick instead of my brain. Asked how I could be so stupid as to trust you again."

Each word landed like a physical blow. "What did you say?"

"I told him the truth. That I care about you. That I understand why you did what you did. That I think you're capable of growth and change. That I'm going into this with my eyes open." He finally turned to look at her. "He didn't buy it. Said I'm setting myself up to be hurt again. That you'll compartmentalize me the moment things get difficult."

"Maybe he's right."

"Don't." Jarod's voice was sharp. "Don't do that. Don't let his anger make you doubt yourself."

"But what if he's right? What if I'm not capable of this? What if I hurt you again and destroy your friendship in the process?"

"Then that's on me. I'm making this choice with full knowledge of the risks." He reached over and took her hand. "But Sadie, I need you to hear this—TJ is not okay with us. At all. He said if I'm going to date you, he needs space from both of us. Maybe a lot of space. Maybe permanently."

The words hung in the air between them, heavy with consequence.

"So you're losing your best friend because of me."

"I'm losing him temporarily because he's hurt and needs to process. That's different."

"Is it?" Sadie pulled her hand away. "Jarod, TJ has been your brother for over a decade. I've been in your life for what—a few months? Most of which I spent lying to you. Why would you choose me over him?"

"Because I'm not choosing between you. I'm choosing to pursue something with you while hoping TJ comes around eventually. That's different than choosing one person over another."

"But if he doesn't come around? If he decides your friendship is over because you're with me?"

Jarod was quiet for a long moment. "Then I'll have to live with that. But Sadie, I can't make my relationship decisions based on what might make someone else comfortable. Even TJ. That's not fair to me, and it's not fair to you."

"But you'll resent me. Eventually. When the friendship is gone and you realize I wasn't worth it."

"Stop putting words in my mouth." His voice was firm but not angry. "Stop deciding what I'm going to feel in the future. Right now, in this moment, I want to be with you. That's all I can control."

Sadie stood abruptly, needing to move. "This is a mistake. We're a mistake. We should end this now before anyone gets hurt worse."

"You mean before *you* get hurt worse." Jarod stood too, crossing to her. "This is what you do, Sadie. The moment things get difficult, you run. You compartmentalize. You decide it's safer to be alone than risk being vulnerable."

"Maybe that's because it *is* safer!"

"Safe isn't living. Safe is existing." He gripped her shoulders gently. "I know you're scared. I know TJ's reaction is triggering every protective instinct you have. But you promised me you'd try. That you'd stay even when it was hard. So I'm asking you—are you going to keep that promise? Or are you going to run at the first sign of conflict?"

Tears pricked Sadie's eyes. "I don't want to hurt you. Don't want to be the reason you lose your best friend."

"You're not. My choices are the reason. I'm choosing this, Sadie. I'm choosing *us*. Now I need you to choose it too."

"I'm scared."

"I know. Me too. But we do it anyway. That's what brave looks like —doing the scary thing even when every instinct tells you to run."

Sadie closed her eyes, feeling tears slip down her cheeks. Everything in her screamed to end this. To protect Jarod from future hurt. To protect herself from the inevitable moment when she'd prove TJ right and mess everything up again.

But a smaller voice—the one that sounded suspiciously like Dr. Chen—whispered: *What if you don't mess it up? What if you're actually capable of being the person Jarod believes you can be?*

"Okay," she whispered. "I'm staying. I'm scared, but I'm staying."

Jarod pulled her into his arms, and she let herself collapse against him. They stood there in the middle of the park, holding each other while the city moved around them, and Sadie felt both terrified and grateful.

"We'll figure this out," he murmured against her hair. "Together. One day at a time."

"What if TJ never forgives us?"

"Then we deal with that when it happens. But Sadie? I need you to stop catastrophizing. Stop jumping to the worst possible outcome and living there. Can you do that?"

"I can try."

"That's all I'm asking. Try." He pulled back to look at her. "Now. Go back to work. Be present there. Don't let this consume you. We'll talk tonight, okay?"

"Okay." She wiped her eyes, probably smearing her mascara. "I look like a mess."

"You look beautiful. Vulnerable and real and brave." He kissed her forehead. "Text me later. Let me know you're okay."

"I will."

She walked back to her office on shaky legs, hyper-aware that people were probably staring at her—disheveled clothes, tear-streaked face, the visible evidence of emotional distress. But for once, she didn't care about maintaining the perfect Corporate Sadie image.

Let them stare. Let them wonder. She had bigger things to worry about.

The rest of the afternoon passed in a fog. Sadie responded to emails, sat through meetings, said the right things at the right times. But inside, she was spinning.

TJ hated her. Hated them. Needed space from both of them. Maybe permanently.

And Jarod—Jarod was choosing her despite that. Choosing her despite the damage she'd caused, despite the risk that she'd hurt him again, despite losing his best friend in the process.

The weight of that choice felt crushing.

At 6 PM, she finally left the office. She should go home, but the thought of sitting alone in her apartment with her thoughts felt unbearable. So she did something she hadn't done in weeks—she drove to the building where the Velvet Room was located.

Not to go in. Just to sit in her car and stare at the entrance, remembering who she'd been when she walked through those doors. The woman who felt powerful and in control and untouchable.

That woman felt like a stranger now.

Her phone buzzed. Jarod: *How are you holding up?*

Sadie stared at the message, then at the building, then back at her phone. She could lie. Could say she was fine. Could go upstairs and lose herself in the old patterns, the old escape.

Or she could be honest.

She took a photo of the building entrance and sent it to him with the message: *Sitting outside the Velvet Room. Haven't gone in. But the urge is strong.*

His response was immediate: *Don't go in. Please. Talk to me instead. I'm coming to you.*

Sadie: *You don't have to do that.*

Jarod: *I want to. Stay in your car. I'll be there in twenty minutes.*

She should have told him not to come. Should have handled this on her own. But the truth was, she didn't want to handle it on her own. Didn't want to sit here alone with the temptation.

So she waited.

Jarod pulled up beside her car nineteen minutes later. He got out and knocked on her window, and she unlocked the doors. He slid into the passenger seat and just looked at her.

"Thank you for telling me instead of going in," he said quietly.

"I almost didn't tell you. Almost went in and pretended it never happened."

"But you didn't. That's growth, Sadie. That's huge."

"It doesn't feel huge. It feels like I'm barely holding on."

"Then let me help you hold on." He took her hand. "Why are you here? What triggered this?"

"Everything. TJ hating us. You losing your best friend because of me. The weight of your choice. The fear that I'm going to prove everyone right and mess this up." She gestured at the building. "This place—it was where I felt in control. Where I could escape from all the pressure and expectations and just... feel good. For a little while."

"And now?"

"Now I know that escape isn't real. It's just numbing. Postponing the feelings instead of processing them. But God, Jarod, I miss it. I miss feeling powerful. Miss not having to worry about hurting people or being vulnerable or any of this."

"I know." His thumb traced circles on her palm. "But you know what? You are powerful. Right now. Sitting here, telling me the truth instead of running, choosing to feel instead of numb—that's real power. Not the performance kind. The actual kind."

"It doesn't feel powerful. It feels exhausting."

"Because growth is exhausting. Healing is exhausting. Being present is exhausting." He shifted to face her more fully. "But you're doing it. Even when it's hard. Even when every instinct tells you to run or escape or compartmentalize. You're doing the work."

"I don't want to let you down."

"You won't. As long as you keep being honest with me. As long as you don't go through that door—" he nodded at the building, "—or any other door that leads back to old patterns. That's all I'm asking."

Sadie looked at the Velvet Room entrance one more time, then back at Jarod. "Take me somewhere else. Anywhere else. I don't want to be here anymore."

"Where do you want to go?"

"Your place. I want to be somewhere that feels safe. Somewhere that's not connected to my old life."

"Let's go." He kissed her hand. "Follow me in your car. We'll order dinner, put on a movie, just be together. No pressure. No expectations. Just us."

They drove to his loft in tandem, and Sadie felt the tension slowly ease from her shoulders with every mile away from the Velvet Room. By the time they arrived, she was exhausted but calmer.

Jarod's loft felt like a sanctuary—warm and comfortable and far removed from both the pressure of Corporate Sadie and the temptation of After Hours Sadie. Here, she could just be... herself. Whoever that was.

They ordered Chinese food and ate it on his couch while a movie played in the background. Jarod didn't push her to talk, didn't ask probing questions. He just let her exist in his space, offering quiet companionship.

Around 9 PM, Sadie's phone buzzed. LaKrecia: *Haven't heard from you all day. Are you okay? Did Jarod talk to TJ?*

Sadie typed back: *It went badly. TJ needs space from both of us. Maybe permanently. I'm at Jarod's place now. I'm okay. Sort of.*

LaKrecia: *Want me to come over? Bring wine and comfort?*

Sadie glanced at Jarod, who was watching her with concern.

"LaKrecia's asking if she should come over. With wine."

"Tell her yes. The more support you have right now, the better. And I'd like to get to know her better anyway."

Sadie: *Come over. Jarod's loft. I'll text you the address.*

LaKrecia: *On my way. Be there in thirty.*

When LaKrecia arrived with two bottles of wine and a bag of chocolate, she took one look at Sadie's face and immediately pulled her into a fierce hug.

"Tell me everything."

They settled in Jarod's living area, and Sadie recounted the day—the lunch meeting between Jarod and TJ, TJ's anger and hurt, the aftermath where she'd almost gone to the Velvet Room, Jarod coming to get her.

"TJ has every right to be pissed," LaKrecia said when she finished. "But that doesn't mean you and Jarod should end things. If anything, it proves you made the right choice being honest with him."

"How does his anger prove we made the right choice?"

"Because now everything's out in the open. No more secrets, no more compartments. TJ knows. He's processing. It sucks, but it's necessary." She poured them all wine. "And Sadie, the fact that you called Jarod instead of going into the Velvet Room? That's huge. That's you choosing growth over comfort. I'm proud of you."

"Everyone keeps saying they're proud of me for basic things like not self-destructing. The bar is very low."

"The bar is exactly where it needs to be," Jarod said. "We all start somewhere. Right now, not self-destructing is a victory. Eventually, it'll become second nature. But for now, we celebrate the small wins."

They spent the next few hours talking and laughing and slowly relaxing. LaKrecia told embarrassing stories about Sadie in college, Jarod reciprocated with stories about his early business failures, and gradually the weight of the day began to lift.

Around midnight, LaKrecia stood to leave. "I'm Ubering home. You two get some rest. Sadie, therapy Wednesday, right?"

"Yes. 6 PM."

"Good. You have a lot to process with Dr. Chen." She hugged Sadie tightly. "You're doing great, baby. Don't let one hard day make you forget that. And Jarod—" she turned to him, "—thank you. For being there for her. For not letting her run. She needs someone who holds her accountable while also being patient. You're doing good work."

"She's worth it," Jarod said simply.

After LaKrecia left, Jarod turned to Sadie. "You should stay. It's late, and I don't want you driving when you're this exhausted."

"I don't have work clothes here."

"So we'll stop by your place in the morning before work. Or you wear something of mine. I don't care. I just want you here. With me. Safe."

The word "safe" did something to Sadie's chest. When had she ever felt safe with someone? Not sexually safe—she'd always been careful about that. But emotionally safe. Vulnerable and exposed but protected anyway.

"Okay," she said. "I'll stay."

They got ready for bed—Sadie borrowing one of his t-shirts, both of them going through their nighttime routines side by side like couples do. Domestic and ordinary and somehow more intimate than any of the sex they'd had.

When they finally climbed into bed, Jarod pulled her close, her back to his chest, his arm secure around her waist.

"Today was hard," he murmured against her neck. "But we made it through. Together."

"Together," she echoed.

"And tomorrow will be easier. And the day after that. Eventually, this becomes normal. Us. Together. Building something real."

"I hope you're right."

"I am. Trust me." He kissed her shoulder. "Now sleep. Tomorrow's a new day."

Sadie closed her eyes, feeling the solid warmth of him behind her, the security of his arm around her waist. She should have felt trapped. Should have felt the urge to escape.

Instead, she felt held.

And for the first time in longer than she could remember, she let herself surrender to it. To the vulnerability of being cared for. To the scary intimacy of sharing space and life with someone who insisted on knowing all of her.

Sleep came slowly, but when it did, she dreamed not of escape or compartments or the Velvet Room, but of standing at the edge of a cliff with Jarod beside her, both of them looking out at an uncertain future.

And instead of feeling terrified, she felt ready.

Ready to jump.

Ready to see if they would fly.

CHAPTER 15
THE ULTIMATUM

THE NEXT TWO weeks fell into an unexpected rhythm. Sadie went to work, went to therapy, spent evenings with Jarod—sometimes at his place, sometimes at hers. They cooked dinner together, watched movies, had sex that was both passionate and tender. They talked about their days, their fears, their hopes for what they were building.

It felt almost... normal. Like a real relationship instead of the compartmentalized arrangement she'd lived for so long.

But underneath the normalcy, tension simmered.

TJ hadn't reached out to either of them. According to Jarod, he'd seen him once at a mutual friend's event, and TJ had been cordial but cold. Polite enough not to cause a scene, but distant enough to make his feelings clear. He was still with Sarah, apparently getting more serious, moving forward with his life.

Without them in it.

Jarod pretended it didn't bother him, but Sadie could see the hurt in his eyes when TJ's name came up. Could feel the weight of what his choice had cost him, even if he refused to acknowledge it.

And that weight settled on her shoulders like a stone.

"You're thinking too loud," Jarod said one evening as they lay on his couch, her head on his chest. It was a Thursday, two weeks after the conversation with TJ, and they'd fallen into the habit of spending weeknights together when schedules allowed.

"Sorry. Just processing."

"About?"

"TJ. Us. Everything." She traced patterns on his chest through his t-shirt. "You miss him. I can tell."

"Of course I miss him. He's my brother. But that doesn't mean I regret my choice."

"Yet."

"Ever." He tilted her chin up to look at him. "Stop waiting for me to resent you. It's not going to happen."

"You don't know that. Right now, you're in the honeymoon phase. Everything feels good. But eventually, the reality will set in—you lost your best friend for a woman who might still hurt you. And you'll wonder if it was worth it."

"Why are you so determined to catastrophize this?"

"Because I'm a realist. Because I know myself. Because—" She sat up, needing space. "Because I don't trust that this is sustainable. We've been together for two weeks, Jarod. Two good weeks. But what happens when it gets hard? When I panic and pull away? When you realize the woman you're betting on isn't actually capable of being who you need her to be?"

"Then we work through it." He sat up too, frustration evident in his posture. "Why do you keep looking for reasons this won't work instead of reasons it will?"

"Because someone has to be realistic!"

"No, because you're scared. And instead of sitting with that fear, you're trying to preemptively end things so you can be the one who leaves instead of the one who gets left."

The observation was too accurate, too sharp. Sadie stood, needing to move. "That's not fair."

"It's completely fair. You're doing exactly what you always do—pushing me away before I can hurt you. Except I'm not trying to hurt you, Sadie. I'm trying to build something with you."

"By sacrificing your friendship with TJ?"

"By making a choice about what I want in my life. TJ is important to me. But so are you. And I'm allowed to want both, even if I can't have both right now."

"But you can't have both. That's the point. You chose me, and you lost him. And eventually, you're going to realize I wasn't worth it."

Jarod stood too, his expression hardening. "Okay. You know what? I'm done having this conversation."

"What does that mean?"

"It means I'm tired of reassuring you every single day that I don't regret choosing you. Tired of watching you sabotage this because you're too scared to believe something good can last. Tired of fighting your fear instead of building our relationship."

"So what are you saying?"

"I'm saying I need you to make a choice." His voice was calm but firm. "Either you're all in—fully committed to making this work, accepting that there will be hard days and trust that we can get through them together—or you're out. But I can't keep doing this halfway thing where you have one foot out the door waiting for everything to fall apart."

Sadie's heart hammered. "That's not fair. I'm trying."

"Are you? Because from where I'm standing, you're still operating in fear mode. Still waiting for the other shoe to drop. Still convinced this is going to fail."

"Because everything in my life has failed! My parents' marriage failed. Every relationship I've ever had has failed. Why would this be different?"

"Because you're different. Or you're supposed to be. You're in therapy, doing the work, learning to be vulnerable. But Sadie, if you don't actually apply any of that work to us—if you keep treating this relationship like it's doomed to fail—then it will fail. Not because it wasn't worth fighting for, but because you gave up before we even really started."

Tears pricked her eyes. "I'm not giving up. I'm being realistic."

"No, you're being a coward." The words were harsh but not cruel. "And I say that with love, but it's true. You're so scared of being hurt that you'd rather destroy this yourself than risk me doing it. That's cowardice, not realism."

"Don't call me a coward."

"Then stop acting like one." He crossed to her, his hands on her shoulders. "I love you, Sadie. I'm in love with you. And I know that terrifies you, but it's the truth. I love you—the ambitious, driven Corporate Sadie and the sensual, free After Hours Sadie and every version in between. I love all of you. But I need you to love me back. Actually love me. Not the compartmentalized version where you keep me at arm's length. The real thing."

The words "I love you" crashed over her like a wave. He loved her. Despite everything—the lies, the compartmentalization, the damage she'd caused—he loved her.

And she had no idea what to do with that.

"I don't—" She struggled to form words. "I don't know if I know how to do that. How to love someone without losing myself."

"Then figure it out. Go to therapy, talk to LaKrecia, do whatever you need to do. But figure it out soon, because I can't keep carrying both of us. I can't love you enough for both of us." His hands dropped from her shoulders. "I need to know you're in this. Really in this. Not just trying it out or testing the waters or seeing if you can handle it. I need you all in."

"And if I can't be? If I'm too broken to give you what you need?"

"Then we end this now. Clean break. Before either of us gets hurt worse than we already are." His eyes were sad but resolute. "I'm not trying to pressure you, Sadie. But I also can't keep building something with someone who's constantly tearing it down out of fear. That's not sustainable for either of us."

"So you're giving me an ultimatum."

"I'm asking you to make a choice. Be all in, or be all out. But no more of this halfway, one-foot-out-the-door thing. I deserve more than that. And so do you."

Sadie felt like the walls were closing in. This was too much, too fast. Two weeks ago, they'd just started trying. Now he was saying he loved her and demanding she be fully committed or end things entirely?

"I need time," she said. "To process. To think."

"How much time?"

"I don't know. A few days? A week?"

"Okay. One week." His expression was unreadable. "Take the time you need. But Sadie, when that week is up, I need an answer. Are you in, or are you out? Because I can't keep existing in this limbo."

"That's not fair. You can't put a timeline on feelings."

"I'm not putting a timeline on feelings. I'm putting a timeline on a decision. Do you want to be with me—really be with me, with all the vulnerability and risk that entails? Or do you want to keep protecting yourself and be alone?" He moved toward his bedroom. "I'm going to bed. You can stay or go—that's up to you. But I need some space right now."

He disappeared into his bedroom, leaving Sadie standing in his living room feeling like the floor had just dropped out from under her.

One week. He'd given her one week to decide if she could love him, be fully present with him, commit to building something real.

Or walk away and go back to being alone.

The choice should have been easy. Jarod was incredible—patient, understanding, challenging her to be better. He loved her. Actually loved her, despite everything.

But the terror that rose in her chest at the thought of fully committing, of being that vulnerable, felt suffocating.

She grabbed her purse and keys and left his loft without saying goodbye.

The drive back to her apartment was a blur. Sadie's hands shook on the steering wheel, tears streaming down her face. By the time she pulled into her parking garage, she was sobbing—ugly, gasping sobs that made her chest hurt.

She made it to her apartment and immediately called LaKrecia.

"Hello?"

"I fucked it up." The words came out broken, barely intelligible. "I fucked everything up."

"Sadie? Baby, what happened? Are you okay?"

"No. I'm not okay. Can you—can you come over? Please?"

"I'm on my way. Hold tight. I'll be there in twenty minutes."

LaKrecia made it in fifteen, letting herself in with the spare key Sadie had given her years ago. She found Sadie curled up on the couch, still crying, mascara streaked down her face.

"Oh, honey." LaKrecia sat down and pulled her into her arms. "Tell me what happened."

Through hiccupping sobs, Sadie recounted the conversation—Jarod's frustration with her constant fear, his declaration of love, the ultimatum he'd given her. One week to decide if she was all in or all out.

"He said I'm being a coward," Sadie finished. "Said I'm sabotaging things because I'm too scared to believe something good can last."

"Is he wrong?"

Sadie pulled back to look at her best friend. "Whose side are you on?"

"Yours. Always yours. But baby, that doesn't mean telling you what you want to hear. It means telling you what you need to hear." LaKrecia brushed hair from Sadie's face. "Are you sabotaging this? Are you looking for reasons it won't work instead of reasons it will?"

"I don't know. Maybe. Probably." Sadie wiped her eyes. "But Krecia, he said he loves me. And I panicked. Because what if I love him back and then he leaves? What if I give him all of me and it's not enough?"

"What if you give him all of you and it *is* enough? What if this actually works?"

"That's what everyone keeps saying. But how do I know? How do I trust that?"

"You don't. That's what faith is—choosing to believe in something you can't prove. Choosing to be vulnerable even though you might get hurt." LaKrecia took her hands. "Do you love him?"

The question hung in the air. Did she love Jarod? She cared about him. Was attracted to him. Felt safe with him. But love?

"I don't know," she whispered. "I don't know what love feels like when it's not mixed with fear."

"Then maybe that's what you need to figure out this week. Not whether you can commit to him, but whether you love him. Because if you do, the commitment becomes easier. The vulnerability becomes worth it."

"And if I don't? If I care about him but I'm not in love with him?"

"Then you let him go. Clean break. You both move on and find people you can love fully." LaKrecia squeezed her hands. "But Sadie,

I've watched you these last two weeks. You light up when you talk about him. You're softer, happier, more yourself than I've seen you in years. That means something."

"Or it means I'm in the honeymoon phase and it'll wear off."

"Stop catastrophizing. For once in your life, just let yourself feel something without analyzing it to death."

They sat in silence for a moment, Sadie's tears gradually slowing. Finally, she asked, "What would you do? If you were me?"

"I'd be terrified. But I'd also be brave enough to try. Because Sadie, you're going to be alone for the rest of your life if you keep pushing away everyone who tries to get close. Is that really what you want?"

"No. But I don't know how to be anything else."

"You learn. You practice. You fall and get back up and try again." LaKrecia stood and pulled Sadie to her feet. "Come on. You're taking a shower, washing off this makeup, and getting into bed. Tomorrow, you're calling Dr. Chen and asking for an emergency session. You have real work to do this week if you're going to make this decision."

"What if I make the wrong choice?"

"There's no wrong choice. There's choosing fear or choosing courage. Both are choices. But only one leads to a life you'll actually want to live."

The next morning, Sadie woke with puffy eyes and a pounding headache. She'd cried herself to sleep after LaKrecia left, and now in the harsh light of day, everything felt overwhelming.

She had six days left to decide. Six days to figure out if she loved Jarod. Six days to determine if she was capable of the vulnerability he was asking for.

She called Dr. Chen's office as soon as it opened.

"This is Sadie Monroe. I have my regular appointment Wednesday, but I need to see Dr. Chen before then if possible. It's urgent."

"Let me check her schedule." A pause. "She has an opening today at 4 PM. One of her patients canceled. Can you make that?"

"Yes. Thank you."

At work, Sadie went through the motions—meetings, emails, conference calls. But her mind was elsewhere. On Jarod. On the ultimatum. On the fact that she had to make the biggest decision of her life in six days.

Her phone buzzed around noon. Jarod: *Hope you're okay. I meant what I said last night, but I didn't mean to upset you. Take the time you need. I'm here when you're ready to talk.*

The text was kind. Concerned. Exactly what she should want from a partner.

So why did it make her want to run?

She didn't respond. Couldn't respond. Not until she had clarity.

Dr. Chen's office felt like a sanctuary when Sadie arrived at 4 PM. She sank into the familiar couch and immediately started crying—a trend that was becoming concerning.

"I'm sorry," she said, grabbing a tissue. "I seem to cry every time I'm here lately."

"That's okay. Tears are information. They tell us what matters." Dr. Chen settled into her chair. "What brings you in today? Marie said it was urgent."

Sadie recounted the conversation with Jarod—the ultimatum, the declaration of love, her panic and subsequent flight. Dr. Chen listened without interrupting, her expression neutral and accepting.

When Sadie finished, Dr. Chen asked, "What are you feeling right now?"

"Terrified. Overwhelmed. Like I'm being asked to choose between being alone forever or risking complete devastation."

"That's quite dramatic. Is that really the choice?"

"Isn't it? Either I commit fully to Jarod and risk him leaving me destroyed like my father destroyed my mother, or I walk away and stay safe but alone."

"Let's unpack that. First, do you actually believe you'd be destroyed if Jarod left? Or is that your fear talking?"

Sadie considered. "I don't know. I've never let myself be vulnerable enough to find out."

"Exactly. You're catastrophizing based on your mother's experience, not your own. You're not your mother, Sadie. You have your own career, your own money, your own identity. If Jarod left tomorrow, would you stop existing?"

"No. But I'd be hurt."

"Yes. You'd be hurt. Hurt and destroyed are different things. Hurt heals. Destroyed means you can't recover. Do you think you're so fragile that heartbreak would destroy you?"

"No," Sadie admitted. "But it would hurt like hell."

"It would. And that's the risk of love. That's the price of admission. You can choose to never pay it—to stay safe and protected and alone. Or you can choose to pay it—to be vulnerable and risk hurt—in exchange for connection, intimacy, love." Dr. Chen leaned forward. "The question isn't whether you might get hurt. You will get hurt, probably multiple times throughout your life. The question is whether the possibility of love is worth the risk of pain."

"Everyone keeps asking me that. Like it's a simple yes or no question."

"It is a simple question. The answer might be complicated, but the question is simple. Is love worth the risk?"

Sadie was quiet for a long time. "I don't know. I want to say yes. But I'm so scared."

"Of course you are. You watched your mother's heart get broken, and you internalized that love equals loss of self. But Sadie, your mother's mistake wasn't loving your father. It was making him her entire identity. You're not going to do that. You're too independent, too driven. You couldn't lose yourself in someone if you tried."

"What if I hurt him? What if I panic and pull away and he realizes I'm not worth the trouble?"

"Then you'll deal with it. Together. Or you won't, and you'll break up. But Sadie, you can't control whether you hurt him or he hurts you. All you can control is whether you show up authentically and try your best. That's all any of us can do in relationships."

"He said he loves me. And I didn't say it back. I just panicked and left."

"Do you love him?"

There it was again. The question everyone kept asking. The question she kept avoiding.

"I think so," she whispered. "I think I might. But I'm not sure what love feels like when it's healthy. All I know is fear-based love. Control-based love. Not this... partnership thing he's offering."

"Then maybe this week is about learning what healthy love feels like. About sitting with your feelings and figuring out if what you feel for Jarod is love or just comfort. And then deciding if it's worth the risk."

"How do I tell the difference?"

"Love challenges you to grow. Comfort lets you stay the same. Love asks for vulnerability. Comfort settles for surface. Love is terrifying and exhilarating. Comfort is safe and eventually suffocating." Dr. Chen smiled gently. "Based on what you've told me, how does Jarod make you feel?"

"Terrified. Challenged. Vulnerable. Like I'm constantly growing and stretching and becoming someone new."

"That sounds like love."

The words settled over Sadie like a blanket. Love. She loved him. Despite the fear, despite the risk, despite everything—she loved him.

And that realization was both liberating and absolutely terrifying.

"So what do I do?" she asked. "How do I tell him that I love him but I'm still terrified?"

"You say exactly that. You tell him the truth—that you love him and you're scared, but you're choosing courage over comfort. Choosing vulnerability over safety. Choosing him over your fear."

"What if I mess it up?"

"You will. Multiple times. That's part of relationships—messing up, apologizing, learning, trying again. The goal isn't perfection. It's showing up consistently, even when it's hard."

They talked for the rest of the session about practical strategies—how to communicate when she felt herself pulling away, how to recognize fear spirals before they took over, how to ask for what she needed without sabotaging the relationship.

By the time Sadie left Dr. Chen's office at 5 PM, she felt clearer than she had in days.

She loved Jarod. She was terrified, but she loved him. And that was enough to make her choice.

She drove to his loft without calling ahead, her heart hammering the entire way. What if he'd changed his mind? What if one day of space had made him realize she was too much work?

She knocked on his door at 5:45 PM.

He answered wearing sweatpants and a t-shirt, looking surprised to see her. "Sadie. Hi. I didn't expect—"

"I love you." The words tumbled out before she could second-guess them. "I'm terrified and I don't know what I'm doing and I'll probably mess this up multiple times, but I love you. And I want to be all in. Fully committed. No more one foot out the door."

Jarod stared at her for a long moment, and Sadie's stomach dropped. Had she misread everything? Was it too late?

Then he smiled—that brilliant, show-stopping smile that had made her fall for him in the first place—and pulled her into his arms.

"Say it again," he murmured against her hair.

"I love you. I'm in love with you. And I'm choosing this. Choosing us. Choosing courage over comfort."

He pulled back to look at her, his hands framing her face. "You have no idea how much I needed to hear that."

"I'm sorry it took me so long. I'm sorry I ran last night. I'm sorry I keep sabotaging—"

"Stop apologizing." He kissed her forehead. "You're here now. That's what matters."

"I'm still going to mess up. Probably a lot. I'm still figuring out how to do this."

"So am I. We'll figure it out together." He kissed her properly then, deep and passionate and full of promise. "I love you, Sadie Monroe. All of you. The scared parts and the brave parts and everything in between."

"I love you too," she said, and this time it came easier. "Even though it terrifies me."

"Especially because it terrifies you. That's how we know it's real."

They went inside and spent the evening talking—really talking, about their fears and hopes and what they needed from each other. About how to handle conflict, how to communicate when things got hard, how to build something sustainable instead of something that burned bright and fast.

It was the most adult, mature conversation Sadie had ever had about a relationship. And while it was uncomfortable at times, it also felt right.

They were building something real. Something that required work and honesty and vulnerability. Something that might actually last.

And for the first time, Sadie let herself believe it was possible.

Not just possible. Probable.

If they both kept showing up. Kept being honest. Kept choosing courage over comfort.

One day at a time.

One choice at a time.

One step toward a future that included love without loss of self, vulnerability without destruction, partnership without dependence.

It was terrifying.

But it was also worth it.

He was worth it.

She was worth it.

They were worth it.

And that, Sadie realized, was the whole point.

CHAPTER 16
THE ERUPTION

THE NEXT THREE weeks were both the best and most challenging of Sadie's life.

She and Jarod fell into a rhythm that felt sustainable—dinners together most nights, staying over at each other's places, integrating their lives in small but significant ways. He met more of her colleagues at a work happy hour. She attended a networking event with him, meeting people from his industry. They were building something real, something public, something that couldn't be compartmentalized.

And it terrified her daily.

But she was learning to sit with the terror. To recognize when fear was making her want to pull away, and to lean in instead. Dr. Chen called it "practicing opposite action"—doing the opposite of what fear told her to do.

It was exhausting. But it was working.

LaKrecia was thrilled, constantly texting encouragement and checking in. Sadie's promotion to Senior VP had been officially announced, and she was settling into the new role with confidence. Everything in her life was finally falling into place.

Except for one glaring problem: TJ.

Three weeks, and he still hadn't reached out. Hadn't responded to

Jarod's attempts to talk. Was completely radio silent, moving forward with his life as if his best friend of over a decade didn't exist.

And Sadie could see it eating at Jarod, even though he tried to hide it.

"I'm fine," he'd say whenever she brought it up. "TJ needs his space. I respect that."

But she'd catch him staring at his phone sometimes, checking for messages that never came. Would see the flicker of hurt in his eyes when mutual friends mentioned TJ's name. Would feel him tense when they ran into someone who asked about TJ's whereabouts.

The cost of their relationship was becoming increasingly clear. And the guilt Sadie carried was growing heavier by the day.

It came to a head on a Friday evening in mid-November.

Jarod had invited Sadie to a dinner party being thrown by one of his business associates—Xavier, a guy he'd known for years. It was at a upscale restaurant, a private room, about twenty people from their industry circles.

"You sure you want me there?" Sadie had asked when he first mentioned it. "Won't it be awkward if people ask about TJ?"

"Let them ask. I'm not hiding you or us. That was the whole point, remember? Full integration. No compartments."

So Sadie had dressed carefully—a burgundy wrap dress that was professional but elegant, her hair in loose waves, makeup polished but not overdone. She looked like herself. Not Corporate Sadie or After Hours Sadie. Just Sadie.

They arrived at the restaurant at 7 PM, and Jarod immediately began introducing her around. "This is Sadie Monroe, my girlfriend. She just made Senior VP at Meridian Capital."

Girlfriend. The word still sent a thrill through her every time he said it. Public claiming. Integration. Everything she'd been too scared to do before.

The party was in full swing—people networking, laughing, drinking wine and enjoying appetizers. Sadie found herself relaxing, engaging in conversations about market trends and investment strategies. This was her element. She could do this.

Around 8 PM, there was a commotion near the entrance to the private room. Sadie looked up and felt her blood run cold.

TJ had just walked in.

With Sarah on his arm.

And based on the shock on Jarod's face, he hadn't known TJ would be here.

The room seemed to freeze for a moment. Everyone who knew the history—and that was most people in the room—went quiet, watching to see what would happen.

TJ's eyes scanned the room and landed on Jarod. Then on Sadie beside him. His expression hardened into something cold and dangerous.

Xavier, the host, rushed over looking panicked. "Rod, man, I'm sorry. I invited TJ weeks ago, before I knew about—I didn't think he'd actually come. He RSVP'd no originally—"

"It's fine," Jarod said, his voice tight. "We're all adults here."

But it clearly wasn't fine.

TJ said something to Sarah, who looked uncomfortable, then walked directly toward them. The crowd parted like water, everyone pretending not to watch while absolutely watching.

"TJ," Jarod said when he reached them. "Good to see you, man."

"Is it?" TJ's voice was ice. "Is it good to see me? Or is it just awkward as hell?"

"Don't do this here. Please."

"Why not? Everyone already knows. Everyone's been talking about it for weeks—how Jarod's whipped over the woman who played us both. How he threw away a decade of friendship for good pussy."

Sadie flinched. Several people gasped. Sarah looked mortified.

"That's enough," Jarod's voice was low, dangerous. "I know you're hurt, but don't disrespect her."

"Disrespect her?" TJ laughed bitterly. "She disrespected us both. Lied to us, manipulated us, kept us in separate boxes like we were interchangeable. But sure, I'm the bad guy for calling it what it is."

"TJ, please." Sadie's voice was quiet but steady. "Can we talk about this somewhere private? Not here. Not in front of everyone."

"Why? Afraid people will know who you really are? Afraid your shiny new VP title will be tarnished when they find out the real Sadie Monroe?"

"That's it." Jarod stepped between them. "You want to be pissed at me? Fine. But you don't talk to her like that."

"I'll talk to her however I want. She's the reason my best friend became a stranger. She's the reason I can't trust you anymore. She's the reason everything's fucked."

"No." Jarod's voice was firm. "I'm the reason. I chose to be with her. I chose to try again despite the risks. I chose our relationship over our friendship, and that's on me. Not her."

"You chose your dick over your brother. That's what you did."

"I chose love over fear. There's a difference."

"Love?" TJ scoffed. "You've been with her for what, a month? That's not love. That's infatuation. That's thinking with the wrong head. And when you finally wake up and realize what you've thrown away for someone who's incapable of actual honesty, don't come crawling back to me."

"TJ—" Sarah touched his arm. "Maybe we should go."

"No." TJ shrugged her off. "I came here to have dinner with people I used to call friends. I'm not leaving because they're uncomfortable with the truth."

Xavier stepped forward, trying to salvage the situation. "Why don't we all just take a breath—"

"I don't need a breath. I need my friend back. But that's not happening, is it?" TJ looked at Jarod with barely contained anger. "You made your choice. You chose her. So don't expect me to stand here and pretend I'm happy for you. Don't expect me to play nice and act like we're still brothers. We're not. Not anymore."

"Don't say that." Jarod's voice cracked slightly. "Please don't say that."

"Why? It's the truth. You threw away ten years of friendship for a woman who's going to hurt you again the moment things get too real. And when she does, when she compartmentalizes you or runs away or does whatever it is she does—don't expect me to be there to pick up the pieces. I'm done."

He turned and walked toward the exit, Sarah hurrying after him.

The room was silent. Everyone staring. The drama they'd all been waiting for had just played out in front of them.

Sadie felt like she couldn't breathe. Every word TJ had said—every accusation, every prediction—felt like a knife. Because what if he was right? What if she did hurt Jarod again? What if she wasn't capable of sustaining this?

"I need air," she managed, and pushed through the crowd toward the exit.

She made it outside to the sidewalk before the panic attack hit. Her chest tightened, her vision blurred, her hands shook. She leaned against the building, trying to remember Dr. Chen's breathing exercises, but nothing was working.

"Sadie." Jarod was there suddenly, his hands on her shoulders. "Baby, breathe. Look at me. Breathe with me."

"I can't—I can't do this—"

"Yes, you can. In through your nose. Out through your mouth. With me."

He breathed with her, slowly, steadily, until the panic began to recede. When she could finally breathe normally again, she looked up at him through tears.

"He's right. About all of it. I'm going to hurt you again. I'm going to panic or pull away or do something that proves I'm not worth what you've sacrificed. And you're going to hate me for costing you your best friend."

"No. Stop. That's fear talking, not truth."

"How do you know? How do you know TJ's not right?"

"Because I know you. I know you're doing the work. I know you show up every day even when it scares you. I know you're not the same person who kept us in separate compartments." He cupped her face gently. "And I know that even if you do mess up—which you will, because everyone does—we'll work through it together."

"But TJ—"

"TJ is hurt. And angry. And he has every right to be. But he doesn't get to decide what our relationship is worth. Only we do." He pressed his forehead to hers. "Do you want to be with me? Despite the cost? Despite his anger? Despite all of it?"

"Yes," she whispered. "God, yes. But I don't want you to lose him because of me."

"I already have. At least for now. And that hurts like hell. But Sadie, I don't regret choosing you. Even after tonight. Even after everything he said. I don't regret it."

"You will. Eventually."

"Stop telling me what I'm going to feel." His voice was firm but not harsh. "I'm a grown man making my own choices. Trust me to know what I want."

"I'm trying."

"Then try harder." He kissed her forehead. "Come on. Let's go home. We don't need to stay here."

"What about Xavier? The party?"

"Xavier will understand. And if he doesn't, then he's not a real friend anyway."

They drove back to Jarod's loft in heavy silence. Sadie kept replaying TJ's words in her head: *She's incapable of actual honesty. She's going to hurt you again. I'm done.*

Done. TJ was done. The friendship was over. And it was all her fault.

When they got to Jarod's place, she went straight to the bathroom and threw up. The stress, the panic, the guilt—all of it too much for her body to handle.

Jarod held her hair back, got her water, helped her to the couch. He didn't try to talk or fix anything. Just held her while she cried.

"I've destroyed everything," she sobbed against his chest. "Your friendship. Your reputation. Everything."

"You haven't destroyed anything. People are going to talk for a few days, then they'll move on to the next drama. And TJ—he'll come around. Eventually."

"You don't know that."

"No, I don't. But I have to believe it. The alternative is living in regret, and I refuse to do that." He pulled back to look at her. "Sadie, listen to me. What happened tonight was bound to happen. TJ and I were going to have this confrontation eventually. Better that it happened and we can all start to heal."

"How is any of this healing? He hates us both."

"Right now, yes. But time changes things. Space changes things. Maybe in six months or a year, he'll be ready to talk. To actually process instead of just being angry."

"And if he's not?"

"Then I'll deal with it. But I'm not going to let fear of what might happen destroy what we're building right now."

Sadie wanted to believe him. Wanted to believe this could all work out. But TJ's words kept echoing: *She's going to hurt you again the moment things get too real.*

And the terrifying thing was, she wasn't sure he was wrong.

They didn't go back to work the rest of that weekend. Jarod called Xavier and apologized for leaving. Xavier was understanding—said TJ had left shortly after them too, that the party had continued but the energy was off.

"Everyone's on your side, man," Xavier had said. "They know TJ's hurt, but they also know he was out of line. Don't worry about it."

But Jarod was worrying about it. Sadie could tell. He was quieter than usual, more withdrawn. She'd catch him staring at his phone, probably wanting to text TJ but knowing it wouldn't be received well.

Sunday afternoon, Sadie's phone rang. LaKrecia.

"I heard about Friday night," she said without preamble. "Are you okay?"

"You heard? How?"

"Girl, it's all over social media. Someone posted about the confrontation. It's been shared like crazy—everyone's talking about it."

Sadie's stomach dropped. "Are you kidding me?"

"I wish I was. Look, it's not as bad as you think. Most people are sympathetic to you and Jarod. They think TJ overreacted. But yeah, it's out there."

"Oh God. My work. What if people at Meridian see it?"

"Then they see it. Sadie, you're not doing anything wrong. You're in a relationship. That's not scandalous."

"But the history—TJ and Jarod both being my—"

"Is messy but understandable. You're human. You made mistakes, and now you're trying to do better. Anyone who judges you for that isn't worth your energy."

After she hung up with LaKrecia, Sadie made the mistake of checking social media. LaKrecia was right—someone had filmed part of the confrontation and posted it. The video had been viewed thousands of times, with hundreds of comments.

Some were supportive: *TJ needs to let it go. They're all adults.*

Others were harsh: *She played them both. Of course TJ's pissed.*

And some were just cruel: *She's climbing the corporate ladder and collecting men like trophies. Classic.*

Sadie felt sick reading them. This was her nightmare—being publicly exposed, judged, reduced to the messy parts of her personal life instead of her professional accomplishments.

"Stop reading those," Jarod said, taking the phone from her hands. "They don't know you. They don't know us. They're just spectators treating our lives like entertainment."

"But what if people at work see it? What if my promotion gets questioned because of this?"

"Then you deal with it. But Sadie, you've done nothing wrong professionally. Your personal life is your personal life. They can't hold that against you."

"You don't know that. Women get judged differently. Especially women in leadership."

"Then fight it. You're a fighter. Don't let fear of judgment make you hide."

But hiding was exactly what Sadie wanted to do. Wanted to compartmentalize again, retreat into Corporate Sadie who kept her personal life completely separate, rebuild the walls that had kept her safe for so long.

She recognized the pattern. Dr. Chen had warned her about this—when things got hard, her instinct would be to retreat into old coping mechanisms. The question was whether she'd recognize it and choose differently.

"I want to run," she admitted. "Every instinct is telling me to end this, protect myself, go back to being alone."

"I know." Jarod pulled her into his arms. "But you're not going to. Because you're braver than your fear."

"Am I though?"

"Yes. You've proven it over and over these last few weeks. And you'll prove it again now."

She wanted to believe him. Wanted to believe she was strong enough to weather this storm. But the doubt was so loud, so insistent.

They spent Sunday night in relative silence, both processing the fallout. Around 10 PM, Jarod's phone buzzed.

He looked at it and his expression changed—surprise mixed with caution.

"It's TJ."

Sadie's heart stopped. "What does it say?"

Jarod read aloud: "I'm sorry for Friday. That wasn't how I wanted to handle things. Can we talk? Just you and me. Tomorrow?"

Hope and fear warred in Sadie's chest. "Are you going to respond?"

"Yeah. I have to." He typed quickly: "Tomorrow works. Time and place?"

TJ: "My office. 11 AM. Just us. No Sadie."

The last two words stung, but Sadie understood. TJ wanted to talk to his friend without her presence complicating things.

"You should go," she said. "This is good. He's ready to talk."

"Are you sure? I don't want you to feel excluded."

"I feel excluded because I am excluded. But that's okay. This is between you and him. I'll be okay."

They went to bed shortly after, but neither of them slept well. Sadie could feel Jarod's tension, his anxiety about the meeting tomorrow. And she felt her own anxiety—what if TJ convinced him she wasn't worth it? What if this was the beginning of the end?

Monday morning, Jarod dressed carefully—business casual but not too formal. He was nervous, she could tell. This conversation could either salvage their friendship or end it permanently.

"Whatever happens," Sadie said as he was leaving, "I love you. Remember that."

"I love you too. And nothing TJ says is going to change that."

But she could see the doubt in his eyes. TJ had been his best friend for over a decade. That kind of bond didn't just disappear. And if TJ really forced him to choose...

Sadie tried to work from home while Jarod was at the meeting, but she couldn't concentrate. Kept checking her phone for updates that didn't come.

11 AM came and went. Then noon. Then 1 PM.

At 2 PM, her phone finally rang.

Jarod.

"How did it go?" she asked immediately.

"Can you come to my place? We need to talk."

The four words every person in a relationship dreads. We need to talk.

"Jarod, what happened?"

"Just come over. Please. I don't want to do this on the phone."

He hung up, leaving Sadie staring at her phone with growing dread.

We need to talk.

Those words never preceded anything good.

She drove to his loft with her heart in her throat, every worst-case scenario playing through her mind. By the time she arrived, she was already preparing herself for the end.

Jarod opened the door before she could knock. His expression was unreadable—not angry, not sad, just... carefully blank.

"Come in," he said.

She followed him inside, her stomach in knots. "What did TJ say?"

Jarod sat on the couch and gestured for her to join him. When she did, he took both her hands in his—a gesture that felt both comforting and ominous.

"TJ and I talked for three hours. Really talked. He got everything out—his anger, his hurt, his feeling of betrayal. And I listened. Didn't defend or explain, just listened."

"And?"

"And... he's willing to try to rebuild our friendship. Slowly. With conditions."

Relief flooded through Sadie. "That's good. That's great. What are the conditions?"

Jarod's expression tightened. "The main one is that he needs space from you. Doesn't want to see you at events, doesn't want to hear about you, doesn't want you integrated into our friend group. He said if I want to be with you, that's my choice. But he can't be around you. At least not for a while. Maybe a long while."

The words landed like stones. "So I'm banned from your life. From your friends."

"Not from my life. From our shared social circle. For now."

"That's the same thing, Jarod. Your friends are your life. Your business connections, your support system—they're all intertwined. And TJ is saying I can't be part of that."

"He's saying he needs boundaries to heal. That's different."

"Is it? Because it sounds like he's asking you to compartmentalize me. Keep me separate from the rest of your life. Which is exactly what I did that started this whole mess."

"It's temporary—"

"You don't know that. He said 'maybe a long while.' That could be years, Jarod. Are you really willing to keep me separate from your friends for years?"

"If that's what it takes to keep both you and my friendship with TJ, then yes."

Sadie stood abruptly. "No. Absolutely not. I'm not going to be the secret girlfriend you hide from your social circle. We agreed—no more compartments. Full integration. That was the whole point."

"Sadie—"

"No. Listen to me. If you agree to TJ's conditions, you're doing exactly what I did. Keeping me in a box. And eventually, you're going to resent me for it. You're going to resent that you can't bring me to events, can't introduce me to people, can't have me be part of your whole life. And then you're going to realize TJ was right—I'm not worth the sacrifice."

"That's not—"

"It is." Tears streamed down her face. "And the worst part is, I understand. I understand why you're considering it. Because TJ is your family. He's your brother. And I'm just... what? The woman you've been dating for a few weeks? Of course you'd choose him."

"I'm not choosing him. I'm trying to find a way to have both of you—"

"By compartmentalizing me. By making me the secret part of your life you keep away from your real life. Sound familiar?"

The accusation hit its mark. Jarod flinched.

"You want me to tell TJ no? To lose my best friend permanently because his boundary is unreasonable?"

"I want you to see that his boundary requires you to repeat my mistakes. And I can't be part of that." Sadie grabbed her purse. "I love you. God, I love you so much. But I won't be the person you hide. I did that to you, and it was wrong. I won't let you do it to me."

"Where are you going?"

"Home. To think. To figure out if there's any way forward that doesn't require one of us to give up everything."

"Sadie, please. Don't leave like this. We can figure this out—"

"Can we? Because right now, it feels like no matter what choice you make, someone loses. If you choose TJ's conditions, I lose. If you refuse them, he loses. There's no winning here."

She walked to the door, her whole body shaking. This was it. The moment TJ had predicted. The moment when everything got too real and too hard and she proved she wasn't capable of sustaining this.

Except this time, she wasn't the one running. She was the one refusing to be compartmentalized.

Growth, she supposed. Painful, devastating growth.

"I need time," she said at the door. "To process. To think. Don't contact me for a few days. Please."

"Sadie—"

"Please, Jarod. I'm barely holding it together. If you push right now, I'm going to fall apart. And I need to be strong enough to make the right decision. Whatever that is."

She left before he could respond, before she could see the hurt in his eyes and change her mind.

The drive home was a blur of tears. By the time she reached her apartment, she could barely see the road.

She made it inside, collapsed on her couch, and called the one person who would understand.

"LaKrecia. I need you. It's all falling apart, and I don't know what to do."

"I'm on my way. Hold on, baby. Just hold on."

CHAPTER 17
THE COUNTDOWN

LAKRECIA ARRIVED WITHIN TWENTY MINUTES, letting herself in to find Sadie curled up on the couch, staring at nothing. The tears had stopped, replaced by a hollow numbness that felt worse somehow.

"Okay," LaKrecia said, setting down two bags—one from the liquor store, one from a Chinese takeout place. "Talk to me. What happened?"

Sadie recounted the meeting between Jarod and TJ, the conditions, the impossible choice. "TJ wants Jarod to keep me separate from their social circle. Indefinitely. And Jarod is actually considering it."

"Fuck." LaKrecia poured them both generous glasses of wine. "That's... complicated."

"It's not complicated. It's compartmentalization. It's exactly what I did to them, and now Jarod wants to do it to me. And I can't—I won't be that person in someone's life. Hidden. Secret. Kept separate."

"But isn't that different? TJ's setting a boundary for his own healing. That's not the same as what you did."

"Isn't it? The effect is the same—I'm kept away from a huge part of Jarod's life. His friends, his business connections, his support system. How is that building a life together? How is that integration?"

LaKrecia was quiet for a moment. "What did you tell him?"

"I told him I needed time. That I couldn't make a decision while I was this emotional. So I have maybe a few days before he expects an answer about whether I can live with TJ's conditions."

"Can you? Be honest."

Sadie thought about it. Really thought about it. "No. I don't think I can. Because even if I agreed, it would poison us. Every time he went to an event without me, I'd feel resentful. Every time he had to explain why his girlfriend wasn't there, he'd feel guilty. Eventually, that resentment and guilt would destroy us anyway. So what's the point?"

"The point would be that you'd have him. And maybe, eventually, TJ would come around and lift the boundary."

"And if he doesn't? If years pass and I'm still the secret girlfriend? What kind of life is that?"

"A compromise. An imperfect solution to an impossible situation."

"Or the beginning of the end. Just slower. More painful." Sadie drank half her wine in one swallow. "I love him, Krecia. I'm in love with him. But I don't know if love is enough when the circumstances are this fucked."

"Love is never enough by itself. It also takes compatibility, timing, circumstances. And right now, your circumstances are working against you." LaKrecia refilled their glasses. "What's your gut telling you?"

"To run. To end it before it destroys me. To go back to being alone where it's safe." Sadie paused. "But that's always what my gut tells me. I'm trying to figure out if that's wisdom or trauma talking."

"What does Dr. Chen say?"

"I haven't talked to her yet. I see her Wednesday. But I know what she'd say—that I need to sit with the discomfort instead of making a decision from panic. That I should figure out what I actually want before I decide what I can live with."

"That sounds right. So what do you actually want? In a perfect world, if you could wave a magic wand?"

"I want Jarod. All of him. Fully integrated into my life and me into his. I want to be able to go to events with him, meet his friends, be part of his whole life. I want what we were building before TJ blew it all up Friday night."

"But that's not available right now. So given the actual options—Jarod with conditions, or no Jarod at all—which do you choose?"

"I don't know." Sadie's voice cracked. "And I hate that I don't know. I should know. I should be able to make a decision. But every option feels wrong."

"Then maybe you're not ready to decide. Maybe you need more time."

"How much time? Jarod's waiting for an answer. TJ's waiting to see what happens. I can't just... indefinitely postpone."

"Why not? Who made up this rule that you have to decide right now? Take a week. Two weeks. A month if you need it. Tell Jarod you need space to process, and then actually process."

"That feels like running."

"It's not running if you're actively working through it. It's only running if you're avoiding." LaKrecia reached over and took her hand. "Sadie, this is a huge decision. It's going to affect the trajectory of your life. Don't make it from a place of panic or pressure. Make it from a place of clarity."

They spent the rest of the evening eating Chinese food and watching mindless TV, LaKrecia staying until nearly midnight to make sure Sadie was okay. When she finally left, Sadie felt marginally more stable, but no closer to knowing what to do.

She pulled out her journal and wrote:

Everything is falling apart. TJ wants me separated from Jarod's life. Jarod is considering it. And I'm stuck between compromising my boundaries or losing the man I love.

LaKrecia says to take time. To not decide from panic. But how much time is reasonable? How long do I make Jarod wait while I figure out if I can live with being compartmentalized?

The irony isn't lost on me. I compartmentalized them. Now TJ wants to compartmentalize me. Maybe this is karma. Maybe this is what I deserve.

But I don't want to live that way. Don't want to be hidden or kept separate. I fought so hard to become integrated, to be whole. And now I'm being asked to go back to pieces.

I don't know what to do. I don't know if love is enough. I don't know if compromise means growth or regression.

I just know that I'm tired. So tired of fighting. Tired of the drama. Tired of hurting people and being hurt in return.

Maybe I'm not meant for this. Maybe I'm meant to be alone.

She closed the journal and went to bed, but sleep was impossible. Her mind kept spinning—replaying Friday night, the conversation with Jarod, imagining futures where she stayed or left.

None of them felt right.

Tuesday morning, Sadie dragged herself to work despite wanting to hide in her apartment forever. She had responsibilities. A new position. People counting on her.

But focusing was nearly impossible. Every meeting was a blur, every email required three attempts to write coherently. By lunch, she was ready to give up and go home.

Her assistant Melissa knocked on her door around 2 PM. "Ms. Monroe? Your 2:30 is here early. Should I send him in?"

"Him? I don't have a 2:30 on my calendar."

"He doesn't have an appointment. But he said it's urgent. His name is TJ Morrison."

Sadie's blood ran cold. TJ. Here. At her office.

This couldn't be good.

"Give me five minutes, then send him in."

Melissa nodded and left. Sadie stood, smoothing down her skirt, checking her appearance in the small mirror behind her door. She looked tired—dark circles under her eyes despite concealer, tension in her jaw. But she looked professional. Controlled.

Corporate Sadie armor in place, even if the woman underneath was falling apart.

When the door opened and TJ walked in, she was struck by how different he looked from Friday night. Less angry, more... weary. Like someone who'd been fighting a battle and wasn't sure if he'd won or lost.

"TJ. This is unexpected."

"I know. I'm sorry for showing up unannounced. But we need to talk. Really talk. Without Jarod, without an audience." He closed the door behind him. "Can you spare twenty minutes?"

"I can spare ten. I have a meeting at 2:30."

"Then I'll be quick." He sat in the chair across from her desk—the same chair Jarod had sat in weeks ago, the same chair TJ himself had sat in when he'd told her about the double date. "I need to tell you something. And I need you to really hear it."

"Okay."

"Friday night, I was an asshole. I said things in public that should have been said in private. I embarrassed you and Jarod and made everyone uncomfortable. That was wrong, and I'm sorry."

The apology caught her off guard. "I... thank you."

"But—" he held up a hand, "—that doesn't mean I was wrong about everything. Because Sadie, I do think you're going to hurt him again. Not because you're a bad person, but because you're still figuring out how to be vulnerable. How to be present. How to sustain a real relationship instead of the compartmentalized version you're used to."

"I'm doing the work. Therapy, self-reflection, showing up even when it's scary—"

"I know. Jarod told me. And that's good. That's growth. But growth isn't linear. You're going to have setbacks. Moments where you panic and want to run. And when that happens, when you hurt him—and you will hurt him—I won't be there to help him pick up the pieces. Because that's my boundary. I can't watch my brother get destroyed by someone who might not be capable of giving him what he needs."

"So you came here to tell me you think I'm going to fail."

"No. I came here to tell you that I understand why Jarod loves you. Despite everything, I get it. You're brilliant, driven, complicated. You challenge him in ways no one else does. And when you're present— really present—you're probably incredible to be with."

"But?"

"But I also came to ask you something. And I need you to be brutally honest." He leaned forward. "Can you actually live with my conditions? With being separated from Jarod's social life indefinitely? Because if you can't—if you're going to resent it and let that resentment poison things —then you need to end it now. Let him go so he can heal and move on."

"You want me to break up with him."

"I want you to be realistic about what you can sustain. I know what my conditions require—they require Jarod to compartmentalize you, which is the opposite of what you've been working toward. And I know that's going to cause problems. The question is whether those problems are worth it to you."

Sadie stared at him, trying to read his expression. "Why are you really here, TJ? What do you want me to say?"

"I want you to admit that you can't do it. That you'll try for a few months, maybe a year, but eventually the resentment will build and you'll either pull away or lash out. And Jarod will be left even more broken than he is now." TJ's voice was quiet but intense. "I'm trying to protect my friend. That's all I've ever been trying to do."

"By pushing me out of his life."

"By giving myself space to heal so I can eventually be in his life again. Without you complicating it."

The honesty was brutal but fair. TJ wasn't being cruel. He was being protective. Of himself, of Jarod, of their friendship.

"I do love him," Sadie said quietly. "I know you don't believe that, but I do."

"I believe you think you do. I'm just not sure you know what love actually requires. Because love isn't just feeling good together. It's sacrifice and compromise and showing up when it's hard. It's putting someone else's needs ahead of your own sometimes. Can you actually do that?"

"I'm trying to learn."

"Trying isn't enough. Jarod deserves someone who's already figured it out. Someone who can give him stability and presence and emotional availability without having to work so hard at it." TJ stood. "I know that sounds harsh. But Sadie, you asked me to be honest. So I'm being honest. I think you love Jarod as much as you're capable of loving anyone right now. I just don't think that's enough for what he needs."

He walked to the door, then paused. "For what it's worth, I hope I'm wrong. I hope you prove me wrong and build something lasting with him. Because he loves you. Really loves you. And if you can be who he needs, then maybe the sacrifice of our friendship was worth it.

But if you can't..." He shook his head. "Just be honest with yourself. That's all I'm asking."

He left, closing the door softly behind him.

Sadie sat at her desk, TJ's words echoing in her head. *Trying isn't enough. You love him as much as you're capable of loving anyone right now. I just don't think that's enough for what he needs.*

What if he was right? What if her version of love—still so new, still so frightening—wasn't enough? What if all her growth and therapy and hard work still left her falling short of what Jarod deserved?

Her phone buzzed. Jarod: *Have you thought more about TJ's conditions? Can we talk tonight?*

Sadie stared at the message. She should respond. Should tell him she needed more time. Should explain that TJ had just been here, saying things that made her doubt everything.

Instead, she turned off her phone and put her head in her hands.

She made it through the rest of the workday on autopilot. When 6 PM rolled around, she drove not home but to Dr. Chen's office, arriving forty-five minutes early for her Wednesday appointment.

The receptionist looked surprised. "Ms. Monroe? Your appointment isn't until tomorrow."

"I know. Is there any chance Dr. Chen has time today? It's urgent."

"Let me check." She disappeared into the back, then returned a few minutes later. "Dr. Chen's last appointment just canceled. She can see you now if you'd like."

"Thank you. God, thank you."

Dr. Chen appeared a moment later, concern evident on her face. "Sadie. Come in. What's happened?"

In the familiar safety of Dr. Chen's office, Sadie finally let herself break down. She told her everything—Friday night's confrontation, the viral video, TJ's conditions, Jarod's consideration of them, TJ showing up at her office today.

"And now I don't know what to do," she finished, her voice hoarse from crying. "TJ says I'm not capable of giving Jarod what he needs. That trying isn't enough. And I'm starting to think he's right."

"Let's examine that," Dr. Chen said calmly. "What specifically did TJ say that's making you doubt yourself?"

"That I love Jarod as much as I'm capable of loving anyone right now, but that's not enough. That Jarod deserves someone who's already figured out how to be emotionally available and stable, not someone who's still learning."

"And do you think that's true?"

"I don't know. I'm doing the work. I'm showing up. But what if I'm fundamentally incapable of the kind of love he needs? What if all my trauma and compartmentalization has broken me in ways I can't fix?"

"Sadie, listen to me carefully. You are not broken. You are a person with trauma who developed coping mechanisms to survive. Those mechanisms aren't serving you anymore, so you're learning new ones. That's not being broken. That's being human."

"But what if I can't learn fast enough? What if Jarod gets tired of waiting for me to become the person he needs?"

"Then that would be his choice to make. Not yours, not TJ's. His." Dr. Chen leaned forward. "Here's what I'm hearing. TJ came to your office and planted seeds of doubt. Made you question whether you're capable of this relationship. And instead of recognizing that as his own fear and protectiveness, you're internalizing it as truth. Why?"

"Because what if he's right?"

"What if he's wrong? What if you are capable of sustaining this relationship, but you're letting his words sabotage it before you've even tried?"

Sadie was quiet for a long moment. "I'm scared."

"Of course you are. This is the most vulnerable you've ever been. The most invested. The most at risk. Fear is a completely normal response." Dr. Chen softened her voice. "But Sadie, you have a choice. You can let fear drive your decisions—which is what TJ is hoping for, consciously or not. Or you can acknowledge the fear and choose courage anyway."

"What about his conditions? About being separated from Jarod's social life?"

"What about them? Can you live with them?"

"I don't know. Part of me says no, that it's compartmentalization and I won't be that person in someone's life. But another part of me says if that's what it takes to keep Jarod, maybe it's worth it."

"Those are two very different answers. So which one is true for you?"

Sadie closed her eyes, trying to access her actual feelings beneath all the fear and doubt. "I don't want to be compartmentalized. Don't want to be the girlfriend who can't come to events or meet his friends. But I also don't want to lose him. So I'm stuck between two bad options."

"What if there's a third option?"

"What do you mean?"

"What if you tell Jarod you need time? Not days or weeks, but real time. Six months, maybe. Time where you continue dating but with lower stakes. Where neither of you makes big decisions about the future until you've both had space to heal and grow."

"He'll think I'm running."

"So explain that you're not. That you love him, but the circumstances are too charged right now. That TJ needs time to heal, you need time to grow, and Jarod needs time to process the cost of his choice. And then you actually use that time productively—therapy, self-work, building your own life independent of the relationship."

"And if he won't wait?"

"Then you have your answer. But Sadie, any man worth having will understand that healthy relationships require time and space. Rushing into decisions from a place of pressure and panic is how people make mistakes."

The session continued for another half hour, Dr. Chen helping Sadie map out what a six-month separation might look like. Not a breakup, but a pause. A chance for everyone to breathe and heal before making permanent decisions.

By the time Sadie left, she felt clearer than she had in days. She had a plan. Not a perfect plan, but a plan that honored her needs and Jarod's and even TJ's.

Now she just had to tell Jarod.

She drove to his loft without calling ahead. It was nearly 8 PM when she arrived, and she could see lights on through his windows.

He answered on the first knock, his expression cycling through relief, concern, and uncertainty.

"Sadie. I've been calling you all day. Your phone's been off—"

"I know. I needed space to think. Can I come in?"

"Of course."

They sat on his couch, the space between them feeling wider than the physical inches.

"I've made a decision," Sadie started. "And I need you to hear me out before you react."

"Okay."

"I love you. I'm in love with you. But I think we need to take a break. Not a breakup, but a pause. Six months where we step back, give TJ space to heal, give me time to continue growing, give you time to process what this relationship has cost you."

Jarod's expression was unreadable. "A break."

"Six months. During that time, we don't see each other. Don't date other people, but don't try to navigate the impossible situation we're in right now. We both focus on ourselves—you repair your friendship with TJ, I continue therapy and self-work. And then, after six months, we reassess. See if the circumstances have changed enough to make this sustainable."

"That sounds like a breakup with extra steps."

"It's not. It's a pause. A chance to let the dust settle and see if we can build something lasting instead of something reactive."

"What if six months isn't enough? What if TJ still doesn't want you around our friend group? What if nothing changes?"

"Then we'll have to decide if we can live with that. But at least we'll be deciding from a place of clarity instead of panic."

Jarod was quiet for a long time. When he finally spoke, his voice was thick with emotion. "I don't want to lose you."

"You're not losing me. I'm still here. Still working on myself. Still committed to becoming the person who can sustain this. I'm just asking for time and space to do that work without the pressure of navigating TJ's conditions."

"What if you decide during these six months that you don't want this anymore? That I'm not worth the complications?"

"Then that's information we both need. But Jarod, if you really love me—if you really think we have a future—then six months shouldn't matter. It's a tiny fraction of a lifetime."

He reached over and took her hands. "I do love you. So much it scares me. But Sadie, this feels like you're running again. Like things got hard and you're choosing safety over risk."

"I'm choosing clarity over chaos. There's a difference." She squeezed his hands. "We've been in crisis mode since the day you told TJ about us. We need space to breathe. To heal. To build something sustainable instead of something reactive."

"And you really think we can do this? Be apart for six months and come back stronger?"

"I don't know. But I think it's our best shot. The alternative is trying to navigate TJ's conditions while resenting them, or you losing your best friend permanently. Neither of those options leads anywhere good."

Jarod pulled his hands away and stood, pacing to the windows. For a long moment, he just stared out at the city, his shoulders tense.

"Okay," he finally said. "Six months. But Sadie, I need a promise from you."

"What?"

"That you actually use this time. That you don't retreat into old patterns or compartmentalize or hide. That you keep going to therapy, keep doing the work, keep growing. Because if we're doing this—if we're pressing pause on us—then it has to be worth it."

"I promise. I'm committed to the work. With or without you."

He turned to face her, and she saw tears in his eyes. "This is killing me. You know that, right? Letting you walk out that door, not knowing if you'll come back?"

"I know. It's killing me too. But I think it's the right thing. For both of us."

"When does the six months start?"

"Tonight. Now. From this moment."

"So this is goodbye. For six months."

"This is see you later. For six months."

He crossed to her and pulled her into his arms, holding her so tightly she could barely breathe. She felt his tears on her neck, felt her own soaking into his shirt.

"I love you," he whispered. "In six months or six years or whenever you're ready—I love you."

"I love you too. So much."

They held each other for a long time, both knowing that the moment they let go, the six months would begin. That they were choosing to be apart in hopes of coming back together stronger.

Finally, Sadie pulled away. "I should go. Before I change my mind."

"Sadie—"

"Don't. Please. If you ask me to stay, I will. And then we'll be right back where we started—in crisis mode, reacting instead of responding."

He nodded, wiping his eyes. "Six months."

"Six months."

She walked to the door, every step feeling like she was walking through cement. At the threshold, she turned back one more time.

"For what it's worth, I think you're incredible. And I think we could have something amazing. I just need to make sure I'm ready to be the partner you deserve."

"You already are. But I understand needing to know that for yourself."

She left before she could second-guess herself, before the magnitude of what she'd just done could sink in.

Six months. One hundred and eighty days. No contact, no seeing each other, no navigating the impossible situation they were in.

Just space to heal and grow and become the people they needed to be.

The drive home was a blur of tears. By the time Sadie reached her apartment, she was sobbing so hard she could barely see.

She'd just walked away from the man she loved.

Chosen to be alone instead of fighting for them.

Let fear—or was it wisdom?—drive her decision.

She didn't know anymore. Didn't know if she'd made the right choice or the biggest mistake of her life.

All she knew was that she was alone again. Back where she'd started, but somehow completely different.

Because this time, she wasn't alone by default. She was alone by choice.

Alone to heal. To grow. To become whole.

And six months from now, she'd find out if that was enough.

If *she* was enough.

If love was enough.

Or if she'd just walked away from her last chance at happiness because she was too broken to hold on to it.

CHAPTER 18
THE ANNIVERSARY

THE FIRST WEEK was the hardest.

Sadie threw herself into work with an intensity that bordered on manic. She arrived at the office by 6 AM and didn't leave until 9 or 10 PM. She volunteered for every project, every presentation, every opportunity that kept her mind occupied and away from the gaping hole where Jarod used to be.

Her team noticed. Melissa brought her lunch one day, concern evident on her face. "Ms. Monroe, you've been here twelve hours. Maybe you should go home? Rest?"

"I'm fine. Just trying to prove myself in this new role."

"You've already proved yourself. That's why you got the promotion." Melissa set down the lunch—a salad Sadie wouldn't eat. "Everyone's worried about you."

"Tell everyone I appreciate their concern, but I'm fine."

Except she wasn't fine. She was surviving. Barely.

LaKrecia called daily, sometimes multiple times a day. Sadie answered about half the calls, gave monosyllabic responses to most questions, and made excuses to get off the phone quickly.

"You're shutting down," LaKrecia said on Day Five. "I can hear it in your voice. You're retreating into work the same way you used to retreat into the Velvet Room."

"I'm not retreating. I'm focusing on my career. There's a difference."

"Is there? Because from where I'm sitting, you're using work to numb the pain. That's not processing. That's avoiding."

"I don't have the energy for this conversation right now, Krecia."

"Then when? When will you have the energy to actually deal with what you're feeling?"

"In six months. When I have clarity. When I've done the work. Just... give me space. Please."

LaKrecia was quiet for a long moment. "Okay. I'll give you space. But Sadie? I'm not going anywhere. When you're ready to actually process instead of just survive, I'll be here."

They hung up, and Sadie felt the loneliness crash over her like a wave. She was pushing away the one person who'd never left. The one constant in her life.

But she didn't have the energy to be a good friend right now. Could barely keep herself together, let alone be present for someone else.

Wednesday rolled around—therapy day. Sadie almost canceled. Dr. Chen had already gotten one emergency session out of her this week. Did she really need to go through another hour of excavating her feelings?

But she'd made a promise to Jarod. To use this time productively. To keep doing the work.

So she showed up.

Dr. Chen took one look at her and said, "You look exhausted."

"I've been working a lot."

"Working, or hiding in work?"

"Does it matter?"

"It does. One is productive. The other is avoidance." Dr. Chen settled into her chair. "How are you feeling about the separation?"

"I don't know. Numb mostly. Like I'm moving through water— everything takes more effort than it should."

"That's grief. You're grieving the relationship, even though it's not technically over."

"It feels over. Six months might as well be forever."

"Why?"

"Because what if in six months, nothing has changed? What if TJ still hates me, Jarod still has to choose between us, and we're right back where we started?"

"Then you'll have that information and can make an informed decision. But Sadie, you're catastrophizing again. You're jumping to the worst possible outcome and living there instead of being present with what is."

"What is feels unbearable."

"I know. Grief does feel unbearable. But it's also temporary. These feelings won't last forever, even if they feel permanent right now."

They spent the rest of the session talking about healthy ways to process grief—journaling, exercise, creative outlets, actually letting herself feel instead of numbing. Dr. Chen gave her homework: write a letter to Jarod that she'd never send, expressing everything she wished she could say. Then write one to herself, from the perspective of who she'd be in six months.

"The letters are about processing," Dr. Chen explained. "About externalizing all the thoughts and feelings swirling in your head so they don't consume you."

Sadie agreed to try, though she had no intention of actually doing it. Writing about her feelings sounded excruciating.

But that night, alone in her apartment with nothing but silence and her thoughts, she pulled out her journal.

Letter to Jarod (that I'll never send):

I miss you. It's only been a week and I miss you so much it physically hurts. I wake up reaching for you. I see things throughout the day that I want to tell you about. I come home expecting to find you here, and the emptiness hits me all over again.

I keep wondering if I made the right choice. If pressing pause was wisdom or cowardice. TJ's words keep echoing in my head—that I'm not capable of giving you what you need. That trying isn't enough.

What if he's right? What if I spend six months doing the work, and I'm still not enough?

But I have to try. I have to believe I can become the person you deserve. The person I want to be. Whole. Integrated. Capable of love without fear.

Six months feels like forever. But it's also nothing compared to a lifetime. And if we're meant to be together, we'll find our way back.

I love you. Even when it hurts. Especially when it hurts.

I hope you're healing. I hope TJ is talking to you again. I hope you're not as miserable as I am.

But also, selfishly, I hope you miss me too. Hope that these six months are as hard for you as they are for me. Because that means it mattered. We mattered.

In six months, I'll either be ready to fight for us, or I'll be ready to let you go. I don't know which yet. I'm just trying to survive until I figure it out.

I love you. I'm sorry. I hope you're okay.

She closed the journal, tears streaming down her face. Writing it out didn't make it hurt less, but it did make it feel more manageable. Like she'd taken some of the weight from her chest and put it on paper where it couldn't suffocate her.

Week two was marginally better. The raw, acute grief had dulled into a constant ache. Manageable, if not comfortable.

Sadie started going to the gym again—not her usual intense runs, but yoga classes that forced her to be present in her body. To breathe. To move through discomfort without running from it.

It helped. A little.

She also started painting. She'd taken art classes in college, before life and career had taken priority. On a whim, she bought supplies from an art store and set up a small studio space in her second bedroom.

She had no idea what she was painting. Just colors and shapes and emotions translated onto canvas. The results were messy and chaotic and probably terrible, but the process was cathartic.

LaKrecia came over one evening and found her covered in paint, staring at a canvas that looked like an explosion of burgundy and deep blue.

"What is it?" LaKrecia asked.

"I have no idea. Grief, maybe? Or love? Or the way they feel the same sometimes?"

"It's beautiful. In a mesmerizing sort of way."

They ordered pizza and sat on Sadie's couch, eating in comfortable silence for a while before LaKrecia asked, "Have you heard from him?"

"No. That's the deal. Six months, no contact."

"That must be hard. Not knowing how he's doing."

"It's torture. But it's necessary." Sadie wiped pizza grease from her hands. "I keep wanting to text him. To call. To just... check in. Make sure he's okay. But I can't. That would defeat the entire purpose of the separation."

"What if he reaches out to you?"

"I don't know. I guess I'd have to decide if responding would help or hurt. But Krecia, part of me really hopes he doesn't. Because if he does, it means he's struggling as much as I am. And I don't want him to hurt like this."

"That's love. Wanting the other person to be happy, even if their happiness doesn't include you."

"Yeah. It sucks."

LaKrecia stayed until late, and when she left, Sadie felt less alone. Less like she was drowning in her own thoughts.

Progress. Small, painful progress.

By week three, Sadie had established a routine. Work from 7 AM to 6 PM—reasonable hours, not the manic twelve-hour days. Gym or yoga from 6:30 to 7:30. Dinner—sometimes cooking, sometimes take-out, occasionally meeting LaKrecia. Painting or journaling from 8 to 10. Bed by 11.

Structure. Routine. Productivity without obsession.

She was functioning. Actually functioning, not just surviving.

Dr. Chen noticed the difference in their Wednesday session. "You seem more grounded this week. More present."

"I'm trying. It's still hard, but I'm not drowning anymore."

"That's significant progress. What's helping?"

"Structure. Having a routine that's about taking care of myself instead of numbing or avoiding. The yoga helps. The painting helps. Even the journaling, as much as I hate it, helps."

"Have you written the second letter yet? To yourself from your future self?"

"No. That one feels harder somehow."

"Because it requires hope. Believing you'll be in a better place in six months. That's scary when you're in the middle of grief."

"Exactly."

"But Sadie, hope is what gets us through. Even tiny, fragile hope. The belief that this pain is temporary, that growth is possible, that we can become who we need to be."

"I want to believe that."

"Then practice believing it. Write the letter. Imagine who you'll be in six months—stronger, more integrated, more whole. Let that version of yourself speak to the version sitting here right now."

That night, Sadie tried. She sat with her journal open for an hour, pen hovering over blank pages, trying to imagine her future self.

Finally, she wrote:

Letter from Future Sadie (six months from now):

Hi. It's me. You. Us. Six months in the future.

I want to tell you it gets easier. And it does. Not all at once, not in a straight line, but gradually. The acute grief fades. The constant ache becomes occasional pangs. You learn to live with the absence instead of being consumed by it.

You're stronger now. More integrated. The compartments you spent years building have mostly dissolved, replaced by something more fluid. More whole. You're not Corporate Sadie or After Hours Sadie anymore. You're just... Sadie. Complex and imperfect and still figuring it out, but whole.

The painting helped more than you expected. So did the yoga. So did LaKrecia's persistent presence, even when you tried to push her away. So did therapy—Dr. Chen helped you see patterns you couldn't see yourself.

You learned that being alone doesn't mean being lonely. That you can be complete without another person. That self-love isn't selfish—it's necessary.

As for Jarod... I don't know yet what happens when the six months are up. That decision is still ahead of me—of us. But I know this: whether you end up with him or not, you'll be okay. Better than okay. You'll be whole.

You're doing better than you think. The work is hard, but it's working. Keep going. Keep showing up. Keep choosing courage over comfort.

You've got this. We've got this.

With love,

Future Sadie

She read it over, tears streaming down her face. It felt like a lie— this optimistic future version of herself. But it also felt like a lifeline. Something to hold onto when the grief threatened to pull her under.

Week four brought an unexpected complication.

Sadie was at a work happy hour—something she'd been avoiding but finally forced herself to attend—when she saw him across the bar.

Xavier. One of her regulars from the Velvet Room.

He didn't see her at first, was laughing with a group of men she didn't recognize. But when he turned to order another drink, his eyes landed on her.

Recognition flickered across his face, followed by a slow smile.

He excused himself from his group and walked over. "Sadie? Is that really you?"

Her stomach dropped. This was her nightmare—worlds colliding, her past catching up with her present. "Xavier. Hi."

"I haven't seen you at the Room in months. People were starting to wonder if you'd disappeared." His eyes traveled over her appreciatively. "You look good. Different, but good."

"I've been busy. Work."

"Too busy for fun? That doesn't sound like the Sadie I knew." He leaned against the bar beside her, too close. "We had some good times, didn't we?"

"Xavier, I—"

"I've thought about you. About those nights. You were always my favorite." His hand found her lower back, a gesture that would have been familiar once but now felt invasive. "What do you say we catch up? Tonight? I could take you somewhere nice, and then..." He let the implication hang.

Every instinct screamed at her to run. To make an excuse and flee. To retreat into safety.

But she'd promised herself no more running.

"I can't," she said firmly, stepping away so his hand dropped. "I'm not doing that anymore. Any of it."

"Not doing what? Having fun? Living a little?"

"Not compartmentalizing my life. Not using physical connections to avoid emotional ones. Not being the woman I was when we knew each other."

Xavier looked confused. "So what, you're in a relationship now?"

"Sort of. It's complicated. But yes, essentially. And even if I wasn't, I wouldn't go back to that life. I'm different now."

"Different how?"

"More integrated. More whole. The Sadie you knew at the Velvet Room—she was only one piece of me. I'm working on being all the pieces at once now."

Understanding dawned on his face. "Well. Good for you, I guess. Hope it works out." He didn't sound sincere, sounded more disappointed than anything.

"Thank you."

He walked away, back to his group, and Sadie felt something shift inside her. She'd just been faced with her past—literally—and she'd chosen differently. Hadn't run, hadn't fallen back into old patterns, hadn't let the temptation pull her backward.

She'd chosen growth over comfort.

It was a small victory, but it felt significant.

That night, she added to her journal:

Ran into Xavier from the Velvet Room today. He propositioned me. Old Sadie would have considered it—maybe even gone through with it, justifying it as just physical, not emotional, not cheating on the technicality of being on a break.

But I didn't. I told him I was different now. And I meant it.

I'm not the woman who needed the Velvet Room to feel powerful. I'm finding power in other ways now—in being whole, in being honest, in choosing growth even when it's uncomfortable.

Dr. Chen would be proud. Hell, I'm proud of myself.

One small victory. But it feels like a big one.

By week five, Sadie had settled into her new normal. The grief was still there, but it had shifted from suffocating to manageable. She could breathe around it.

She'd started having coffee with colleagues outside of work. Had accepted an invitation to join a book club. Was building a social life that existed independent of Jarod, independent of any romantic relationship.

LaKrecia noticed the change. "You seem lighter. Less like you're carrying the weight of the world."

"I feel lighter. Not happy exactly, but... stable. Like I'm not constantly on the verge of falling apart."

"That's huge. I'm proud of you."

"Everyone keeps saying that. I'm just doing what I have to do to survive."

"No, you're doing more than surviving. You're building a life. There's a difference."

Sadie considered that. Was she building a life? Or was she just filling time until the six months were up and she could find out if Jarod still wanted her?

She didn't know. But either way, she was moving forward. One day at a time. One choice at a time.

Progress.

Painful, slow, imperfect progress.

But progress nonetheless.

Week six brought news she didn't expect.

She was having lunch with a colleague from another department when the woman mentioned, "Oh, I saw your ex at a charity gala last weekend. He was there with someone—not sure if it was serious or just a date. But they looked cozy."

Sadie's heart stopped. "My ex?"

"Jarod, right? Tall, gorgeous, runs that security software company? I remember you brought him to that work happy hour a while back."

"He's not my ex. We're just... on a break."

"Oh. Sorry. I thought—well, he looked pretty into whoever he was with. So I assumed."

The woman continued talking, but Sadie couldn't hear her over the roaring in her ears. Jarod was at a gala. With someone. Looking cozy.

Was he moving on? Had the six months become too much for him? Was this his way of signaling he was done waiting?

Or was it innocent—just networking, just a colleague, nothing romantic?

She didn't know. Had no way to know without breaking the no-contact rule.

That night, she almost called him. Almost texted. Almost broke her own boundary because the not-knowing was torture.

But she didn't.

Instead, she painted. Angry slashes of red and black across canvas. Grief and jealousy and fear made visual.

And when she was done, covered in paint and exhausted, she wrote in her journal:

Heard Jarod was at a gala with someone. Don't know if it means anything. Don't know if he's moving on or if it was innocent.

The not-knowing is killing me.

But I can't reach out. Can't break my own boundary just because I'm jealous and scared. That wouldn't be growth. That would be regression.

If he's moving on, I have to accept that. Have to trust that if we're meant to be together, six months won't matter. And if we're not, then knowing now versus knowing in four more months changes nothing.

I'm choosing to trust the process. Even when it hurts.

Even when I want to break every rule I set for myself.

Even when I don't know if he's waiting for me or forgetting me.

I'm choosing to trust.

God, I hope I'm not making a mistake.

She closed the journal and stared at the angry painting on her easel. It was ugly and beautiful and honest.

Just like this entire process.

Ugly and beautiful and honest.

And maybe that was enough.

Maybe that was growth.

CHAPTER 19

THE BREAKING POINT
THREE WEEKS EARLIER

JAROD SAT in his loft the night Sadie left, staring at the door she'd walked through. Six months. One hundred and eighty days. No contact.

It felt like a death sentence.

His phone sat on the coffee table, Sadie's contact photo staring back at him—a candid shot he'd taken of her laughing at something he'd said, her guard completely down, looking happy and free and whole.

He wanted to call her. To tell her this was a mistake. To beg her to come back.

But he'd agreed. Six months. Space to heal and grow.

So instead, he called the one person who might understand.

"Hey, man." TJ's voice was cautious when he answered. "Everything okay?"

"No. Can I come over?"

"Yeah. Of course."

Twenty minutes later, Jarod was sitting on TJ's couch, a beer in his hand that he wasn't drinking, staring at nothing.

"She left," he said finally. "Asked for a six-month break. Said we need space to heal and grow before we can figure out if this is sustainable."

TJ was quiet for a long moment. "How do you feel about that?"

"Like my chest has been ripped open. Like I can't breathe. Like I just made the biggest mistake of my life by agreeing to it."

"So why did you agree?"

"Because she's right. We've been in crisis mode since I told you about us. We need space. Time. Perspective. But knowing that intellectually and feeling it emotionally are two different things."

TJ sat down in the chair across from him. "I'm sorry, man. I know I'm part of why this happened. My conditions—"

"Your conditions were reasonable. You were protecting yourself. I don't blame you for that." Jarod finally took a sip of his beer. "I blame myself for not seeing this coming. For thinking love would be enough. For believing we could make this work despite everything."

"You still can. Six months isn't forever."

"It feels like forever. What if she uses that time to convince herself she doesn't need me? What if she's so good at being alone that she decides it's easier than being with me?"

"Then you'll deal with it. But Rod, you can't control what she does during this time. You can only control what you do. So what are you going to do?"

Jarod looked at his best friend—his brother—and felt the weight of everything that had happened crash over him. "I'm going to try to repair what I broke with you. I'm going to focus on work. I'm going to give her the space she asked for, even though it's killing me. And I'm going to hope like hell that in six months, she comes back ready to fight for us."

"And if she doesn't?"

"Then I'll have lost the woman I love. But at least I'll have you back. That has to count for something."

TJ's expression softened. "For what it's worth, I don't hate her. I'm angry at the situation, at how everything went down. But I don't hate her. And I don't want to be the reason you lose her."

"You're not. She made this choice. I'm just trying to respect it."

They talked for another hour—really talked, for the first time in weeks. About the hurt and betrayal TJ had felt. About Jarod's conflicted feelings. About how to rebuild their friendship while honoring Sadie's need for space.

By the time Jarod left, he felt marginally better. Not good, but less like he was drowning.

Week One

The first week was brutal. Jarod threw himself into work, taking on projects he'd been putting off, meeting with clients at all hours. Anything to keep his mind occupied.

But every quiet moment, Sadie flooded back. Her laugh. The way she looked at him when she thought he wasn't paying attention. The vulnerability in her eyes when she told him she loved him.

He missed her with an intensity that surprised him. They'd only been together for a few weeks—shouldn't he be able to handle a separation better than this?

But it wasn't about the length of time. It was about the depth of connection. Sadie had gotten under his skin in a way no one else ever had. She'd challenged him, pushed him, made him want to be better.

And now she was gone.

TJ called several times that week, checking in. They met for basketball on Saturday, falling back into their old rhythm. It felt good. Almost normal.

Except TJ carefully avoided mentioning Sadie, and Jarod was grateful for the omission. He didn't want to talk about her. Didn't want to examine his feelings. Didn't want to acknowledge how much he was hurting.

Week Two

Eric—the friend who'd hosted the disastrous dinner party—reached out about a business opportunity. A potential partnership between their companies, something that would require frequent meetings and collaboration.

It was exactly what Jarod needed—a project to pour himself into, something meaningful that would occupy his time and energy.

They met several times that week, hashing out details, and Eric didn't mention Sadie once. Jarod appreciated the professional boundary, the implicit understanding that the topic was off-limits.

But at their Friday meeting, Eric's date from the dinner party showed up—Olivia, a corporate attorney with a sharp mind and sharper wit.

"Jarod, good to see you again," she said warmly. "How have you been?"

"Busy. Work."

"I heard about you and Sadie. I'm sorry it didn't work out."

Jarod's jaw tightened. "It's not that it didn't work out. We're just... taking time."

"Oh. That's different then." Olivia sat down across from him. "For what it's worth, I thought you two seemed good together. At the party, before everything exploded. You looked at her like she was the only person in the room."

"She was. To me, she was."

"Then I hope the time apart gives you both what you need to make it work."

The conversation moved on to business, but Olivia's words stuck with him. *You looked at her like she was the only person in the room.*

Because she had been. She still was.

Week Three

TJ invited Jarod to a charity gala. "Sarah's firm is hosting it. I know social events are probably the last thing you want right now, but it might be good to get out. Network. Pretend to be normal for a few hours."

Jarod almost said no. But sitting alone in his loft another Saturday night sounded worse than pretending to be social.

"Okay. I'll go."

"Good. And Rod? Bring a date if you want. Or come solo. Either way, you've got a seat at our table."

"I'll come solo. I'm not ready to date."

"Even casually?"

"Especially casually. Sadie might be okay with me seeing other people during this break, but I'm not. I made a commitment to her. I'm keeping it."

"That's honorable. Probably stupid, but honorable."

The gala was exactly as Jarod expected—overdressed people drinking overpriced wine and pretending to care about the charity while actually networking and posturing. He hated these events, but he showed up and played the part.

Sarah had seated him next to one of her colleagues—Natasha, a litigator with model looks and impressive credentials. It was clearly a setup, TJ and Sarah's awkward attempt at helping him "move on."

Natasha was smart, funny, and made it clear she was interested. Under different circumstances, Jarod might have been interested back.

But all he could think about was Sadie. How she would have hated this event, would have made sarcastic comments under her breath that only he could hear. How they would have left early and gone back to his place, and she would have complained about uncomfortable heels while he rubbed her feet.

"You're clearly not over her," Natasha said about an hour in, her tone more amused than offended.

"What?"

"Whoever she is. The woman you're thinking about instead of actually listening to me drone on about antitrust law."

"I'm sorry. That's rude—"

"It's honest. Which I appreciate more than polite pretending." She smiled. "For what it's worth, she's lucky. Not many men stay this devoted during a separation."

"I'm not sure it's devotion. Might just be stupidity."

"There's a fine line between the two."

They spent the rest of the event talking about work, carefully avoiding personal topics. When it was over, Natasha gave him her card. "If you ever get over her and want to grab coffee, call me. But I'm not holding my breath."

Someone had filmed part of their conversation—the part where they were laughing, sitting close, looking to outside observers like they might be on a date. That video ended up on social media, tagged with Jarod's company name.

He didn't see it until Monday, when Eric texted him: *Bro, there's a video of you and some woman from the gala circulating. Might want to check it out before it gets back to Sadie.*

Jarod's stomach dropped. He found the video—grainy cell phone footage showing him and Natasha talking and laughing, her hand briefly touching his arm. Completely innocent, but it looked intimate to anyone who didn't know the context.

Had Sadie seen it? Would someone tell her?

He wanted to text her, to explain. But that would break the no-contact rule. And what would he even say? *Hey, I know we're on a break, but just so you know, I wasn't actually on a date with that woman. We were just talking.*

It would sound defensive. Guilty.

So he did nothing. Posted nothing, said nothing, let the video circulate and hoped Sadie wouldn't see it or wouldn't care if she did.

But the thought that she might be hurting, might think he was moving on—it ate at him all week.

Week Four

Jarod was having lunch with TJ when his phone buzzed with a notification. His therapist—Dr. Raymond Foster, whom he'd been seeing since before he met Sadie—had an opening that afternoon.

"I should take this," he said to TJ. "Therapy. Been going twice a week since the separation started."

"That's good. Healthy." TJ paused. "How's it going? The therapy?"

"Brutal. He keeps asking me if I think the relationship is worth fighting for, given the cost. Keeps pushing me to examine whether I'm holding onto Sadie because I actually love her or because I'm stubborn and don't like losing."

"What do you tell him?"

"That I love her. That it's worth it. That I'm willing to wait six months or six years if that's what it takes."

"And what does he say to that?"

"That I need to also be willing to let her go if that's what's best for both of us. That sometimes love means releasing someone, not holding on tighter."

TJ was quiet for a moment. "Do you think you can do that? Let her go if she comes back in six months and says she can't do this?"

"I don't know. I like to think I'm evolved enough to want her happiness above my own. But the truth? If she walks away permanently, it's going to destroy me. And I don't know how to be okay with that."

"Maybe you don't have to be okay with it. Maybe you just have to survive it."

"Survival isn't living, man. I don't want to just survive losing her. I want to not lose her at all."

"Then you wait. You do the work. You hope she's doing the same. And you trust that if it's meant to be, six months is nothing."

"You sound like a greeting card."

"Fuck you, I'm trying to be supportive."

They both laughed—genuine laughter that felt good after weeks of heaviness.

Maybe this was progress. Maybe he was healing. Maybe by the time the six months were up, he'd be in a better place to actually be the partner Sadie needed.

Or maybe he was deluding himself, and six months from now, he'd be just as broken as he was today.

Only time would tell.

Week Five

Dr. Williams gave Jarod homework similar to what Dr. Chen had given Sadie: write a letter to her that he'd never send. Express everything he couldn't say during the separation.

Jarod resisted for days. The thought of putting all his messy feelings on paper felt exposing, even if no one would ever read it.

But finally, late one night when sleep wouldn't come and his loft felt too empty, he opened his laptop and wrote:

Dear Sadie,

It's been five weeks. Thirty-five days. Eight hundred and forty hours. I'm counting. Is that pathetic? Probably. But I can't help it.

I miss you. Not just the physical stuff—though I miss that too, God, I miss that—but the other things. The way you challenged my assumptions about everything. The way you made me want to be better. The way you looked at me when you thought I wasn't paying attention, like you couldn't quite believe I was real.

TJ and I are rebuilding. It's slow, awkward sometimes, but we're getting there. So I guess the separation is working in that regard. I'm getting my best friend back.

But I'm losing you in the process, and I don't know if that trade-off was worth it.

Someone filmed me at a gala with a woman—completely innocent, just conversation—and I heard it circulated online. I wanted to text you immediately, to explain. But that would have broken our agreement. So I'm sitting here hoping you didn't see it, or if you did, hoping you know me well enough to know I wouldn't move on. Not from you. Not from us.

I'm not dating. Not even casually. People have asked. TJ and Sarah tried to set me up. But I can't. Because even though we're apart, you're still the only person I want. The only person I think about when I wake up and the last person I think about before I sleep.

Is that healthy? Dr. Williams says probably not. Says I should be using this time to figure out if I can be happy alone, independent of you. And I'm trying. I'm going to therapy twice a week. I'm working out. I'm spending time with friends. I'm doing all the things you're supposed to do to heal.

But I don't want to heal from you. I want to heal WITH you. I want to do the work together, not apart. I want to face our challenges as a team instead of as individuals hoping to come back together stronger.

But you needed this. You needed space to grow without the pressure of us. So I'm giving it to you, even though it's killing me.

Four and a half more months. One hundred and thirty-five more days. I can do this. I will do this. Because you're worth waiting for. Because what we had—what we could have—is worth fighting for.

I love you. I'm not moving on. I'm not dating. I'm not doing anything except waiting and hoping and working on myself so that when the six months are up, I can be the partner you deserve.

Please be doing the same. Please be growing and healing and becoming whole. Please don't be using this time to convince yourself you're better off alone.

Please still want me when this is over.

I love you,

Jarod

He read it over three times, then saved it in a folder on his laptop labeled "Things I'll Never Send."

It didn't make him feel better, exactly. But it made the feelings more manageable. Less like they were consuming him and more like they were just... there. Part of him. Part of this process.

Week Six

Eric called with news about their business partnership. "We've got approval from both boards. This is happening. We're officially partners."

It should have been exciting news. A major business win. Proof that Jarod could still focus on his career despite the personal chaos.

But all he felt was hollow. Like he was going through the motions of his life instead of actually living it.

"That's great," he said, trying to inject enthusiasm into his voice. "When do we start?"

"Next month. We'll need to have regular meetings, coordinate our teams. You good with that?"

"Yeah. Of course."

After he hung up, Jarod sat in his loft and took inventory of his life. His business was thriving. His friendship with TJ was healing. He was doing the therapeutic work. He was checking all the boxes.

But he felt empty.

Because none of it mattered without Sadie.

And that realization terrified him. Because it meant Dr. Williams was right—he'd made her too central to his happiness. Had let his identity become too wrapped up in being her partner.

He needed to figure out how to be whole on his own, independent of her. Otherwise, when the six months were up, he'd just be bringing his emptiness back to the relationship, expecting her to fill it.

That wasn't fair to either of them.

So he made a decision. He called Dr. Williams and asked to increase his therapy to three times a week. Started volunteering at a youth basketball program, finding purpose outside of work and relationships. Reconnected with friends he'd been neglecting.

He started building a life—a real life, not just a placeholder until Sadie came back.

Because whether she came back or not, he needed to be whole. For himself. For any future relationship. For the possibility of being the partner she needed if she did choose to try again.

It was hard work. Uncomfortable work. Work that required him to examine all the ways he'd made Sadie responsible for his happiness.

But it was necessary work.

And slowly—painfully slowly—he started to feel less empty. Started to find moments of genuine happiness that had nothing to do with her.

He was still counting down the days. Still missed her with an ache that never fully went away.

But he was also building something sustainable. Something that didn't require her presence to be real.

And maybe that was growth.

Maybe that was what these six months were really about—both of them learning to be whole independently so they could come together as complete people instead of broken ones seeking completion in each other.

He didn't know if it would be enough. Didn't know if Sadie was doing the same work, or if she was using this time to convince herself she was better off alone.

But he knew this: when the six months were up, he'd be ready. Ready to fight for them if she wanted to try. Ready to let her go with grace if she didn't.

Ready to be the man she deserved, whether that meant being her partner or being strong enough to wish her well from a distance.

It wasn't what he wanted. What he wanted was her. Now. Always.

But sometimes love meant doing the hard thing. The uncomfortable thing. The thing that felt like death but was actually growth.

So he kept going. One day at a time. One therapy session at a time. One choice at a time.

Building a life. Becoming whole. Hoping.

Always hoping that in four and a half more months, she'd come back ready to try.

And terrified that she wouldn't.

CHAPTER 20

THE DECISION
MONTH FIVE

SADIE STOOD in front of her latest painting—an abstract piece that had taken her three weeks to complete. Layers of deep purple fading into lighter lavender, with streaks of gold cutting through like hope breaking through darkness. It was the first piece she'd created that felt genuinely good, not just therapeutic.

"It's beautiful," LaKrecia said from behind her. She'd come over for their weekly dinner—a tradition they'd established two months ago. "You're really talented. Have you thought about showing these somewhere?"

"God, no. They're just... processing. Not real art."

"They're real to you. That makes them real art." LaKrecia moved closer, studying the canvas. "This one feels different than the others. Less angry. More... hopeful?"

"Maybe. I don't know. I started it the day I realized I actually liked who I was becoming. That I wasn't just surviving anymore—I was building something."

"That's huge, Sadie."

Five months. One hundred and fifty days. Sadie had stopped counting weeks ago, but the date still lived in the back of her mind. One more month until the six months were up. One more month until she had to decide what happened next.

The thought filled her with equal parts anticipation and dread.

"Have you thought about what you're going to say to him?" LaKrecia asked, reading her mind as usual. "When the six months are up?"

"Constantly. But I still don't know." Sadie moved to the couch, where they'd spread out Thai food. "Some days I'm sure I want to try again. Other days I'm convinced I'm better off alone. And most days I'm just confused."

"What does Dr. Chen say?"

"That I need to figure out what I actually want, not what I think I should want. That I need to be honest about whether I'm ready for the vulnerability a relationship with Jarod requires."

"And are you? Ready for that vulnerability?"

Sadie considered the question. Five months ago, the answer would have been a definite no. But now?

"I think so. I'm not the same person I was when this started. I'm more integrated, more whole. I can sit with discomfort instead of running from it. I can be alone without feeling like I'm dying. I've built a life that doesn't require another person to be meaningful."

"So what's the hesitation?"

"What if all this growth I've done—what if it's only sustainable when I'm alone? What if the moment I'm back in a relationship, I fall into old patterns? What if I hurt him again?"

"What if you don't? What if all this work has actually changed you fundamentally?"

"That's what terrifies me. The not knowing. I've spent five months learning to be comfortable with uncertainty, but this—this is the biggest uncertainty of all."

They ate in silence for a while before LaKrecia asked, "Do you still love him?"

"Yes." The answer came without hesitation. "God, yes. I think about him constantly. Wonder how he's doing, if he's happy, if he's moved on. I miss him so much sometimes it physically hurts."

"Then you have your answer."

"Do I? Because love alone isn't enough. We established that five months ago."

"No, but love plus growth might be. You're not the same person who started this break. You've done the work. Now you just have to trust that it was enough."

After LaKrecia left, Sadie pulled out her journal. She'd been writing in it almost daily, documenting her journey, tracking her progress. She flipped back through the entries, seeing the evolution—from the raw, desperate grief of the first few weeks to the more measured, thoughtful entries of recent months.

She'd changed. Fundamentally, undeniably changed.

The question was whether that change was enough.

Three Weeks Before the End

Dr. Chen announced in their session that she thought Sadie was ready to start thinking concretely about the future.

"We have three weeks left before your six-month mark. I think it's time to start processing what you want to happen when that date arrives."

"I've been thinking about it constantly."

"I know. But thinking and processing are different. Thinking is circular—you go around and around the same questions. Processing is linear—you work through the questions methodically until you reach clarity." Dr. Chen pulled out a notepad. "So let's process. Start with this: If Jarod wasn't a factor—if you'd never met him—what would your life look like right now? Who would you be?"

Sadie thought about it. "I'd be... pretty much who I am now, actually. I like my life. I like my job, my friendships, my painting. I like who I've become. The work I've done—I didn't do it for him. I did it for me."

"That's important. You're not dependent on him for your sense of self or happiness."

"No. I'm genuinely okay alone. Not just surviving, but actually okay."

"Good. Now, second question: What would adding Jarod back into your life give you that you don't already have?"

"Partnership. Someone to share things with. Physical intimacy. Emotional intimacy. The challenge of being seen fully and loved anyway. The opportunity to practice vulnerability in a safe relationship."

"Those are good reasons. Not neediness or desperation, but genuine additions to an already full life."

"So what's the problem?"

"You tell me. What's holding you back?"

"Fear. Pure, simple fear. Fear that I'll fall back into old patterns. Fear that the growth won't stick under pressure. Fear that I'll hurt him again and confirm everyone's worst predictions about me."

"And what's the evidence for those fears? Have you fallen back into old patterns during these five months?"

Sadie thought about Xavier at the bar, about the moments when she'd wanted to compartmentalize or numb, about all the times she'd chosen growth over comfort. "No. I've been tested multiple times, and I've chosen differently every time."

"Then trust that pattern. Trust that the work has fundamentally changed you, not just temporarily modified your behavior."

"What if I'm wrong?"

"Then you'll handle it. You'll make amends, learn from it, and try again. But Sadie, you can't let fear of future mistakes prevent you from taking present risks. That's not growth—that's another form of self-protection."

The session ended with homework: write a pros and cons list about trying again with Jarod. Not from fear, but from clarity.

That night, Sadie pulled out her journal and made two columns:

PROS:

- I love him
- I genuinely miss having him in my life
- We challenged each other to grow
- The relationship pushed me to become more integrated and whole
- I'm ready to practice the vulnerability I've been learning
- Partnership, intimacy, shared life
- I believe we could build something sustainable now

CONS:

- TJ's conditions might still be in place
- The history—we've hurt each other deeply
- Risk of falling back into old patterns under stress
- My growth might not be sustainable in relationship
- The public nature of our drama might continue
- Fear of disappointing him and myself

She stared at the lists. The pros outweighed the cons. But the cons were heavier, weightier with consequence.

What did that mean?

Two Weeks Before the End

Sadie was at a work dinner—a celebration of successfully closing a major deal—when she overheard two colleagues talking.

"Did you hear Jarod Morrison is launching a new partnership with that security firm? Supposed to be huge."

"Good for him. I heard he's been killing it lately. Focused, driven. Someone said he's dating again too."

Sadie's stomach dropped. Dating? Had someone told her that before? Had she just forgotten?

No. This was new information.

Or was it? She'd heard about the gala months ago. Maybe this was connected to that. Maybe it was nothing.

Or maybe he'd moved on.

She excused herself from dinner early, claiming a headache that wasn't entirely fabricated. At home, she pulled out her phone and did something she'd avoided for five months—she looked at Jarod's social media.

His profiles were mostly professional—updates about his company, industry news, networking events. But there were a few personal posts scattered through. Photos from the charity gala. Pictures from basketball games with TJ and other friends. A shot of him at what looked like a volunteer event with kids.

He looked good. Happy. Healthy. Like someone who'd moved on.

Was that what she wanted? For him to be happy without her?

Yes and no. She wanted him to be happy. But she also selfishly wanted him to be waiting for her.

The contradiction made her head hurt.

She almost texted LaKrecia, but it was past midnight. Instead, she opened her journal and wrote:

Heard Jarod might be dating. Don't know if it's true or just rumors. Two weeks left until I can ask him directly. Two weeks of not knowing if he's moved on or if he's still waiting.

Part of me hopes he's happy. Hopes he's built a life that fulfills him. But part of me—the selfish, vulnerable part—hopes he's as miserable without me as I've been without him.

Is that terrible? To want someone you love to suffer because you're suffering?

Probably.

Dr. Chen says I need to trust the process. Trust that if we're meant to be together, we'll find our way back. And if we're not, then these five months of growth will have prepared me to handle that loss with grace.

But I don't want grace. I want him. I want us. I want the chance to prove we can do this right.

Two more weeks. Then I'll know.

One Week Before the End

Sadie was painting in her makeshift studio when her phone rang. An unfamiliar number.

She almost didn't answer, but something made her pick up.

"Hello?"

"Sadie? This is Sarah. TJ's girlfriend."

Sadie's heart stopped. "Sarah. Hi. Is everything okay?"

"Yes. Well, sort of. I'm calling because—look, I know this is weird, and I'm probably overstepping. But I felt like someone should tell you."

"Tell me what?"

"TJ and I have been talking. About you and Jarod. About the six months and what happens when they're up. And TJ—" She paused. "TJ's conditions. About keeping you separate from their social circle. He's willing to lift them."

The world tilted. "What?"

"He's been going to therapy. We both have, actually, as a couple. And his therapist helped him see that those conditions were about control, not healing. That he was trying to punish you and Jarod for hurting him, when what he really needs is to process his feelings and move forward. So he's willing to lift the conditions. If you and Jarod want to try again, TJ won't stand in the way."

Sadie couldn't speak. The biggest obstacle—the thing that had seemed insurmountable—was gone.

"Why are you telling me this?" she finally managed.

"Because I've watched TJ struggle with losing his best friend. And I've watched Jarod struggle with losing you. And honestly? Life's too short for this much self-inflicted misery. You and Jarod love each other. You've both done the work. TJ removing his conditions is the last piece. Now you just have to decide if you're brave enough to try."

"Does Jarod know? About TJ lifting the conditions?"

"Not yet. TJ's planning to tell him this weekend. But I wanted to tell you first. Give you time to process before the six months are up."

"I don't know what to say. Thank you?"

"Don't thank me. Just... think about it. Really think about whether you want this. Because if you're not all in, if you're going to hurt him again—it's better to let him go now. TJ and I will help him move on. But if you are all in, if you're ready to fight for this—then don't let fear or pride or stubbornness stop you."

After they hung up, Sadie sat in stunned silence.

TJ had lifted his conditions. The external obstacle was gone.

Which meant the only thing standing between her and Jarod now was her own fear.

She called LaKrecia.

"I need you. Can you come over?"

"I'm on my way."

Twenty minutes later, LaKrecia was sitting across from her, listening to everything Sarah had said.

"So what are you going to do?" LaKrecia asked when she finished.

"I don't know. The conditions are gone. TJ's okay with us trying. All the external obstacles are removed. But Krecia, I'm still scared."

"Of course you are. But scared doesn't mean wrong. Scared just means it matters."

"What if I mess it up again?"

"Then you mess it up and learn from it and try again. But Sadie, you've spent five months doing the work. Five months becoming someone who can handle a real relationship. Don't let fear of potential failure prevent you from taking the risk."

"When did you get so wise?"

"I've been taking notes from Dr. Chen." LaKrecia smiled. "But seriously, baby. You love him. He loves you. You've both done the work. The circumstances have changed. What more do you need?"

"Certainty. A guarantee. A promise that this will work out."

"Life doesn't come with guarantees. You know that better than anyone. So you have to decide—is the possibility of happiness with Jarod worth the risk of potential hurt? Because those are your options. Risk or safety. Love or fear. Which one are you choosing?"

Sadie thought about the last five months. The painting, the therapy, the growth. The woman she'd become—integrated, whole, capable of vulnerability.

She thought about Jarod. His patience, his challenge, his love for all of her—even the messy, complicated parts.

She thought about the life they could build together. Not perfect, but real. Not easy, but worth it.

"I'm choosing love," she said finally. "I'm choosing risk. I'm choosing him."

"Then you have your answer."

"I guess I do."

"So what are you going to do? Wait for him to reach out when the six months are up? Or take initiative?"

Sadie considered. Six days left. Six days until the official end of the separation.

She could wait. Let him make the first move. See if he even still wanted to try.

Or she could be brave. Could show him that she'd changed, that she was ready to fight for them.

"I'm going to his loft. Tomorrow. I'm not waiting six more days. I'm done waiting."

"That's my girl." LaKrecia pulled her into a hug. "I'm proud of you. Whatever happens, I'm proud of you."

The Next Day

Sadie stood outside Jarod's building, her heart hammering so hard she thought she might pass out. She'd rehearsed what she wanted to say a hundred times. But now that she was here, everything felt inadequate.

She pressed the buzzer for his unit.

"Hello?" His voice through the intercom made her chest ache.

"Jarod. It's me. Can I come up?"

Silence. Long, agonizing silence.

Then: "Yeah. Come up."

The elevator ride felt eternal. By the time she reached his floor, she was shaking. She knocked on his door, and it opened almost immediately.

Jarod stood there, looking exactly the same and completely different all at once. Same handsome face, same intense eyes. But there was something lighter about him. More grounded.

"Sadie." Her name on his lips felt like coming home.

"Hi. I know I'm six days early. I know we agreed to six months. But I couldn't wait anymore. I had to see you. I had to tell you—"

"Come in. Please."

She stepped inside his loft—the space that had become so familiar five months ago. It looked different. Lighter. There were new plants by the windows, new art on the walls. Evidence of a life being lived, not just endured.

"You redecorated," she said.

"I needed change. Needed to make this space feel like mine again instead of just the place I was waiting for you to come back to."

The words hit her. Had he moved on? Was she too late?

"Jarod, I—"

"Let me go first," he interrupted. "Please. I need to say something."

"Okay."

He took a deep breath. "These five months have been the hardest of my life. But they've also been the most important. I've learned that I made you too central to my happiness. That I was expecting you to complete me instead of being whole on my own. So I've done the work —therapy, volunteering, rebuilding my life independent of you. And I've realized that I can be happy alone. That I don't need you."

The words felt like a knife. "Oh. Okay. I understand—"

"But—" He stepped closer. "Just because I don't need you doesn't mean I don't want you. I want you, Sadie. So fucking much. I want to build a life with you. I want partnership and challenge and all the messy, complicated beauty that comes with loving someone who's as strong and stubborn as you are."

Hope bloomed in her chest. "I want that too. That's why I'm here. Sarah called me. Told me TJ lifted his conditions. And I realized that the only thing standing between us now is my fear. And I'm done letting fear drive my decisions."

"So what are you saying?"

"I'm saying I love you. I'm saying I've done the work. I'm saying I'm ready to be vulnerable with you, to be all in, to fight for us. I'm saying—" Her voice cracked. "I'm saying please give us another chance. Let me prove I can be the partner you deserve."

Jarod closed the distance between them, his hands framing her face. "You already are. You did the work. You became whole. You showed up here six days early instead of waiting. That's growth, baby. That's courage."

"So is that a yes? To trying again?"

"It's a hell yes. To trying again. To being all in. To building something real and sustainable and messy and beautiful."

He kissed her then—deep and passionate and full of five months of longing. Sadie felt tears streaming down her face, mixing with the kiss, tasting of salt and hope and second chances.

When they finally broke apart, both breathing hard, Jarod rested his forehead against hers.

"I missed you so much," he whispered.

"I missed you too. Every day. Every moment."

"So what happens now?"

"Now we try. We take it slow. We communicate. We're honest even when it's hard. We build something sustainable instead of something reactive."

"I can do that."

"Me too."

They stood there holding each other, and Sadie felt something settle in her chest. This was right. They were right. Not perfect, but right.

"Stay," Jarod said. "Tonight. Tomorrow. As long as you want."

"I'll stay tonight. But Jarod—I need my own space too. We need to build this right, not just fall back into old patterns. So I stay tonight, but tomorrow I go home. And we date. Really date. Take our time building something lasting."

"Slow and steady."

"Exactly."

"I can do slow and steady. As long as it's with you."

They spent the rest of the evening talking—really talking, about the last five months, about what they'd learned, about what they wanted from a future together. They ordered food, curled up on his couch, and just... existed together.

It felt easy. Natural. Right.

And when they finally went to bed—just sleeping, holding each other, no pressure for anything more—Sadie felt peace for the first time in five months.

She'd done it. She'd become whole. She'd chosen courage over fear. She'd fought for love instead of running from it.

And tomorrow, they'd start building their future.

One day at a time.

One choice at a time.

Together.

CHAPTER 21
THE DEPARTURE

SADIE WOKE to sunlight streaming through Jarod's floor-to-ceiling windows and the solid warmth of his body beside her. For a moment, she felt disoriented—was this real? Had she actually shown up at his door yesterday? Had they actually agreed to try again?

Then Jarod stirred, his arm tightening around her waist, and she knew it was real.

"Morning," he murmured, his voice rough with sleep.

"Morning."

They lay there in comfortable silence, neither wanting to move, both savoring the simple intimacy of waking up together.

Finally, Jarod propped himself up on one elbow to look at her. "I keep thinking I'm going to wake up and you'll be gone. That this was just a really vivid dream."

"I'm real. This is real." She reached up to touch his face. "We're really doing this."

"We are. And it's terrifying and wonderful at the same time."

"That seems to be our specialty."

He kissed her then—slow and sweet, nothing like the desperate passion of last night. This was about connection, about being present, about choosing each other in the clear light of morning.

When he pulled back, his expression turned serious. "So. Ground rules. How do we do this right?"

"We already talked about this. We take it slow. We date. We don't just fall back into living together or being constantly together. We build something sustainable."

"Right. But what does that look like practically? Do we see each other every day? A few times a week? Do we tell people we're back together or keep it quiet until we're sure?"

Sadie thought about it. Five months ago, she would have wanted to keep it quiet, to protect herself in case things fell apart. But she'd done the work. She was choosing courage.

"We tell people. No more secrets, no more compartments. We're together, we're trying, and we're not hiding it." She paused. "But we don't rush back into the intensity we had before. Maybe we see each other three or four times a week? Maintain our own lives, our own spaces, while building something together?"

"I can do that. What about TJ? Sarah said he lifted his conditions, but I haven't actually talked to him yet. Do we wait to tell him, or...?"

"We tell him. Soon. Together, if he's willing. We don't hide or avoid. We face things head-on."

"When did you get so brave?"

"Five months of therapy and self-work. It's amazing what you can accomplish when you're not running from your feelings."

They got up and made breakfast together—a domestic intimacy that felt both familiar and new. Jarod made coffee while Sadie scrambled eggs, both moving around his kitchen with easy coordination.

"This feels good," Jarod said, watching her plate the food. "Normal. Like we've been doing this for years instead of just starting over."

"It does. But Jarod—" She set down the spatula and turned to face him. "We need to talk about what happens when it doesn't feel good. When we fight or one of us panics or old patterns try to resurface. How do we handle that?"

"We talk about it. Immediately. No letting it fester. And if we can't work through it alone, we bring in help—our therapists, LaKrecia, whoever we need."

"And if I pull away? If I feel myself compartmentalizing or wanting to run?"

"Then you tell me. And I don't let you run. I hold space for whatever you're feeling, but I also hold you accountable to staying and working through it."

"That sounds terrifying."

"It is. For both of us. But that's how this works—we make ourselves vulnerable and trust the other person to handle it with care."

They ate breakfast on his couch, and Sadie found herself studying him. He really had changed. There was a groundedness to him that hadn't been there before, a sense of being comfortable in his own skin regardless of whether she was there or not.

"What are you thinking?" he asked, catching her staring.

"That you seem different. Lighter, somehow."

"I feel different. The work I did these last five months—it wasn't just about waiting for you. It was about becoming the kind of person who can be in a healthy relationship. Someone who's whole on their own."

"I did the same work. And I think—I hope—we're both in a better place to actually do this right now."

"We are. I believe that." He set down his coffee. "So when are you leaving? Going back to your place?"

"After breakfast. I need to shower, change, get ready for the week. And we need to practice being apart without panicking that the other person is disappearing."

"I'm not going to lie—my instinct is to ask you to stay. To spend the whole day together. But you're right. We need to pace ourselves."

"How about dinner tomorrow? You come to my place, I cook, we ease back into seeing each other regularly?"

"That sounds perfect."

Sadie left Jarod's loft around noon, and the drive home felt surreal. She'd gone there yesterday on a whim, terrified he'd reject her, and come away with a second chance. It felt too good to be true.

The moment she walked into her apartment, her phone rang. LaKrecia.

"Well? Don't leave me hanging. What happened?"

Sadie filled her in on everything—showing up at Jarod's door, the conversation, the decision to try again, the ground rules they'd established.

"I'm so proud of you," LaKrecia said when she finished. "You didn't let fear stop you. You showed up and fought for what you wanted. That's huge."

"It is. But Krecia, I'm still scared. What if the growth doesn't stick? What if we fall back into old patterns?"

"Then you'll recognize it and course-correct. But babe, you're not the same person you were five months ago. Neither is he. Give yourselves credit for the work you've both done."

"I'm trying."

"Good. Now, when do I get to see you two together? Because I need to assess whether he's still worthy of my best friend."

Sadie laughed. "Soon. Maybe next week? Dinner at my place?"

"Perfect. I'll bring wine and my list of very important questions for him."

"Don't scare him off."

"If he scares that easily, he doesn't deserve you."

After they hung up, Sadie walked through her apartment. It looked different somehow. Or maybe she was different, and that changed how everything else looked.

The paintings she'd created over the last five months lined one wall—a visual representation of her journey from grief to acceptance to hope. She studied them, seeing the progression from dark, angry colors to lighter, more hopeful ones.

Growth. Visible, tangible growth.

Her phone buzzed. Jarod: *Missing you already. Is that pathetic?*

Sadie: *Only if it's pathetic that I'm missing you too.*

Jarod: *Then we're both pathetic. I can live with that.*

Sadie: *See you tomorrow night. 7 PM?*

Jarod: *I'll be there. Should I bring anything?*

Sadie: *Just yourself. And maybe wine.*

Jarod: *Done. I love you.*

The words on her screen made her smile. He'd said them so easily, so naturally. Like they were just a fact, not a declaration that required courage.

Sadie: *I love you too.*

She set down her phone and pulled out her journal. She'd been writing in it almost daily for five months—it felt strange not to have a crisis to document.

Day one of trying again. It feels good. Scary, but good. We're taking it slow, building something sustainable instead of just falling back into intensity.

I'm different now. He's different. We're both more whole, more grounded. I think we can actually do this.

Dr. Chen would be proud. I showed up six days early instead of waiting. I fought for what I wanted instead of letting fear keep me safe and alone.

This might work. For the first time, I actually believe this might work.

And even if it doesn't—even if we try and it falls apart—I'll be okay. I've learned that I can be whole on my own. That I don't need someone else to complete me.

But God, I want him. Want us. Want the messy, complicated, beautiful thing we could build together.

Here's to second chances. Here's to growth. Here's to choosing courage over comfort.

Monday morning, Sadie returned to work with a lightness she hadn't felt in months. The promotion had settled in, she had a good team, and for the first time, her personal life wasn't a source of constant stress.

Melissa noticed immediately. "You seem happy, Ms. Monroe. Good weekend?"

"Very good. Thanks for asking."

"It's nice to see you smiling again. You've been so serious lately."

Had she? Sadie supposed she had been. The weight of the separation, the work of growth—it had all been so heavy. But now, with Jarod back in her life, with hope for the future, everything felt lighter.

Around 10 AM, her phone buzzed with a text from an unknown number.

Hi Sadie. It's TJ. Sarah told me she called you. Can we meet for coffee? Just the two of us. I'd like to talk.

Sadie's stomach dropped. This was it. The conversation she'd been dreading and anticipating in equal measure.

She typed back: *Yes. When and where?*

TJ: *Today at 1 PM? There's a coffee shop near your office—Grounds. You know it?*

Sadie: *I know it. I'll be there.*

The rest of the morning was a blur. She couldn't focus on work, couldn't stop thinking about what TJ would say. Was this about lifting his conditions? About apologizing? About warning her not to hurt Jarod again?

At 12:45, she left the office and walked to Grounds. TJ was already there, sitting at a corner table with two coffees waiting.

He stood when he saw her. "Sadie. Thanks for meeting me."

"Of course." She sat down, accepting the coffee he'd ordered—oat milk latte, her usual. He'd remembered. "How are you?"

"Good. Better. Sarah and I have been doing therapy together, and it's helped a lot." He took a breath. "I owe you an apology. Several, actually."

"TJ—"

"No, let me say this. Please." He looked at her directly. "I was an asshole to you. At the dinner party, at your office, in general. I blamed you for everything—for playing Jarod and me, for destroying our friendship, for all of it. And while you definitely made mistakes, so did I. I made Jarod's relationship decisions about me. I tried to control who he could be with because I was hurt."

"You had every right to be hurt."

"I did. But I didn't have the right to try to control Jarod's life. Or yours. The conditions I set—about keeping you separate from our social circle—they weren't about protecting myself. They were about punishing you both. My therapist helped me see that."

"Sarah mentioned you lifted them."

"I did. And I want you to know—if you and Jarod want to try again, I won't stand in the way. I won't make him choose between us. I'm working on separating my hurt from his happiness."

Sadie felt tears prick her eyes. "Thank you. That means more than you know."

"But I also need to say something else." His expression turned serious. "I don't fully trust you yet. I understand you've done work, that you've grown. But trust is rebuilt slowly. So if you hurt him again—if you fall back into old patterns or compartmentalize him or run when things get hard—I won't forgive you a second time. And I'll be there to help him pick up the pieces and move on."

"That's fair."

"Is it? Because I'm basically saying I'm waiting for you to fuck up."

"You're saying you're protecting your friend. I respect that. And TJ? I'm not going to fuck up. I've spent five months doing the work to make sure of that. But if I do—if I somehow mess this up despite everything—then you absolutely should be there for him. He deserves that."

TJ studied her for a long moment. "You really have changed, haven't you?"

"I have. Five months ago, I would have been defensive, would have told you to mind your own business. But I've learned that accountability isn't the enemy. That people who call me on my shit are doing me a favor, not attacking me."

"Dr. Chen sounds like a miracle worker."

"She is. But she'd say the miracle was me showing up and doing the work."

They talked for another thirty minutes—not about the past, but about the present and future. About Sarah and their relationship. About Jarod's business ventures. About building toward something healthier for everyone involved.

By the time they parted ways, Sadie felt lighter. TJ wasn't her friend—might never be her friend. But he was no longer her enemy. He was just someone who loved Jarod and wanted to protect him.

She could respect that.

That evening, she called Jarod to tell him about the meeting.

"How did it go?" he asked.

"Good. Really good, actually. He apologized for being an asshole, said he's lifted his conditions, and basically gave us his cautious blessing."

"That's huge. I'm meeting him for drinks Wednesday. We're working on rebuilding."

"How do you feel about that?"

"Relieved. Hopeful. Like maybe we can actually have it all—you and him and a functional friendship."

"We can. I believe that now."

"Me too. So tomorrow night? You're still cooking for me?"

"I am. Hope you like chicken parmesan, because that's about the extent of my culinary skills."

"I like anything that involves spending time with you. The food is just a bonus."

After they hung up, Sadie pulled out ingredients and started prepping for tomorrow's dinner. It had been so long since she'd cooked for someone—since she'd done anything domestic and intimate like this.

It felt good. Normal. Like building a life instead of just surviving one.

Tuesday Evening

Jarod arrived at exactly 7 PM, holding a bouquet of purple flowers —irises and lavender, her favorites. The gesture made her chest tight.

"You remembered."

"Of course I remembered. Purple, like twilight." He handed them to her. "These are for choosing courage. For showing up at my door. For fighting for us."

She kissed him—deep and passionate, right there in her doorway. When they finally broke apart, both breathing hard, she pulled him inside.

"Come on. Dinner's almost ready."

They ate at her small dining table, talking easily about their days, their work, their lives. It felt remarkably normal—no drama, no crisis, just two people enjoying each other's company.

After dinner, they moved to her couch with wine, and Jarod studied the paintings on her wall.

"These are incredible. LaKrecia mentioned you'd been painting, but I didn't realize you were this talented."

"They're just therapy. Ways to process feelings."

"They're more than that. They're art." He pointed to the purple and gold one. "This one especially. It's... hopeful. Beautiful."

"That's the most recent one. I painted it the week I realized I actually liked who I was becoming."

"I like who you're becoming too." He pulled her close. "Actually, I love who you're becoming. And I'm so proud of you for doing the work."

"I'm proud of you too. You really did become whole on your own. I can see it—the way you move through the world now. More confident. More grounded."

"We both did the work. Now we get to see if we can maintain it together."

They talked for hours—about therapy, about growth, about what they wanted their relationship to look like moving forward. About being honest when things were hard, about asking for what they needed, about building something sustainable.

Around 11 PM, Jarod stood reluctantly. "I should go. Let you get sleep before work tomorrow."

"You could stay." The words came out before Sadie could stop them.

"I could. But we said slow and steady. If I stay tonight, we'll end up in bed together, and then we'll wake up together, and before we know it we're back to the intensity without building the foundation first."

"When did you get so wise?"

"Five months of therapy. Dr. Williams drilled into me that sustainable relationships are built on friendship and communication, not just chemistry."

"He's right. As much as I hate it right now."

Jarod kissed her at the door—slow and deep and full of promise. "Tomorrow night? My place? I'll cook this time."

"You can cook?"

"I make a mean pasta carbonara. It's literally the only thing I can cook well, but it's impressive as hell."

"Then yes. Tomorrow night."

He left, and Sadie found herself smiling as she cleaned up dinner. This was what healthy looked like—wanting to be together but respecting boundaries. Building toward intimacy instead of rushing into it.

It felt right.

The next few weeks fell into a comfortable rhythm. They saw each other three or four times a week—dinners, movies, walks through the city. They kept their own spaces, maintained their own lives, but slowly integrated each other into those lives.

Sadie introduced Jarod to more of her work colleagues. He brought her to his volunteer basketball program, where she watched him interact with kids and fell a little more in love with him.

They had their first real fight three weeks in—about something stupid, Jarod leaving dishes in the sink overnight, Sadie making a sarcastic comment that hit harder than intended. But instead of letting it fester, they talked about it. Really talked. Apologized, explained their perspectives, and moved forward.

Progress.

LaKrecia came over for dinner and interrogated Jarod thoroughly, but by the end of the night, she pulled Sadie aside and whispered, "He's good for you. Really good. Don't fuck this up."

"I'm trying not to."

"I know. And you're doing great."

TJ and Jarod rebuilt their friendship slowly. They started with basketball games, then moved to occasional dinners with Sarah and Sadie. It was awkward at first—careful conversations, avoiding certain topics—but gradually it became easier.

One night, about six weeks after Sadie and Jarod had gotten back together, the four of them were at dinner when TJ raised his glass.

"I want to make a toast. To second chances. To growth. To everyone at this table doing the hard work of becoming better people." He looked at Jarod. "To my brother, who taught me that sometimes love requires sacrifice." Then at Sadie. "And to someone who proved that people really can change."

They clinked glasses, and Sadie felt tears threaten. This was what healing looked like. Messy and imperfect, but real.

After dinner, as they were leaving, TJ pulled Sadie aside.

"I was wrong about you," he said quietly. "I didn't think you could change. Didn't think you'd do the work. But you have. And Jarod's happy—really happy. So... thank you. For proving me wrong."

"Thank you for giving me the chance to prove it."

"Don't make me regret it."

"I won't. I promise."

That night, lying in Jarod's arms (they'd started occasionally staying over at each other's places, maintaining the balance between intimacy and independence), Sadie felt something she hadn't felt in years.

Peace.

Real, genuine peace. Not the numb safety of compartmentalization, but the deep contentment of being whole and being loved for it.

"What are you thinking about?" Jarod asked, his fingers tracing patterns on her shoulder.

"That I'm happy. Really, truly happy. And I don't think I've ever been able to say that before."

"Me too." He kissed the top of her head. "We did it, baby. We actually did it. We're building something real and sustainable."

"We are. It's not perfect—"

"Fuck perfect. Perfect is boring. This is real. And real is so much better."

Sadie closed her eyes, listening to his heartbeat, feeling the steady rise and fall of his chest. She'd spent so many years running from this—from vulnerability, from connection, from the terrifying beauty of being known and loved anyway.

But she wasn't running anymore.

She was staying. Building. Growing.

Choosing courage over comfort.

Choosing love over fear.

Choosing wholeness over compartments.

One day at a time.

One choice at a time.

One moment at a time.

And it was enough.

More than enough.

It was everything.

CHAPTER 22

THE UNRAVELING
THREE MONTHS LATER

SADIE STOOD in front of her closet, trying to decide what to wear. It was ridiculous—she was a Senior VP who commanded boardrooms without breaking a sweat. But choosing an outfit for Jarod's family reunion had her second-guessing everything.

"Just pick something," she muttered to herself, finally settling on a sundress in deep purple. Casual but put-together. The kind of thing that said "I'm not trying too hard" while actually trying very hard.

Today was significant. Jarod had invited her to his family's annual reunion in Atlanta—the first time she'd be meeting his parents, his sisters, his extended family. It was a big step. A statement that this was serious, that they were building toward something permanent.

And it terrified her.

Her phone buzzed. Jarod: *On my way to pick you up. You ready?*

Sadie: *As ready as I'll ever be.*

Jarod: *They're going to love you. Stop panicking.*

Sadie: *How do you know I'm panicking?*

Jarod: *Because I know you. Breathe. It's just a family BBQ, not a firing squad.*

She smiled despite her nerves. Three months together—really together, building something sustainable—and he could read her like a book.

When he arrived, looking relaxed in khakis and a polo shirt, he immediately pulled her into a hug. "You look beautiful. And terrified. Mostly beautiful though."

"I'm not terrified. I'm just... appropriately anxious."

"That's one way to put it." He kissed her forehead. "Come on. We've got a flight to catch."

The flight to Atlanta was smooth, but Sadie's anxiety ratcheted up with every mile. She'd met important people before—clients, executives, investors. But this was different. This was personal. These people mattered to Jarod, which meant they mattered to her.

"Tell me again who I'm meeting," she said as they landed.

"My parents—Michael and Patricia. My older sister Jordan and her husband David—yes, same name as my friend, it's confusing. My younger sister Alexis, who's in med school. And probably about thirty cousins, aunts, uncles, and family friends."

"So no pressure."

"None at all." He squeezed her hand. "But seriously, Sadie. They know about you. They know we had a rough start but that we've both done work to make this sustainable. They're not going to judge you. They just want to meet the woman who makes me happy."

"What if they don't like me?"

"Impossible. You're brilliant, successful, beautiful, and you make me laugh. What's not to like?"

"The fact that I played you and your best friend like a fiddle? The fact that our relationship started as a disaster?"

"That's in the past. We're building a future. Focus on that."

The reunion was at his parents' house—a beautiful colonial in a quiet Atlanta suburb. As they pulled up, Sadie could see the backyard full of people, hear music and laughter carrying through the air.

Jarod's hand found hers as they walked to the back gate. "Hey. Look at me."

She did.

"I love you. My family is going to love you. And if they don't, we'll deal with it together. But they will. I promise."

"Okay. I trust you."

"That's my girl."

They walked into the backyard, and immediately people descended. Jarod's mother—a beautiful woman in her sixties with warm eyes and an even warmer smile—pulled Sadie into a hug before she could even introduce herself.

"You must be Sadie. I'm Patricia. It's so wonderful to finally meet you. Jarod talks about you constantly."

"It's wonderful to meet you too, Mrs. Morrison."

"Please, call me Patricia. Mrs. Morrison makes me feel ancient." She linked her arm through Sadie's. "Come on, let me introduce you to everyone."

The next hour was a whirlwind of names and faces. Jarod's father, Michael, with his firm handshake and kind eyes. His sisters—Jordan, who was warm and funny, and Alexis, who peppered Sadie with questions about corporate finance. Countless cousins and aunts and uncles, all welcoming and curious.

It was overwhelming but in a good way. This was what a functional family looked like—loud and chaotic and full of love.

Around 3 PM, as Sadie was helping set up the dessert table, Jordan pulled her aside.

"Can we talk? Just for a minute?"

"Of course."

They walked to a quieter corner of the yard, away from the crowd.

"I want to thank you," Jordan said. "For making my brother happy. I've never seen him like this—so grounded, so content. Whatever work you both did, it's paying off."

"Thank you. That means a lot."

"But I also need to say something else." Jordan's expression turned serious. "TJ called me. A few months ago, when you and Jarod were separated. He told me everything—about how you played them both, about the compartmentalization, about the conditions he set."

Sadie's stomach dropped. "Oh."

"I'm not telling you this to shame you. I'm telling you because I want you to understand something. Jarod is the best man I know. Kind, loyal, genuine. He's been hurt before—his ex-fiancée cheated on him, destroyed his trust. It took him years to open up again."

"I didn't know he'd been engaged."

"He doesn't talk about it much. But that betrayal—it changed him. Made him more cautious, more guarded. Until you." Jordan looked at her intently. "You got past his walls. He loves you completely. And if you hurt him again, if you break his trust again, I don't think he'll recover. So I need to know—are you all in? Really all in? Because if you're not, if there's any doubt, you need to let him go now before it destroys him."

The words were harsh but fair. Protective older sister energy at its finest.

"I'm all in," Sadie said firmly. "I know I made mistakes at the beginning. Terrible mistakes that hurt him and TJ. But I've spent the last eight months doing the work to make sure I never make those mistakes again. I love him. And I'm not going anywhere."

Jordan studied her for a long moment, then nodded. "Good. Because he deserves happiness. And if you're the one who can give it to him, then welcome to the family."

They hugged, and Sadie felt a lump form in her throat. She was being accepted. Not just by Jarod, but by his family. It felt like coming home.

The rest of the afternoon passed in a blur of food and conversation and laughter. Sadie found herself genuinely enjoying the chaos, feeling more relaxed than she'd felt in weeks.

Around 6 PM, as the sun was starting to set, Jarod found her talking to his younger cousins and pulled her aside.

"Walk with me?"

They walked to a quiet corner of the property, away from the crowd, where a small garden overlooked a pond.

"Your family is wonderful," Sadie said. "Thank you for bringing me."

"Thank you for coming. I know this was scary for you."

"It was. But it was also... healing? Is that weird? To say that meeting your family was healing?"

"Not weird. It makes sense. You're building connections, integrating into my life. That's what we wanted."

They sat on a bench overlooking the pond, and Jarod pulled her close. For a moment, they just sat in comfortable silence, watching the water reflect the sunset.

"Sadie, I need to ask you something," Jarod said finally, his voice serious.

"Okay."

"These last three months—they've been incredible. Better than I could have imagined. We've built something real and sustainable. We communicate, we're honest, we handle conflict well. You've met my family, I've integrated into your life. We're doing everything right."

"We are. So what's the question?"

He turned to face her, taking both her hands in his. "The question is—where do you see this going? Long term. Because I need you to know—I'm not interested in casual. I'm not interested in dating just to date. I want a future with you. Marriage, kids someday, building a life together. And I need to know if that's what you want too."

Sadie's heart hammered. This was it. The moment she'd been simultaneously anticipating and dreading. The moment when she had to decide if she was really ready for forever.

"I—" She paused, trying to organize her thoughts. "Jarod, I love you. And yes, I want a future with you. But marriage and kids—that's a big conversation. One I think we should have over time, not in the middle of your family reunion."

"I'm not proposing right now. I'm just asking if we're on the same page about what we're building toward."

"We are. I want a future with you. I want to keep building what we've started. I just—I need time. To make sure the foundation is solid before we start talking about forever."

Something flickered in his expression. Disappointment? Frustration?

"How much time?"

"I don't know. A few more months? A year? I just want to make sure we can sustain this before we make permanent commitments."

"We've already sustained it. Eight months of work—five apart, three together. How much more time do you need?"

"I don't know, Jarod. I just know I'm not ready to talk about marriage yet. Can that be okay?"

He was quiet for a long moment. Too long.

"It has to be okay. Because I can't pressure you into something you're not ready for." He stood, releasing her hands. "But Sadie, I need you to understand something. I'm thirty-four years old. I've done the casual dating thing. I've waited for people who weren't ready. And I'm at a point in my life where I know what I want. I want you. Forever. And if you're not ready for that—if you don't know if you'll ever be ready for that—then we need to have a different conversation."

"Are you giving me an ultimatum?"

"I'm being honest about what I need. Just like you're being honest about not being ready. Those things might not be compatible."

Fear spiked through Sadie's chest. This was it. The moment she'd been afraid of. The moment when her inability to fully commit would drive him away.

"So what are you saying? That if I can't promise you marriage right now, we're done?"

"No. I'm saying I need to know that we're working toward the same goal. That you're not just treading water, waiting to see if something better comes along."

"That's not fair. I'm not looking for something better. I just need more time to be sure."

"Sure of what? Sure that I won't hurt you? Sure that this will last? Sadie, there are no guarantees in life. At some point, you have to take a leap of faith."

"I took a leap of faith when I showed up at your door. When I chose to try again. When I've spent three months rebuilding this with you."

"I know. And I appreciate that. But I also need to know there's an end goal. That we're building toward forever, not just toward comfortable."

They stared at each other, the tension thick between them. This was their first real conflict since getting back together—not about dishes or schedules, but about fundamental compatibility.

Before either could say more, Jarod's phone rang. He looked at it, then at her. "It's TJ. I should take this."

"Okay."

He walked a few feet away, and Sadie sat on the bench trying to process what had just happened. Was he right? Was she treading water? Or was she just being realistic about needing more time?

She couldn't tell anymore.

Jarod's conversation seemed tense. She could hear snippets—"What do you mean?... When?... Fuck. Okay. Yeah, I'll call her."

He hung up and turned back to her, his expression unreadable.

"That was TJ. He needs to talk to both of us. Says it's urgent."

"About what?"

"He wouldn't say. Just said to call him when we're both available." Jarod looked at his phone. "He sounded weird. Stressed."

"Should we call him now?"

"Let's wait until we're back at the hotel. Don't want to deal with whatever this is in the middle of family time."

They returned to the reunion, but the easy joy of the afternoon was gone. Sadie could feel the distance between them—not hostile, but careful. Like they were both protecting themselves from whatever was coming next.

They left the reunion around 8 PM, citing an early flight the next morning. The drive to their hotel was silent, both lost in their own thoughts.

Once in the hotel room, Jarod immediately called TJ, putting it on speaker.

"Rod. Thanks for calling back. Is Sadie with you?"

"I'm here," Sadie said.

"Good. Because you both need to hear this." TJ took a deep breath. "I got a call today from Kilo. The one from the Velvet Room."

Sadie's blood ran cold. "What? Why would he call you?"

"Because apparently, you gave him your real name. And he's been following your career. Saw the social media posts about you and Jarod getting back together. And he's... concerned."

"Concerned about what?" Jarod asked, his voice tight.

"He called to warn me. Said he knows things about Sadie's past that you might not know. About her time at the Velvet Room. About the other men. About—" TJ paused. "About the fact that she was there just five months ago. Right before you two got back together."

"That's not true," Sadie said immediately. "I haven't been to the Velvet Room since before we started dating the first time. He's lying."

"He says he has proof. Photos, time stamps. Says he saw you there, talked to you. That you told him you were taking a break from someone but weren't sure if you'd go back."

"That's bullshit, TJ. I ran into him at a work event months ago, and he propositioned me. But I turned him down. Told him I was different now. I didn't go to the Velvet Room."

"So why would he lie?" TJ asked.

"I don't know. Maybe he's bitter. Maybe he's trying to cause problems. But I'm telling you—I haven't been there."

Jarod had been silent through this exchange, his expression unreadable. Now he spoke, his voice carefully controlled. "What kind of proof does he say he has?"

"Photos. He's sending them to my phone now." A pause. "They're coming through. I'm looking at them."

The silence stretched. Sadie's heart hammered so hard she thought it might break through her chest.

"TJ?" Jarod prompted.

"Fuck. Rod, man... these photos. They're of Sadie. At what looks like the Velvet Room entrance. Time stamp says March fifteenth."

March fifteenth. That was the night she'd almost gone in. The night she'd sat in her car, staring at the building, texting Jarod instead of going inside.

"I can explain—"

"You were there," Jarod said flatly. "March fifteenth. That was week five of our separation."

"I was outside the building. In my car. But I didn't go in. I texted you instead, remember? Told you I was tempted but didn't go in."

"You told me you were sitting outside. You didn't tell me you actually drove there. That you were that close to falling back into old patterns."

"Because I didn't! I resisted! I chose to reach out to you instead of going in. That was growth!"

"Growth would have been not driving there in the first place." His voice was cold, distant. The warmth she'd come to rely on completely absent.

"TJ," Sadie said desperately. "Tell him. You were there when I texted him. You know I didn't go in."

"I know you told him you were sitting outside somewhere. I didn't know it was the Velvet Room." TJ's voice was careful. "Sadie, Kilo is claiming you went in. That you were there for several hours."

"He's lying! Why would I lie about this? Why would I risk everything we've built?"

"Maybe you didn't think we'd find out," Jarod said quietly. "Maybe you thought you could compartmentalize this too. Keep your relapse separate from our relationship."

"There was no relapse! Jarod, please. You know me. You know I've changed."

"Do I? Because right now, I'm learning that you drove to your old hunting grounds during our separation and didn't think that was worth mentioning. What else haven't you mentioned?"

"Nothing! There's nothing else!"

"TJ, send me those photos," Jarod said.

"Rod, maybe you should take some time—"

"Send them. Now."

A moment later, Jarod's phone buzzed. He pulled up the photos, and Sadie watched his face as he looked at them.

They showed her car in the parking garage. Showed her walking toward the building entrance. Showed her standing at the door.

But they didn't show her going in. Because she hadn't.

"These don't prove anything," she said. "They show me at the building. They don't show me going inside."

"They show you close enough to go inside. Close enough that you were tempted." Jarod's voice was flat, emotionless. "You drove there, Sadie. To the place where you used to escape, where you used to compartmentalize, where you used to be someone else. And you didn't think I needed to know that?"

"I told you I was tempted! I told you about having urges and choosing differently!"

"You said you were sitting outside 'somewhere.' You specifically didn't tell me it was the Velvet Room. Why?"

"Because I knew you'd react like this! Knew you'd assume the worst!"

"Maybe I'm assuming correctly." He set down his phone. "TJ, I need to go. I'll call you tomorrow."

"Rod, wait—"

But Jarod had already hung up. He stood and walked to the window, his back to her.

"Jarod, please. Look at me."

"I can't right now."

"Why? Because you've already decided I'm guilty?"

"Because I'm trying very hard not to say something I'll regret." His voice was tight with controlled emotion. "You drove to the Velvet Room. During our separation. When you were supposed to be doing the work, becoming whole, proving you'd changed. And you drove there."

"And I didn't go in! I chose differently! That's the whole point!"

"The point is you were tempted enough to drive there. That when things got hard, your instinct was still to escape to your old patterns. That maybe you haven't changed as much as we both wanted to believe."

"That's not fair. Everyone has moments of temptation. The growth is in choosing differently, which I did!"

"But you didn't tell me the full truth. You gave me a sanitized version—'I was sitting outside somewhere feeling tempted.' You knew saying 'I drove to the Velvet Room and stood at the entrance' would make me question everything. So you lied by omission."

"I didn't lie—"

"You absolutely did." He finally turned to face her, and the coldness in his eyes made her stomach drop. "You did exactly what you used to do. You compartmentalized. Kept parts of your truth from me because it was easier than being fully honest."

"That's not—I was trying to protect you from worrying about nothing!"

"It's not nothing. It's you, five months into doing the work, still having impulses to escape to your old life. And me not knowing about it. That's a pretty fucking significant omission, Sadie."

"So what are you saying? That one moment of temptation that I resisted means I haven't changed? That all the work was for nothing?"

"I'm saying I don't know anymore. I thought I knew you. Thought I knew where we stood. But finding out you were at the Velvet Room—that you kept that from me—it makes me question everything."

"Don't do this. Don't let Kilo manipulate you into doubting us."

"Kilo didn't do this. You did. By not being fully honest. By still keeping pieces of your truth separate."

They stared at each other across the hotel room, and Sadie felt everything they'd built start to crumble.

"I love you," she said desperately. "I know I should have been more specific about where I was that night. But I didn't go in. I chose you. I chose us. That has to count for something."

"It does. But it also doesn't erase the fact that you went there in the first place. Or that you didn't trust me enough to tell me the full truth." He grabbed his jacket. "I need air. I need to think."

"Where are you going?"

"I don't know. For a walk. Just... I need space."

"Jarod, please don't leave like this. We need to talk about this."

"We will. Tomorrow. But right now, I can't—I need to process." He stopped at the door. "For what it's worth, I believe you didn't go inside. But the fact that you went there at all, that you didn't tell me—Sadie, that's exactly the kind of compartmentalization we've been working to overcome. And finding out you still do it, even in small ways, even when you're scared—it makes me wonder if you really have changed. Or if you've just gotten better at hiding the parts of yourself you don't want me to see."

He left, the door closing behind him with terrible finality.

Sadie sank onto the bed, her whole body shaking. This couldn't be happening. Not now. Not after everything they'd built.

Her phone rang. She grabbed it desperately, hoping it was Jarod.

But it was TJ.

"Sadie. I need to tell you something."

"What?" Her voice came out broken.

"Kilo just called me again. He wants money. Says if we don't pay him twenty thousand dollars, he's going to the media with a story about you—about the Velvet Room, about 'playing' Jarod and me, about your secret life. He's blackmailing us."

Sadie felt the room spin. "Oh my God."

"I told him to go fuck himself. But Sadie, he's serious. He's got photos, probably has more evidence. If he goes to the press—"

"My career is over. The promotion, my reputation, everything." She closed her eyes. "What do I do?"

"I don't know. But you need to tell Jarod. Right now. Before this gets worse."

"He just left. He's furious. He thinks I lied to him about the Velvet Room."

"Did you?"

"No! I didn't go inside! But I didn't tell him I actually drove there, and now he thinks I'm still compartmentalizing, still keeping secrets."

TJ was quiet for a long moment. "Are you? Still keeping secrets?"

"No. I swear. That night at the Velvet Room—that was my lowest moment. But I didn't go in. I called Jarod instead. That was real growth."

"Then you need to make him believe that. Because right now, with Kilo's blackmail and these photos—it looks really bad, Sadie."

"I know. God, I know."

They hung up, and Sadie sat in the silent hotel room, trying to figure out how everything had gone from perfect to disaster in the span of two hours.

This morning, she'd been meeting Jarod's family, being welcomed, building toward a future.

Tonight, everything was falling apart.

Her phone buzzed. A text from an unknown number.

Hi Sadie. It's Kilo. I think we need to talk. Call me.

She stared at the message, her hands shaking.

This was her nightmare. Her past coming back to destroy her present. Everything she'd worked for—her career, her relationship, her reputation—hanging by a thread.

And Jarod was out there somewhere, questioning everything they'd built.

Questioning her.

Questioning them.

She needed to fix this. Needed to make him understand. Needed to—

The hotel room door opened. Jarod stood there, his expression unreadable.

"We need to talk," he said. "Right now. Because I just got a call from Kilo too."

TO BE CONTINUED IN BOOK TWO...